MUSCLEBOUND

LIZA CODY

MUSCLEBOUND.

THE MYSTERIOUS PRESS

Published by Warner Books

A Time Warner Company

mys

 Mysterious Press books are published by Warner Books, Inc.,
1271 Avenue of the Americas, New York, NY 10020.

 A Time Warner Company

The Mysterious Press name and logo are registered trademarks of Warner Books, Inc.

Printed in the United States of America

First Printing: September 1997

10 9 8 7 6 5 4 3 2 1

Library of Congress Cataloging-in-Publication Data

Cody, Liza.
     Musclebound / Liza Cody.
         p.   cm.
     ISBN 0-89296-601-7
     I. Title.
   PR6053.0247M87   1997
   823'.914—dc21
                                                                97-10122
                                                                CIP

I'm very grateful to: Angus, Felicity Bryan, Mike Lewin, Peter Lovesey, Charlotte Nassim, Kate Nowlan and Sara Paretsky. Thank you.

MUSCLEBOUND

Chapter 1

It's a porking joke. I can't help laughing. I'm sat here, in the back of a van with my thermos full of hot tea, protecting a car park. Me—the greatest living motor-borrower of all time. There ain't a single one of these poncy rich-men's playthings I couldn't have away. Before you could say, "Eva's a genius," I'd be in there, snick-snack, and off, vroom-vroom.

But no—I'm not doing that, am I? I'm watching over them, aren't I? I'm sat here with my thermos, saying, "Off you go, you swollen, fat-walleted bastard—off you go to America or Bonn—make a few more million. See if I care. Take the missus and the kiddies to Disneyland—waste your dosh on the spoiled little dwarves. I don't give a wet pooh. And don't you worry none. 'Cos Eva's here making sure your Mercedes is waiting safe and sound for when you come home with your nose peeling and all them plastic bags full of cheap booze hanging off your arm."

See, this here's a private car park for the three car, gold card, platinum watch, eat-my-shit brigade. They get security and full-wax valeting all in one go. They don't have to drive to the long-stay car park at the airport and then climb in a bus with the rest of the hoi polloi. Oh no—they get chauffeured from one fancy location in London to a first class lounge in the terminal of their choice. And they get petted and portered and called sir all the way along the line. Yes, *sir.*

No, sir, Eva Wylie wasn't stuck here on God's earth to lick fat farts' arses.

Except when she's down on her luck. When you got no luck, you lick. No lick, no lucre. No lucre, no luck. It's all one big barbed wire circle. It keeps them who's got nothing in their place—which is saying sir to them who's got it all.

Don't you sneer at me, though. A girl's got to survive. Surviving's an honourable profession where I come from. I'm big. I got to eat. I got three dogs, and they're big too, and they got to eat. So who's going to feed us? You? Don't make me laugh. The last time I got fed for free I was in pokey, and believe me, no free meal's worth that price.

It doesn't bear thinking about.

I stopped thinking and said, "C'mon, Milo, shake yer legs." And I opened the van door.

Milo is my third dog, my youngest. He's hand-reared. And if I say it myself, he's turning out totally monster. He's got a head like a bull and feet like a camel and he ain't full grown yet.

He woke up from his twitchy sleep and went, "Herf?"

"Shut up," I said, and I laid my hand on his snout. I'm teaching him to be quiet, see, to speak only when it counts. You can't have an attack dog who yaks for no reason. Besides, his voice hasn't broken proper yet. And sometimes I can't help laughing when he goes, "Hip-herf," and looks all flummoxed at himself. And I mustn't laugh, 'cos when I laugh he thinks I'm soft. Which I ain't. I'm the boss. And that's a fact he better not forget.

"Siddown!" I said. I walked away. I'm also teaching him to stay where he's put. I don't want him following me around like a lapdog. A guard dog is not a pet, but Milo hasn't got the hang of it yet.

I walked away into a row of Audis, BMWs, Rovers and other shiny motors. I went where I could see him but he couldn't see me.

"Ramses!" I shouted. "Lineker!"

Milo stirred and strained like he was tied up. But he didn't come to me. I was stone chuffed. I only want him to come when I call *his* name. I didn't call his name. I called my other two dogs. But they didn't come because they ain't here. They're at home guarding the breaker's yard where we live.

I was well pleased because it means Milo is learning their names as well as his own.

I went away even further and then I yelled, "Milo!"

"Herf-hip," he shouted—stupid pup. He came bounding along, all feet and knees, and ran full tilt into my thighs.

"Shut up," I said. "Sit."

"Herf?" he said. But he sat down, grinning from ear to ear like he'd told a really good joke.

"Shut up, you soppy devil," I said. But I gave him half a Bow Chow and a pat 'cos I was pleased with him even if he does talk too much.

I put him on my left-hand side and we walked in and out of the Audis making sure no thieving little crow had nicked any hubcaps, telephones or radio cassettes.

See, this is supposed to be a secure lock-up for top people's motors, but it isn't as secure as the owners say. There's been some pinching going down, and that's why me and Milo are spending the night in a van. And when you think about it, I'm the best you can get for this kind of job. What I don't know about driving away in some other bastard's motor you can stuff in a flea's left lug-hole. Believe.

It was cold and it was dark. London was snoring—like it

3

does. The blob of light from my torch bounced along ahead of us, and Milo's breath steamed out of his nostrils like dragon-puff.

Just me and Milo, out walking, watching and working. Me and Milo. Milo and me. Everyone else all cosy and comfy, kipped down in their sweaty cots, snoring and farting. All safe and tucked up with Eva guarding the family Ferrari.

Go on—laugh. But this time last year you wouldn't have laughed—you'd have had more respect. 'Cos I was the London Lassassin. I was a wrestler of repute. I was fighting in halls and rings all over the south of England. I was a comer. The London Lassassin, the biggest, meanest villain on the circuit.

And then it all went turd-shaped. I got dumped on. I won't tell you how, 'cos that's another story and I don't want to think about it. But it wasn't my fault. It was those other arse-holes' fault, only I got the blame. As usual.

This time last year I'd walk into a hall and hear the crowd shout my name—"Eva, Eva, Bucket Nut, Bucket Nut." They'd scream and roar. They'd boo and hiss and spit. No one ever ignored me. No, not ever. Because I was someone, and I had my name on posters. I had cash in my pocket, I had my picture in programmes.

But that was last year. Now I'm nobody. Now I'm trudging round under the cold moon with my hands balled up in my sleeves, and only Milo to care if I live or die.

Is it any wonder The Enemy takes advantage? There's people like that. They wait till you're down and then they walk all over you in hobnail boots. They say, "You doing anything this week, Eva?" When they know for sure you're doing sweet fuck-all 'cos no one wants you no more.

That's what The Enemy says. She says, "Because if you're free I've got a job for you."

If I'm free! She knows I got nothing. She knows I can't say,

4

"Bugger off, ferret face. Find some other mug." Which is what I want to say.

You think I *want* to spend the night watching Rovers and Rollers? Don't be so sodding feeble-minded. Me? The London Lassassin? The ex-London Lassassin. Oh no. I was born for better.

Well, no. I wasn't born for it, except in me heart. I made myself better. With me own sweat.

And now I'm back where I started. And The Enemy takes advantage. She makes me play nanny to a load of fat farts' motors and she thinks I ought to be grateful. A lot she knows!

"Lay off the beer," she says. As if it's any of her business. "Stay awake," she says. Do this, do that, don't do the other.

In case you don't know, The Enemy is Anna know-it-all Lee of Lee-Schiller Security. She's politzei, and a right royal ache in the arse. But she's got coin, and I ain't. So she can say, "Stay awake," and then climb into her warm soft kip to snooze while I do her dirty work in the cold and dark. That's what coin does. If you got it you can laugh. If you don't got it you have to jump when them that's got it say "Jump."

And she can say, "It'll do you good, Eva. You're getting out of condition."

And in my head, I say, "You talking? Or are you chewing breeze blocks? I ain't listening." But I got to stand there like she's talking sense, 'cos she's got coin and I ain't.

And it's a dark cold night out here in this executive playpen. And it's a dark cold night in my heart.

"Herf?" said Milo. And I smacked his muzzle and made his eyes water.

"Hip!" he said, like I was the world's number one bastard. Which I ain't.

The world's full of much bigger bastards than I'll ever be. I ain't even bastard number six zillion.

5

"You think I'm a bastard," I said to Milo. "But I'm only doing it for your own good. If I let you speak every time you fancy speaking you'll be no sodding good as a guard dog. You'll be out on your ear with no one to feed you or keep Ramses and Lineker from chomping your no-good tail."

Milo blinked the tears out of his eyes and trotted on.

"You want a bastard?" I said. "I'll show you a bastard. I'll show you Mr. Deeds."

Milo doesn't know, 'cos he's too young to remember, but Mr. Deeds, Mr. Dirty Deeds, was the one who kicked me out of my world. Mr. Deeds of Deeds Promotions said to me, "You're out, Eva. You're barred. I don't never want to see your ugly mug again. Not ever. You're through. You won't never fight on any of my bills again."

Yes, he said that. To me. After I'd filled a hall for him. And had the crowd going ballistic—screaming and swearing and wanting my autograph.

"I'll see you never work again," he said.

And I ain't.

He put the whammy on me. I couldn't get no fights after that.

So if you want a bastard, I'll give you Mr. Dirty Deeds. For free. He kicked me out of my own world. And I can't get back in. I can't get back to the lights and the heat of the ring. I can't hear the clapping and oohs and ahs. I can't hear the grunts and groans, or the thuds as bodies hit the canvas, or the referee counting, one, two, three.

It's all there still. Out there. Somewhere. But I ain't allowed in. It's lost. And without it, I'm lost. How'm I going to be rich and famous without I'm the London Lassassin? Tell me that?

Milo stuck his wet nose into my hand, and I let him. He's only got me. He was a motherless prawn, barely a week old when I took him in. I stuffed him up my jumper for warmth

6

and I took him home, and I've been a mum and dad to him ever since. I fed him on Whelpie and saved him from Ramses and Lineker countless times. And for why? 'Cos I'm soft-hearted. That's for why. It'll be ages before he starts earning his keep, and meanwhile he's eating me out of house and home, and costing me time and trouble. He'd better turn out to be the best guard dog ever—that's all I can say. 'Cos if he isn't, I'll skin him and make a fur waistcoat out of his useless hide.

"Hear that?" I said. "A waistcoat. So you better buck up your ideas."

"Hip?" he said. But he said it quiet. So I let it go. Like I said, I'm soft hearted—I've got a dog who talks too much, but do I complain?

Let me tell you something. Last week I was in a normal poor folks' car park. I won't say why—it's none of your business. But it was late and it was cold and I wanted a ride home. And, just sitting there, all alone, was this little red Vauxhall Astra. So I thought, well, the owner's too pissed to drive it and probably took a cab home anyway. And someone who can afford to get drunk and pay for a cab ain't gonna grudge me a ride. So I borrowed the Astra.

Now, normally, I just borrow a car. You can have your stereo, you can keep your coat, your umbrella, your bag and your briefcase. I ain't a thief. And I don't do no damage neither—just what it takes to get in and get started. What's more I usually leave it cleaner than when I find it. A borrowed car needs a bit of a wipe down afterwards.

But this time was different. I got in all clean and tidy, and I started up without totally wrecking the steering—well, what do you expect if you don't fit an immobiliser? Everything was as it always is—except the owner had left a tape in the slot. And you know what came blasting out the speakers? What made the hair

7

on the back of my head pop up? It was that music. My music. "Satisfaction."

It's *my* music. It *is*.

When I was in the ring. No, when I was outside waiting to come on, that was the music I was waiting for. I didn't hear it in my ears—I heard it through the soles of my feet. I heard it in the pit of my stomach. *Ba-ba ba-ba-baaa da bad'n bad'n*. Just like that. And I'd come crashing out snarling and howlin' like a wild animal. And the crowd'd turn and snarl and howl back at me.

It's mine, that music.

Well it was mine.

But you know the weird thing? I hadn't ever heard the song. I only knew the *ba-ba ba-ba-baaa da bad'n bad'n* bit, 'cos that's what they played over and over for me while I got to the ring. They never played the words. And I never thought to find out because, if you must know, if it ain't Heavy Metal, it ain't music, and that's a fact. Mr. Dirty Deeds chose that music for me, and he's an old man with no taste. He's the wrong generation.

So there I was, freezing my arse off in a high-rise car park, all set to do a quick quiet exit, and all of a sudden, out of the speakers comes this *ba-ba ba-ba-baaa da bad'n bad'n*. It frightened the life out of me. I was banjaxed. It was like a sign. A sign from Hell.

I should of turned it off, 'cos when you're borrowing an Astra you don't drive it off with a million mega-decibels honking out the sun-roof, do you? You do not. Well, maybe *you* do—but then you ain't got my brains. But I didn't turn it off. Well, I couldn't find the right knob quick enough. But then when I did find it I didn't want to. Because, you know what I found out? I found out it wasn't a song about satisfaction at all. It was a song about *no* satisfaction.

Which showed me what a floppy dick Mr. Dirty Deeds was. He chose me a song called "Satisfaction" which was all about frustration and "Baby, better come back later next week, 'cos you see I'm on a losing streak . . ." And it was really angry and bitter. And so was I. So I kept it playing till it was over.

Later, when I dropped the motor off, I kept the tape just in case there was another sign from Hell for me.

And there was one. Really truly. It was called "Jumpin' Jack Flash," and it was all about *me*. Except I'm not Jack. I'm Eva.

But Jack and Eva both got hags for mothers. We both got the strap. And now we're both drowned and washed up and got spikes through our heads.

But we're all right.

Well, *I'm* all right. Bugger Jack. 'Cos in the song, he doesn't whine and he doesn't cry. He yells and carries on, but he's all right. And that's me too.

"Herf," said Milo.

"Shurrup," I said.

"Eva," said Anna Lee.

"Shit," I said. "What you doin', creeping up on me like that?"

"Creep?" she said. "I opened the gate and walked in. You didn't hear me. Milo did. You didn't."

Talk about creeps—Milo was all busy kissing her hand and wagging his no-good tail.

"Eva," she said, "you're drinking on the job."

"Kiss my arse," I said. "This ain't drinking. This is just a slurp to keep the cold away." Well, if you get caught with a can of Special Brew halfway to your gob you can't say it's coffee cake, can you?

"I'm taking you home," said Anna Lee, The Enemee.

"You're takin' me nowhere."

"Home," she said.

"Now," she said.

"Get a move on," she said.

9

And somehow me and Milo found ourselves in the back of her white Peugeot speeding down Jamaica Road and she was saying, "I'm sorry."

"What?"

"It's the end of the line. You blew your last chance."

"I blew nothing," I said. "Stop the car."

"What for?"

"Stop!"

I almost fell out into the gutter. And I couldn't stand it no more. I couldn't stand for that tight-arsed hoity-toity to see me throw up.

I ducked round a corner and threw up over the hood of an XRI.

But I didn't go back. I'd had it with The Enemy. She thought she was giving me the boot. She wasn't. I was giving her the boot. Work for her? I'd rather stick my head under a commuter train.

I should of thrown up in her Peugeot. I should of thrown up down the back of her neck. In her handbag.

Fancy that! Giving a sick person the boot. Some people got no heart. No heart at all. I wouldn't go back if she begged me.

Chapter 2

I left Milo in The Enemy's car. He didn't come with me. I said, "No-good fuckin' pup."

What use was he anyway? He was too young and green to work, and he ate like a horse.

"She can keep you," I said. "I never wanted you anyway."

I walked on. I didn't care. I DID NOT CARE. *NOT*.

But the pavement was rocking, and the walls were waving like a flag in the breeze. And before I knew it, I didn't know which way was home. Well, sneer if you like, but that happens. Even when you're stone cold sober. You schlep along thinking of this and that or nothing at all. You turn this way and that, or you forget to turn at all, and there you are—lost.

Lost is what I was.

I came out on a main street but it didn't mean nothing to me. It could of been any old street. It was well lit, but the lights were blurry and swinging in the wind. Except there wasn't no wind. I thought I was going to puke-up again but I saw a garage, still open, on the other side. And I thought maybe they'd have a can of Special Brew to settle me guts.

I crossed. Slowly. Even at four in the morning there were cretins whizzing by—zip-zap. Not one of them keeping to the speed limit. And I thought this here road's a dangerous place when you've had a little drink and you aren't feeling too hot.

And then, woo-eee, a bright red Carlton swooped round me like I didn't exist and swung into the garage. It came so close it nearly took the coat off my back.

"Bastard!" I yelled. But no one heard. No one cared. I might as well have shouted at a post.

"Bastard," I said, and I hopped onto the pavement.

"I'll have you," I said, and I stepped over the chain into the garage forecourt.

I was going to have it out with the driver of the Carlton. I was going to pick him up by the armpits and say, "Oy, pus-bottom, watch where you're going." But by the time I got up off the floor and kicked the chain for tripping me up, I saw the driver wasn't in the Carlton no more. He'd gone inside the booth, and he'd left the driver's door open and his motor running. Which is exactly the same as saying, "C'mon, Eva, here's a nice red Carlton all warm and ready to take you home."

So I said, "Ta, very much. Sorry I called you a pus-bottom." I jumped in and shoved the stick in first.

At the same time, the driver stuck his head out of the booth and shouted something. I didn't catch the exact words because I was too busy revving up and moving out. But what happened next was very weird. As I swung past the booth, the passenger door slammed shut. I hadn't noticed a passenger. And then another man, who I hadn't seen before, walked out from the booth and pointed a stick at me.

I thought, "Why's that dink pointing a stick at me?" And I'd hardly finished thinking that when the passenger-side windows shattered. Kerash-kerunch. Glass everywhere. I was so startled I nearly whacked into one of the petrol pumps.

I went, nought to sixty, out of the forecourt, right under the nose of a Safeway truck. I was sweating and swearing but, do you know, I was half a mile up the road before I realised what shattered the windows.

The dink wasn't pointing a stick at me. He was pointing a sawn-off shotgun. The windows didn't just shatter. The dink shot them out.

Can you believe that? Some bastard shot at me. Me. Just for borrowing a Carlton. Who the hell'd do a thing like that?

If he didn't want his motor borrowed, why didn't he just remove the keys like a sensible person?

Shit. He could of killed me. Fancy that. Ex-Wrestler Shot. What a headline that'd make.

Suddenly, I was so shook up I couldn't drive no more. I pulled into the kerb.

There could of been a bleeding stump where my head should be—think of *that* next time you pick your nose and worry about hair-loss.

By now I was feeling sick but sober. The cold air from the smashed windows whistled straight through one ear and out the other. There wasn't nothing to be done about that, but I jacked the heater up to max which at least warmed my toes.

I drove off again. Slowly. I'd have to dump the motor fairly smartly. Even politzei with only half a brain cell would notice two missing windows and pull me over. I checked the mirrors. No politzei. Yet. It was a nasty night, but even nasty nights can be made nastier. All you need is one nosy copper. A nosy copper'd bounce me into jug quicker than you could spit—slightly flibbed on the boozometer, driving a borrowed Carlton without insurance or a license—you name it and I could get bounced for it.

The important thing was to get off the main road and a bit closer to home—wherever that was.

I got off the main road.

And then I began to wonder. What was the shit with the shooter doing in a petrol station booth at four in the morning? Well, you don't need a sawn-off for ten gallons of unleaded and a packet of cheese and onion crisps, do you? And you don't leave your engine running when you fill up. Or your doors open.

You only leave your doors open and the engine running if you want to make a very sharp exit.

I braked hard. It was worse than I thought—I'd borrowed hot wheels, and there would be two *very* pissed off villains not a million miles away. And at least one of them had a shooter.

I sat for a minute. My head was spinning. And then it occurred to me to sniff around and find out exactly what I'd borrowed.

And what did I find? Oh man! You'll never guess. Never—'cos I'd never of imagined it, even in a six-pack fantasy.

I found a Puma sports bag, and man oh man oh man, had those two cowboys had a good night? Had they *ever!*

The Puma bag was stuffed to the zip with dosh. Money. Just money. Big, big money. More than I'd ever seen in my life. Thousands and thousands. Hundreds of thousands. Thousands of hundreds of thousands. Smackeroos times a zillion.

I gaped at it. I gawped at it.

I stuck my nose in the bag and nuzzled it. It smelled sweeter than chocolate ice cream.

I stroked it and it was softer than a cat's belly fur.

I crooned to it and it answered back. It said, "Take me. I'm yours. I'm all yours, babe."

Well, what's a girl supposed to do? What would you have done? And don't tell me you'd of done any different to what I done. Don't. 'Cos I'll never believe you in a month of Sundays.

I didn't even think about it. I mean, what was there to decide? I'd just lost another job. I was down on my luck. So was I going to leave a bagful of zillions lying around for some bugger who didn't need it half as much as me? Was I going to let it sit there, getting cold, so it could say, "Take me, I'm yours," to someone else?

You don't know me very well if you think that.

Chapter 3

My two big dogs, Ramses and Lineker, have a wooden shed and a wire pen all to themselves. In the daytime, when the men are working in the yard, when all the crushers and cutters and lifting gear are whining and clunking away, I'm asleep in my pit. Then Ramses and Lineker snuggle down in their shed and kip too. But if any one of those men goes a step too close to that pen Ramses wakes up and goes bounding out to the wire, hackles up, gnashers bared, and tells me all about it.

"Ro-ro-ro," he goes, like a bass guitar. And that wakes Lineker who goes, "Yak-yak." And that wakes Milo, who says, "Hip-herf." And that wakes me.

So what I've got is a totally fool-proof warning system against anyone coming too close to me and my dogs.

At night, when the men have gone and the machinery's closed down, Ramses and Lineker roam free. And I pity anyone who climbs over the gate or crawls through the fence into our yard. Dogs is territorial animals. And so am I. If you want your throat mangled, come on in. Go on, I dare you.

It took just two nails and a hammer. I nailed the Puma bag high up on the wall of the dogs' house. I nailed it high in case that fool Lineker took it into his cretin head to have some chewing practice.

My teeth were chattering—rat-a-tat-tat. I felt smashed again. I couldn't walk in a straight line.

I was rich. I was stinking dirty filthy rich.

It was what I'd always wanted.

I cried like a baby.

Go on, laugh. But I sat on the dogs' bedding and howled.

Every crisp crinkly crunchy note in that Puma bag was mine. Mine, all mine.

If you haven't ever been on your uppers, if you haven't ever lived in hunger-town, if you haven't ever really truly *wanted*— you won't understand. So go away and suck on fish food.

It was nearly morning, nearly the time when the yard comes alive. I went to bed, but I couldn't sleep. There was almost as much in my head as there was in that Puma bag—and I was counting it.

But at last the rhythm of the crusher took over. *Bad'n, bad'n,* it said. Just the same as "Satisfaction." And I went to sleep with *bad'n, bad'n* thumping in my brain like a headache.

Which really did turn into a headache when I woke up—a bad'n. But I almost enjoyed it, because I was thinking, "Now I can straighten everything out. I can buy me own gym and get fit again."

It wouldn't be the same as Sam's gym, where I used to work out—the one Mr. Deeds kicked me out of. It'd be better. I'd have a personal trainer and a sauna kept 'specially for me. I'd sweat the poison out of my system. I'd sweat the extra weight off. I'd be lean and hard. I'd be mean and tough. And I'd be in charge. Oh I'd be a bad'n alright. Believe. A lean, mean, bad machine.

I went down Mandala Street market for my breakfast. It was three in the afternoon, cold and grey. But I had a bunch of twenty-pound notes in my pocket to keep me warm. I bought a couple of burgers and a bag of chips at John's Burger Bar.

"In the money?" John said, when he took my twenty.

"What's it to you?" I said. People can never keep their snouts out—always got to comment.

"Only I ain't seen you around lately," he said. "The girls was saying you'd had a thin time."

"Times change," I said. "And you can tell those toms to keep their snouts out an' all."

"Always nice doin' business with you, Eva," he said. Fart-face.

I'd take my custom elsewhere. That's what I'd do. I'd go up West and eat at the Café Royal off of china plates and tables with tablecloths on. No more styrene cups and greasy fingers for Eva Wylie. Eat my dirt, fart-face, you won't see me again.

But stuffing my face with burgers reminded me of Milo. Last I saw of him he was sitting all warm and stupid in The Enemy's car. He betrayed me and she drove off with him. But now I was ready to forgive him. If The Enemy thought she could drive off with the dog I'd hand-reared from a sprat she had another think coming.

Besides, she owed me money.

Just because I had millions and zillions of my own didn't make her owe me any less. I don't freeze my arse off all night in a car park for nothing, you know. I ain't stupid.

So I went round to see her.

To look at, her gaff is just like a dentist's office. There's a cream door with a plate that says Lee-Schiller Security. You walk in and there's a secretary sitting behind a big office desk. There's a waiting room with a sofa and two comfy chairs.

So I walked in and the old secretary bird said, "Good afternoon—oh, it's you, Eva. Have you come to collect Milo?"

And that's the trouble with old secretary birds—they want to know all your business.

"Where is she?" I said.

"Anna?" she said. "She's with Mr. Schiller. But don't go in. They're busy."

So I gave the top of her desk a little tap—just to remind her she wasn't anyone. She jumped, and said, "I wish you wouldn't hit things, Eva."

"I wish you wouldn't stick your beak in my breakfast," I said, and I went past her.

"Please," she said. "They're busy."

But I wasn't mad really. I was too rich to be mad. Money soothes. Have you noticed that? There ain't much a little dosh can't cure. I could of bawled at her the way I usually do, but I only said, "Fuckin' shut up," quite sweetly, as a reminder. Gelt is good for your disposition.

I walked straight into The Enemy's office and found her and Mr. Schiller sitting side by side, drinking tea and studying ledgers.

"Afternoon, Eva," Mr. Schiller said. He's sort of all right, but you can tell by the way he holds his mug that he used to be politzei too.

"Oh bugger," said The Enemy.

"Hip-herf," said Milo.

"Shurrup," I said, "and get over here where you belong." He had been sitting at The Enemy's feet, looking, for all the world, like he was her dog. That *really* gets up my nose—when people suck up to my beasts. She wouldn't have a hope in hell with Ramses. Ramses'd rip her foot off.

Milo didn't even move—the sod.

Suddenly I was a fist on two feet. I said, "Gimme my pup."

"Take him. He's yours," The Enemy said, "but if you think you can walk in here shouting the odds you can walk right out again."

19

"You'd love that," I said. "You owe me money." I had her there. She couldn't deny it.

"I'll pay you. When haven't I?"

"Now *you're* shouting," I said. I was stone happy.

"And why not?" she shouted. "You're so full of shit your eyes have turned brown."

"Please!" said Mr. Schiller. "Calm down, both of you." He paid me in cash out of his own pocket. Which shows what kind of bloke he is. But The Enemy looked like she was having a tooth pulled. Which shows what kind of a cow she is. It almost made my headache go away.

"Call this money?" I said. "Exploiting the worker, I call it."

"You call what you did work?" she said. "I call it getting drunk on the job and snoring."

"Who the fuck cares what *you* call it," I said. "I did as much work as you paid me for." And I turned on my heel and did a smart exit.

The only trouble was I forgot Milo. Which spoiled it a bit. I had to go back in and drag him out by the scruff of his neck.

"Just get over yourself," The Enemy said. "Come back when you've straightened up."

"Don't hold your breath," I said, and I went.

Who the hell did she think she was—telling me to straighten up? Me. I had more oil in my oilcan than she'd ever see in three of her miserable lifetimes. I had it nailed to the wall of my dogs' shed. It made me somebody. Somebody she couldn't touch.

She'd never make me sit out in a car park all night again. Never. She'd never take my time like that no more. She'd never steal my precious hours, minutes and seconds out of that little bag of time which is my life and throw them away like they was rubbish. Tick, tock. They may be tick-fucking-tock to her, but they're chunks of my life to me. And now I've got dosh, I can spend all my tick-tocks how I like, not how she likes.

"It's all your fault," I said to Milo. Because it was. If he hadn't stayed with The Enemy instead of coming with me I'd never of had to go and get him. And if he'd left when I left I'd of never had to go back. Then I wouldn't have had to hear her say, "If you got paid every time you cocked up, Eva, you'd make a very nice living. As it is . . ."

But I didn't wait to hear the rest. Who needs it? I don't.

Chapter 4

There's no point in having so much moolah that it oozes out your ears unless you can swank about it. That's why I went to see my ma.

My ma isn't hard to swank to 'cos she doesn't have a pot to piss in. Anyone'd look good compared with her—'specially when she's suckin' on a jar. Which is practically all the time.

But she *is* my ma, and I've got family feeling for her. She's different, though. She's got about as much family feeling as she's got savings in the bank—which is none at all. And if I've got a grudge against her, *that's* for why—look no further.

Do you know I've got an elder sister I haven't seen since I was eleven? Yes I do. People think I'm all on me own—no family. Well that shows how wrong you can be. I got a sister. Simone's her name. It's a pretty name—as pretty as she was last time I saw her. And as I say, I ain't seen her since I was a nipper.

Why ain't I seen her? Good question. It's a good question with a bad answer. My ma—our ma. That's the bad answer.

My ma is such a bad ma she couldn't keep a home together for more than a couple of weeks at a time, and she didn't give goolies for her own kids. So we got took off of her. And did she care? Did she—bollocks. Out of sight, out of mind—that's

Ma's motto. Never mind we was sleeping eight to a room. Never mind we was getting our legs strapped, never mind the food was cat vomit, never mind it was so cold you could see your breath *indoors*. No, never mind all that, so long as she could suck on a bottle and score a few quid off of man-trash.

Well, now I'd scored more than a few quid. I was jumpin'.

Ma thinks I'm a downer. She thinks I'll never make nothing of meself 'cos I ain't a looker. She could of been proud of me for being the London Lassassin. But was she? She was not. She was shamed. That's my ma. I make myself tough, I win fights, I give the crowd what it pays for. And my ma is shamed. She didn't never come to watch me fight. Not once.

"Ooh no," she says, "I don't mind seeing the blokes if they've got nice bods. But I don't want to see no daughter of mine make a spectacle of herself. Not with a bod like yours, Eva. It ain't for display."

Encouraging, huh? I don't think about it. If I thought about that crap I'd top myself. I'd die on my feet.

I stopped. Milo bumped into the back of my legs.

I said, "Why'm I thinkin' crap, Milo?"

"Hip?" said Milo.

"I'm on a roll," I told Milo. "I'm on the up. It ain't never happened before but this time there's *good* mojo working. And I'm going to ride it. Believe."

And I walked straight into Value Mart and bought a lottery ticket with one of my brand new silky smooth twenty quid notes.

I know what you're thinking. You think I'm crazy. I got squillions, so what do I want with more? Know what? I ain't crazy. Okay, I got squillions. But clever folk like me *keep* their squillions. They make their squillions work for them. And that's what I was doing. Because, with good mojo buzzing, my lottery ticket would win for sure. And I wouldn't of wasted a quid, would I? I'd of bought more dosh for a quid. Geddit? So now who's crazy?

You think—that Eva, she never had no jack before, she don't know what to do with it, she'll just wave it and waste it. Shows how much you know. 'Cos now I got it, it's mine and I'm keeping it. So don't you think you can get your grubby paws on it. Me and my three dogs say you can get stuffed. What's mine's mine. What's yours is yours, and if you ain't got none—tough. I'll give you exactly what you gave me when I had none. And you can guess how much that'll be. Let's all see how smart *you* are.

By now I'd got to that high-rise hen coop my ma calls home. I walked fast, and young Milo was huffing and puffing behind me.

I didn't even bother with the lift—it only works one time in fifty. I trudged up five floors in that vertical pisser of a stair-well. The people who live here are huns. Give 'em a flight of steps and the first thing they do is come over all unnecessary and wee on them. I dunno what they're thinking of. Give me a flight of stairs and I go up 'em—or down 'em. Simple.

Milo stopped on the third floor, his eyes oozing and pleading.

I said, "Don't look at me like that. I ain't carrying you."

"Herf," said Milo with a broken heart. He's young. His muscles ain't hard. But he's too big to carry up toilet stairs. And he's so dumb he wants to take a breather right where breathing poisons you stone blind.

"C'*mon*," I said. And we came out onto the outside walkway where the wind tore our ears off.

It was my day for nasty surprises.

My ma was moving out. She was doing a bunk and she **wasn't** leaving no forwarding address. Not even for her own **daughter.** That shows you. Does that ever show you what sort of ma I got? Cuddle up to a brick and call it Ma—you'll get more satisfaction.

"Where the cockin' hell you off to?" I said when I got my breath back.

"Cop a hold of this," Ma said, and dumped a box full of frocks and crockery in my arms. "You'll have to use the stairs. I got me bed in the lift."

She disappeared back indoors and left me holding her crud. When she came out again it was with another armful of her gaudy tat.

"Get a move on," she said, "I got to load this in the van. The rent man's due."

"Where you going?" I said. "Why didn't you tell me?"

"Don't just stand there like a lump in the gravy," she screamed. "I told you—the rent man's coming."

"You was flitting," I said. "And you wasn't going to tell me."

She said, "All right—you stand there shouting if you like. It's all you're bleeding good for. I'm off. The rent man's coming and he'll have me in court."

"You just don't care, do you?" I said. "How're we ever going to get together—me and Simone—if you just bugger off and don't tell us. How can anyone be a family if your ma just buggers off? Tell me that!"

"Oh shut up, will you!" she yelled. "I *told* you—the rent man's coming."

"You wasn't even going to tell me," I said. "I'd of come here and found you gone, you puke-coloured old bag."

"About time too," she said, "I'm fucking fed up of you going on and on and on about Simone. Why can't you get it through your thick skull? You just ain't someone Simone wants to know."

How about that, eh? Ain't that a fine way for a ma to carry on? It's enough to make your gums bleed.

25

"Oh fuck!" Ma said. "Now look what you've gone and done. He's here."

I turned and saw a big bloke, all blue in the face from the stairs, hanging off the railing, panting his lungs out. He was carrying a baseball bat.

He staggered over and said, "Going somewhere?"

"Not me," said Ma. "I was just tidying up."

Ma. Tidying up. Not even a toddler who believed in Father Christmas'd believe that one. The rent man didn't. He said, "I've come for me money, Mrs. Smith."

Mrs. Smith. That's another good one.

"Right," said Ma from behind her bundle of tart-rags. "Why don't you go in and have a sit down. You look all wore out. I'll be in in a sec to put the kettle on."

Sit down on what? Her settee was probably already on the van. You had to hand it to her. The rent man nearly handed it to her on a baseball bat. He said, "Just the money, Mrs. Smith. *Now.*"

"Herf!" said Milo. The hackles went up. He was only a kid in dog years but he knew when stuff was going critical.

Me too.

"*The rent,*" the rent man shouted. He thumped the baseball bat in the palm of his hand. Whack! If he'd thumped Ma's peroxide head that way she'd of ended up on the floor below. I grinned. It was no more than she deserved.

Ma said, "You said you'd give me till next week. I ain't got all of it. You said."

"I said today."

"Next week. You *said.*"

"Now!" he shouted. "I ain't letting you off no more. You ain't even a *cheap* screw. I been looking at the books—it's four months you owe. Four fuckin' months. You're getting me in lumber."

26

So now you know how a woman with no readies pays the rent.

It made me sick.

I said, "Oy, you, balls for brains."

"What?" He turned his baseball bat in my direction.

"You heard her," I said. "She ain't got your money. Come back tomorrow."

"I ain't coming back tomorrow," he said, "'cos I ain't leaving today. Not without my money."

He flicked his bat at me. I stepped aside. He flicked his bat at Ma. She was too slow. The bat swiped her hands. The armful of frocks and undies went flying out over the balcony. They went tumbling like horrible confetti into the wind.

"Woo-hoo-hoo," went Ma, sucking on her knuckles.

"Herf," went Milo and took a chomp at the rent man's crotch.

I dropped my box of crud and got down in a crouch.

The rent man whacked Milo. I took a jump at him. He whacked me. I went down. Clean and simple.

"Wow-wow-wo!" cried Milo.

"Woo-hoo-hoo!" cried Ma.

A dog and a bitch, both howling.

I said nothing. My arm was dropping off and my teeth were clenched so tight they hurt.

"Just the bleedin' MONEY!" said the rent man.

I could of had him. I *could* of. If I hadn't got all tangled up in Ma's suspenders. No one whacks my pup and gets off light. No one. But there I was—on the deck with no feeling in my right arm and Ma and Milo woo-hooing in my lug-holes. And the poxy rent man—he was looming and smacking his bat in the palm of his hand. I dunno how it happened—really I don't. It wasn't supposed to happen that way.

I said, "Want your money, eh?"

LIZA CODY

"What d'you think I want?" he said. "A tango lesson?"

"You got a frigging polite way of asking," I said. "How come I ain't heard the word 'please'?"

"When did that ever earn me the price of a dry fart?" he asked. Then he bent over bawling Ma, grabbed a fistful of her hair and shouted, "Gimme my fucking money, you cheap tart. PLEASE."

"All you had to do was ask nicely," I said, because there was bugger all else I could say. I reached in my pocket. I had to do it with my left hand 'cos the other one felt like it went AWOL. And I gave the bastard a wodge of twenties.

"Keep the change, my man," I said. Well, what was I going to do, on the deck with only one arm? "And next time," I said, "MIND YOUR TURDING MANNERS."

The look on his face was almost worth what it cost.

"Wha'?" he said.

"Fuckin' cock off," I said, "and don't come back."

"Wha'?" said Ma, mascara dripping off her chin. The look on her face was almost worth what it cost too.

"Wo-wo-wo," went Milo. I couldn't of said it better meself. 'Cos, when you look at it—I lost. The rent man won and I lost. Just like that. Without putting up any kind of show at all. I took a jump at him. He walloped me. I crashed. Just like that. Biff—crash.

It ain't never happened before. Of course I lose sometimes. In the ring, I'm the villain and villains ain't supposed to win all the time. Blue-eyes is supposed to beat the villain sometimes. Blue-eyes is supposed to beat the devil in black. And sometimes, in the ring I was given such piss-poor opposition I had to work a lot harder at losing than winning. But I never went down without I did damage. Dirty damage. Never jump-biff-crash, just like that. Never.

"Get up," Ma said. "Get up and help."

When I opened my eyes, I saw the rent man had gone. Milo was standing, all lopsided and shivering, with his tail between his legs. Ma's underwear was blowing about in the wind and she was trying to catch it. I couldn't stand to watch.

"Get off your lard-arse and help me," Ma said. But I couldn't stand to touch it. I rubbed my shoulder. It was okay. It went dead for a while and then it hurt. But it was okay.

"Come *on*," Ma said.

But I couldn't stand to look at her neither.

I got up. I picked Milo up in my arms. I walked away.

"Oy!" said Ma. "Where you off to?"

But I was too gutted to talk. I walked away with Milo in me arms.

Chapter 5

The vet said Milo had a dislocated femur. He jolted it back in place and made Milo cry. He said Milo was young and strong—he'd not notice it in the morning. And that was true.

But I ain't a pup. I got memories and feelings and stuff that a pup ain't got. I can't go to the vet with them and be all right the next day. I got them for keeps, and they hurt.

I s'pose you'll say, "Who cares? You're flush now, Eva. You're laughing. Take some of that crinkly stuff you got nailed up on the doghouse wall and rub it on what hurts. That's what loaded folk do." Well, that goes to show what a big help *you* are. It shows how unfeeling people become when they know you got lots of dosh. I won't come to you again.

No. Harsh was who I needed. Harsh knows everything. Harsh has all the answers. He's a god, and an ace good wrestler too. But unless you know your onions, like me, you won't appreciate him. It takes someone who knows what's what in the ring to appreciate a wrestler like Harsh. He's what we call a shooter—a straight shooter. What's more, he's got brains—which is more than I can say for most of the thickos I know.

But it'd been a bit of a stretch since I seen him last. I hadn't seen him 'cos he trains at the gym I got kicked out of. The one

Mr. Dirty Deeds barred me from. Harsh is still in my ex-world and I didn't want to see him 'cos it reminded me of what I ain't got.

And I didn't want to walk into the gym just to hear those heavyweights, Gruff and Pete, say, "Here comes the has-been." 'Cos they would, you know. Gruff and Pete are the worst fungus-farts in the world. They know what hurts and they hurt what hurts. They enjoy it. I didn't want to face them.

So I waited outside in the mizzle. I waited and watched out for Harsh. I waited a long time on the other side of the road where I could see the gym door. I waited in the doorway of the tobacconist till the owner moved me on and then I hunkered down next to a boarded-up shop. And, would you believe it, I hadn't been there twenty minutes when some little old woman gave me ten pence. I mean, shit, she must of thought I was homeless or something. She just walked past and dropped a ten-pence coin on the ground in front of me like I was a beggar. I should of shouted at her. I should of said, "Oy, you soppy old wrinkly, don't you know a squillionaire when you see one?" I should've given her back her pitiful ten pence. But I never. I was narked, but I also thought, ain't that weird—when I had fuck-all, nobody gave me fuck-all. Now I've got loads, people are falling over to give me more. Loot attracts loot.

See what I mean? That's what made me feel hot about the lottery ticket I bought. I couldn't wait for Saturday to find out how much I'd won. I was so hot, I couldn't not win. So I picked up the coin and stashed it. I'd keep it as my lucky piece.

Just as I was doing that I saw Harsh come out the gym door. And I was really glad he didn't see me picking up a coin off the street 'cos he looked so clean and beautiful. He's got the perfect body—strong, muscled, but not overcooked. Every bit of him's useful. None of it's for show.

And that's why I nearly didn't go over to talk to him. 'Cos he looks how I ought to look. But I suddenly knew that nosy cow, The Enemy, had a point—I *had* slurped a bit too much of the sauce. I *had* let myself go. And that's why the rent man decked me. Of course it was Ma's fault too—her upsetting me, her and her tarty underwear. And it wasn't so much that the rent man actually decked me—no—it was him looking at me and knowing he could. A year ago he would of looked at me and said to hisself, "Uh-oh, trouble, back off." This year he looked at me and said to hisself, "Ho-ho, easy meat. I can have this." And he did.

So I didn't want clean beautiful Harsh looking at me and seeing what the rent man saw.

But I didn't have no other choice. And besides, I told myself as I crossed the road, he hadn't seen the old bird drop me a coin, and he hadn't seen me pick it up. So I walked as tall as I could and I called out his name.

"Harsh!" I said.

He spun round, easy and graceful, on the balls of his feet. "Eva," he said. "Well, well, well."

"Harsh," I said, "you got to help me."

"Do I?" he asked.

It had came out all wrong. Why does it *always* come out wrong?

"This bloke yesterday," I said.

"Excuse me?" said Harsh.

"Yeah. He knew he could clobber me."

"Eva," Harsh said. "Give me some space. Let go of my coat."

"And he clobbered me. He did. But it's 'cos he *knew* he could."

"Eva," Harsh said. "This may mean a lot to you, but, so far, it means very little to me. Let go of me and explain yourself clearly."

"I got to get back."

"Get back where?"

"Where I was," I said. "Fit. Hard."

"Ah," said Harsh. "I see."

Harsh saw. I felt like bawling my eyes out.

"I can pay you," I said, because I didn't want to bawl.

"Where did you get all that money?" Harsh said. "Don't brandish it out here where everyone can see."

I stuffed fistfuls of wedge back in my pockets. I said, "I wanted to show you—so's you'd believe."

"I believe you," Harsh said. "You don't have to wave it around. Where did you get it?"

"It's mine," I said.

"All right, don't shout."

"So I'll pay you," I said. "And you'll get me fit again."

"You will not pay me," Harsh said. "You do not need money to be fit. You need the will to do the work. You need the will to stop drinking."

"I ain't drinking."

"I can smell it."

"I gave it up."

"Then you need to use your toothbrush. How much money will that cost you?"

"What're you ravin' on about?" I shouted. I was so let down. "Are you blind or what? I want to be the London Lassassin again. I can pay. And you're going on about a fuckin' stupid toothbrush."

"It is a journey," Harsh said. "And in your case it should begin with a toothbrush."

He turned away and left me standing. Can you believe it? When I opened my eyes again, he was gone. Gone. He left me standing with all that wedge balled up in me pockets. Me! A squillionaire.

I could of run after him and throttled him.

"I'll give you a toothbrush," I said. "I'll give you a toothbrush so hard it'll come out the other end."

I mean, I'm talking quads, pecs, deltoid, trapezius—and he's talking toothbrush. That's way past dumb. I thought Harsh understood, I really thought he *knew*, but he told me squat, treated me like a tadpole.

And then two geezers walked up and one of them swatted me on the shoulder. I whisked round.

"Oy," the black-haired geezer said. "Oy, Eva, don't thump me."

It was Flying Phil. I said, "What you done to your hair?" He used to streak it blond. Now it was blue-black and spikey.

"Ain'tcha heard?" he said. "Dad's retired. I've gone solo. I'm Firefly Phil, the Giant Killer now. What you doing shouting the odds out here? Mr. Deeds'll go ape. He told you what he'd do if he caught you within a mile of the gym."

"Fuck Mr. Deeds," I said. "And fuck you too." I was too upset about Harsh to talk to a moron like Phil.

"Know what?" Phil said. "You're turning into one of those bag women."

"Fuck off."

"Yeah, next you'll be pushing a trolley and collecting carrier bags. You're already doing the bit where you shout at strangers."

"I ain't," I said. "I was talking to Harsh. He's going to get me back in the ring."

"Harsh?" Phil said. "Don't make me laugh. He's retiring too."

"What?"

"Yeah, Eva. You're really out of the loop. He got his degree or whatever it was, and he's going back to Wog Land or wherever it was he came from."

"He's never!" I said. Well, I knew Harsh was studying for something 'cos he's such a brainy bloke. But he'd never leave the wrestling. He'd never, never walk out on me when I was all set to get back.

"He's never," I said again. "He's going to be my personal trainer."

"Dream on," said Phil. "He's going to be a personal assistant to some fuckin' economical adviser in Wog Land."

"What do you know about fuck-all?" I said.

"More than you do," Phil said. "I know Harsh is leaving, and I know he ain't interested in you. And I know a boozy fantasy when I hear one."

"Shows how brain damaged you are," I said.

"You were always such a gark, Eva, and you ain't improved." Phil turned to the strange bloke he was with and said, "She always had the hots for Harsh. She thinks he's a Zen-master or something."

"He ain't a bad middleweight," the bloke said, which made me look at him proper. 'Cos he couldn't be as pill-panned as Phil if he said that.

"Boring," Phil said. "Zen wrestling don't pull in the punters."

"Someone got to do it," the stranger said. He had screwy hair and toffee-coloured skin. He looked like a heavyweight to me. Usually my natural enemies are heavyweights. That's what Gruff and Pete are. But this bloke looked like he had more in his crow's nest than bird droppings. So I said, "Who're you when you're at home?"

"Keif," he said. "You?"

"Eva, the great big beaver," Phil said. "You don't want to be seen talking to her. She's crazy."

"*You're* talking to her."

"I'm bullet-proof. I'm a star. I ain't on probation with the boss like you are."

"Sod that," said Keif. "He can tell me work stuff. He can tell me when to show up and where. He can't tell me who to talk to on a public highway. He ain't God."

"He thinks he is," Phil said. "Same difference. Anyway, *I'm* telling you. She's bother. Who's been showing you the ropes this last month?"

"You have."

"So?"

"So?" said Keif.

"So you been letting a blue-bummed ape show you round the zoo," I said.

"Personal trainer!" Phil sneered. "You couldn't afford a personal piss-pot."

"A lot *you* know," I said. "I've been doing really well lately."

"See?" Phil said to Keif. "Ditzyland. Pure Ditzyland. She never had two beans to rub together. Anyway it'd take more than Harsh to get her in shape—it'd take a fucking jack hammer. And when she *was* in shape you shoulda seen the shape—God-fuckin'-zilla looked like Miss World beside her."

"Yeah?" I said.

"Yeah."

"See," I said to Keif, "some of us do a bit more than dye our hair when we want to get on in the fight game."

And with that, I trotted off. I told them, see. I got the last word in. You don't mouth off to Eva Wylie and get away with it.

But by the time I got round the next corner I was out of breath and cursing Harsh.

"Fuckin' toothbrush," I said. It was such a letdown. But then, just to prove I couldn't really lose, I saw a dented white Ford just sitting there. The driver's side door so badly aligned that I hardly had to pop the lock. It was just waiting to take me home. Well I couldn't refuse that, could I?

And I couldn't refuse a little drink when I got home either.

All right, I know I told Harsh I'd given it up—you don't have to nag at me—but it was the end of the bottle, see. Waste not, want not. And then I had a couple of tinnies. But then, beer isn't really booze, is it? Beer's as weak as gnats' piss so it doesn't count, does it? Well, does it?

But I couldn't find my toothbrush. I looked everywhere, but it'd went missing. I turned the Static upside down, and then I thought, screw it—it wasn't even bedtime, and I could buy a whole hundredweight of sodding toothbrushes before then. I could hire someone to clean my teeth for me. I could say, "Oy you, number four servant, clean my teeth and be quick about it. I got Harsh coming round for drinkies on the patio and you know what he's like about scummy gnashers—he's Pillock from Planet Prat." That's how rich people act, don't they? You don't think rich people brush their own teeth, do you? Get *over* yourself.

Chapter 6

It was just after six in the evening. The yard went dead, which reminded me it was time to lock the gate and let the dogs out. So I got up and went to the gate. It was raining and the wind sliced strips off me. I should of worn my padded coat but I couldn't find it.

I was fumbling with the chains and padlocks when I saw a little Renault Clio pulled up to the pavement opposite. I didn't take much notice 'cos I was cold and wet and I wanted to go back indoors away from the weather. But the padlock kept slipping and I couldn't seem to get the chain link into the keeper.

So when this soft voice out of the night said, "Eva, is that really you?" I dropped the keys again and said, "Fuck off. Can't you see I'm busy?"

But I shouldn't have. No. Because this was the only person in the whole wide world I really, truly wanted to see.

I said, "Fuck off, can't you see I'm busy," and she said, "Sorry, didn't mean to interrupt."

I picked the keys up and wiped the rain from my eyes.

She was stood there in a long, slick raincoat with a small umbrella to keep the rain off of her hair. The street lamp behind made it look like she had diamonds falling on her. And she was looking at me like she'd been waiting a long time. For me.

She said, "Is that really you?"

And I said, "Who?" And I sat down in the wet 'cos my legs went stringy. And my guts went thin and stringy too, 'cos I knew who it was.

I said, "Simone." And I shut my eyes and screwed my eyelids down. I knew, when I opened them, she'd be gone. I knew it was the booze seeing her—not me. Because I used to dream for years that she'd come back out of the night. Sometimes I'd dream that I'd walk into Ma's gaff and there she'd be, sitting on the sofa. I'd dream she was round the next corner, and if I could only get there quick enough, I'd see her standing, just looking into a shop window. I'd dream she was in a car, going by, and I couldn't quite see her face through the reflection in the glass.

The thing that was different, the thing that was wrong, was that when I dreamed her coming out of the night she looked like she did the last time I saw her. That was when she was twelve and I was eleven. I don't know why. I know she had to grow up like I did. But I always saw her small and pretty. Not a grown-up woman in a long, slick raincoat.

And the other thing wrong was that when I dreamed her, she was small and I was the London Lassassin. I was in my glory. Famous. Strong. Popular. I was not sitting on my duff in an oily puddle. That was not part of my dream. Shit, no.

So I opened my eyes. And there on the other side of the gate was this little pair of high-heeled shoes. And above that was Simone with diamonds falling on her umbrella.

I said, "Is it really you?"

So I let her into the yard. And I forgot to let the dogs out. For the first time in my life I forgot about the dogs.

In my dream she always said, "Eva, is that really you?" That was in the dream, and that's what she said. So I knew it was really Simone.

But the Static was a tip. I hadn't realised till she went in. And that wasn't in the dream. In the dream I had everything in place so she could see how well I was doing.

"I was looking for my toothbrush," I said.

"Never mind," she said. "Let me look at you."

So she looked at me and I looked at her. There was only torch light and lamp light, see, because I don't believe in electricity bills. So I had to look hard. And the more I looked the more I could see the old Simone. But it was queer because it was like this grown-up woman kept stepping in front of *my* Simone—now you see her, now you don't. And I kept wanting to push the grown-up woman out the way. "Clear off," I wanted to say, "you're standing in front of my sister."

She hardly came up to my chin. Well, that was okay, she was always smaller than me even though she was a year older. But her face had changed. She used to have a fairy face—great big blue eyes looking out at you from behind silky fine hair. You always saw those eyes first 'cos they were dark and the rest of her face and hair was silvery. The rest of her face was little. And when she was little, her face seemed to say, "help me." And I always did. I always looked out for her and took her with me when I bunked off.

But now there was too much colour. The silvery skin was pink on the cheeks. The pale mouth was red. The eyelids and eyelashes were black. The hair was gold. My Simone was still there but she was wearing a grown-up mask, and I couldn't see what her face was saying.

"Eva," she said, "you grew so big."

"Yeah," I said. And I turned away. I turned away because I didn't know what she was looking for in me after all these years, and I didn't think she'd like what she was seeing. They called us

40

Beauty and the Beast, even in the old days. And I wasn't at my best that night. I wanted to be in my prime like I was when I dreamed about this meeting, but I couldn't find me toothbrush.

I couldn't keep still neither. My heart was a spitball on a skillet—jumping, sizzling. There was so much I wanted to say but it all got stuck in my guts—it wouldn't come up past my gullet.

It was choking me, so I said, "How'd you find me?"

"Mother," she said.

"Who?" I said.

"Our mother," she said.

"Ma?" I couldn't understand her using the word mother for Ma.

"Yeah," she said. "I've been overseas for quite a while, and when I came back I wanted to get in touch. My other mother knew where she was—you know, sent her photos and things."

Another huge subject for conversation. I couldn't deal with it. Her other mother. Why had she let them adopt her? Why had she changed her name? One time I thought she betrayed me by doing that. But she was only a little kid then, and I don't s'pose she was given any selection, so I forgave her. Almost. I couldn't think about it.

"I'm a wrestler," I said.

"A wrestler?" she said. I couldn't see if the face behind the mask was saying "wow" or "shit."

"Din't Ma say?"

"It was as much as I could do to get your address out of her," she said. "She isn't very helpful, is she?"

"Helpful!" Something went off bang in my chest and I found myself sitting on the floor again. "I've been on at her for years," I said. "Years. Fuckin' years. I *knew* she knew where you were. But would she tell me? She'd rather stuff a hungry rat in her knickers. Don't call her mother. She ain't a mother."

41

"Oh Eva," she said. "Never mind." She handed me some tissues. "We're together now," she said.

Together, she said. It nearly crashed me. I blew my nose.

"Let's not spoil it by talking about Ma," she said. "Let's go out for a drink. Let's celebrate."

That was the right thing to say. I couldn't wait to get out of the Static, out of the yard. It all looked like a pit full of garbage now she was here. And besides I was thirsty—I needed something to steady me nerves.

She found my padded jacket. There was something sad about that—for one thing I always thought, when we found each other again, it'd be me helping her, not her sorting me out. And for another, I wish it'd been me lovely leather jacket, the one with all the biker fringes and metal I lost somewhere. That jacket made me look the business, not like I'd been made in Taiwan.

Outside the rain came like bullets that nearly took our heads off and we ran all the way up Mandala Street to the Fir Tree. It was only when we got there I remembered she had a car. But she just shook the rain out of her hair and laughed. "I was so excited I forgot," she said. "Remember how I used to be scared of storms when we were little? Remember how we used to get under the bed? You weren't scared though."

"Nah," I said. "I like thunder and lightning." I do. I did. I like a lot of banging and crashing. And in them days I liked it even more. Ma couldn't score when the weather was really filthy, and we wouldn't wake up to find some scraggy tart-raker reeling around in a string vest with a fag hanging out of his gob. Or hear those sounds we didn't want to hear. But I didn't want to think about that.

"Weren't you ever scared of anything?" she asked. "I can't remember you *ever* being scared."

And that made me feel big and strong again. Because Simone

was remembering me right. Well, nearly. 'Cos even if I was scared I'd of died before I showed it. If you showed it you got mashed. There was one kid—and this was the first time we got sent away, so we was very little—well, this one kid, he had the horrors about elastic bands. Don't ask me why—it's the weirdest thing to get the horrors about. Elastic bands, can you credit it? What's wrong with elastic bands? But this one kid, he'd just get the shakes if he even saw one through a window. And he was too thick to pretend, so all the other kids . . . Well, you get the picture. He'd find elastic bands in his pockets, in his bed, even in his dinner. When he couldn't take it no more, he ran away. But they brought him back. 'Cos it was a place of safety, see, and they always bring you back. Joke, huh?

So they brought him back and it looked like all the other kids had saved up every fuckin' elastic band they could lay their sticky paws on.

"What's the matter?" Simone said. "You've gone all grim."

"Nuffin'," I said. "I was just thinking about that kid who was scared of elastic bands. I wonder what happened to him."

"You *know* what happened to him," Simone said. "You *saw* what happened to him. He hanged himself from a coat peg in the cloakroom. We all saw. With a belt. And all the big kids laughed and said it should've been an elastic belt. But it was leather."

"Oh yeah," I said. But I couldn't remember. You'd think I'd remember a thing like that. But I never.

What I remember was going to her dormitory in the dead of night and saying, "I want to go home." And her saying, "You can't." But I made her get up and come with me. That was the first time we bunked off together. But they brought us back. It didn't stop me trying again, though. And again. And again.

I went to the bar to get the drinks in—a white wine spritzer, whatever that was, for her, a pint for me. But I knocked back a shot of dark rum while I was there—for me nerves, see, and for the cold.

"Oh Eva," she said, when I got back to the table. "You've got to tell me everything. I feel very . . ."

Very what? Very out of it? Drowning in yesterdays? Angry about the time we lost—the time they took away? Scared? No, not scared. That ain't me—I ain't never scared. But the little round table between us looked like the north pole. Like it was a million miles of ice over a million miles of deep dark water and I didn't know if I could drag her back across it to where we started. I wanted her back. Well, I had her back but it was like waving to her across the ice, waving to her across the time they took her away. I wanted her back like we was then, sharing a bed in a thunderstorm, creeping out of a back door, just us two against the world, the universe.

My tongue was a blob of foam rubber in my mouth.

"Pardon?" she said.

"Nuffin'," I said. "I'm a wrestler now. I'm the biggest and best on the circuit. I got a personal trainer and everything. You ought to come an' see me some time. I'll get you ringside seats. The promoter's a friend of mine. He'll treat you like royalty when he knows you're my sister. Nuffin's too much bother for my sister."

"I'd love to come," she said. "Of course I would. Oh Eva, don't get so excited. Of course I'll come. It's all right. It's all right, really."

" 'Course it's all right," I said. "It's just . . . it's just I made something of meself, Simone. I did."

"Of course you did," she said. "And I'm proud of you."

There. She said it. What I wanted to hear. "I'm proud of you." Just like that.

"You want another one of those whatsits?" I said, and I went back to the bar.

This time it was the landlord's missus serving. I chucked back another dark rum, and she said, "You want to watch that, Eva. You make a scene like you did last week and you're out of here. I mean it. My old man's keeping an eye on you."

"What scene?" I said. "Your old man can keep his eye on the noodles growing out your arse for all I care."

"Don't be so bleedin' lippy, Eva. I got more time for you than most round here. If I hadn't you'd of been barred months ago."

"You can't bar me," I said. "My money's as good as anyone else's."

"An' that's another thing," she said, "where . . . ?"

But I didn't want to hear her other thing. There's always another thing from those dried up old quackers, always, *always* another thing.

When I got back to the table I found my seat taken by the bloke who sells china in the market. He was putting the move on Simone. Which was no more than you'd expect, but it narked me, and I said, "Fuck off, arse-sniffer. Time for old men like you to go home to the wife."

He said, "Where didja find a sister like this, Eva?"

I said, "Hit the road, humpity back." But I was quite chuffed actually, because Simone had owned up to me. If she'd of taken after our ma she'd never of done that. Ma *never* owns up to me if she can help it.

"Men," Simone said after he'd slid away. "Always want something."

"Are you married?" I asked. I don't know where that came from. Fancy not knowing if your own sister's wed.

"Well . . ." she said, and I held my breath. I didn't want her to be wed. I did not.

"I was," she said, "but it didn't work."

That was a relief, I can tell you. I didn't want to get her back just to find out she was someone else's. She didn't ask me if I was married.

"It only lasted a couple of months," she said.

"What happened?" I said.

"Nothing," she said. "It was a mistake. I'm not cut out for keeping house."

"What are you cut out for?" It was so weird. When we was together I wouldn't of had to ask. She was cut out for something big. Everyone liked her. She could of been anything except maybe a brain surgeon—we was neither of us much good at school work.

"Well," she said, "I tried a lot of things. But it was hard, though. My other family . . ."

"What about them?"

"Take it easy, Eva," she said. "It can't be helped. You know it wasn't down to us. We were just kids. You know we had to go where we were put."

"You didn't have to get yourself adopted," I said. "You didn't have to make it fucking permanent. No one *forced* you."

"There's force and there's force."

"What's that supposed to mean?"

"Oh Eva," she said. "Don't shout. Please don't shout. I hate it when you shout."

True. She cried when she got shouted at. That's why she never got the strap half as much as me. They only had to shout and she cried.

"You didn't have to make it permanent," I said.

"They had carpets on the floor," she said. "And central heating. They gave me my own room. They wanted me. They gave me a home, Eva."

"*I* wanted you," I said. "You *had* a home."

"No," she said.

"You *did*," I said.

46

"I didn't," she said. "And nor did you. Be honest. And don't shout at me. If you shout at me I'm leaving."

"We had each other," I whispered. It had been enough for me. Why wasn't it enough for her? I didn't need fitted carpets when I had her.

"We were always in trouble, always on the run."

"But we was together. It was okay when we was together."

"Shshsh!" she said. "You were tougher than me."

"Yeah, an' who looked after you?"

"You're shouting again."

"*Not* shouting!"

"I'm leaving," she said. And she left.

Chapter 7

I couldn't believe it. One minute she was there, and then she wasn't. Blink, I had a sister. Blink, she was gone. Just like that.

I stood up.

The landlord came over. He said, "Pick that bloody chair up, Eva. You can't just waltz in here and throw the bloody furniture around."

"Tell you what," I said, "you find a dog and get dog-knotted."

I'm not quite sure what happened after that, but I found myself outside in the rain, in the gutter. Come to think of it, I'd spent a lot of the last couple of days on my arse. There was a bunch of blokes by the Fir Tree door and they was all cackling.

I got up and went home.

I couldn't believe it—she blew. Just blew without leaving no forwarding address.

I didn't shout at her. Did I shout at her? Well, maybe just a tiny rant, but that ain't shouting. What'd she want—blowing out like that?

There was no Renault Clio sitting by the kerb. It was like I'd made it all up in my head.

But I didn't. Simone *was* here. She was.

The dogs were going crazy, and I remembered I forgot them. So I let them out.

Ramses was so disgusted he took a lump out of my padded jacket. I had to keep him off with my boot or he'd of had a lump out of me too. Lineker just sneered.

"Fuck off," I said. "You don't understand. I don't know where to find her. You're just bloody hounds, you don't know what it's like."

"Herf?" said Milo.

"Shurrup," I said. "I don't want you neither." And I didn't. I didn't want no half-grown pup. I wanted Simone.

"Hip," said Milo, and Ramses took a lump out of him too.

"She's too sensitive," I said. "She always was too sensitive."

"Hip?"

"I gotta find her. She's too sensitive—she can't look out for herself."

"Hip-herf?"

"Shurrup," I said. "Stop interrupting. I *never* shouted. She just *thought* I shouted."

Milo ran away.

"Go on," I said. "You blow too. All of you. See if I care."

I was holding Ramses off with a broom handle. He had his back up and his head down. He looked mean enough to spike kittens and then start a world war for dessert.

"You want my throat," I said, prodding him back. "You always want my throat. Well, you ain't having it tonight. Hear me?"

He heard. He backed off and then lunged away, blood-hounding over to the gate. He was restless and frustrated and hungry. So was I.

I went to the Static and rummaged but I couldn't lay my hands on any food. Maybe I forgot to buy any or maybe I mislaid it when I was turning the place over looking for my toothbrush.

I sat on the bunk and wrapped the sleeping bag round my shoulders. I couldn't find *anything*—not my food, not my toothbrush, not my sister. A lesser woman would of wept.

Next thing I knew it was morning. The dogs were barking hard enough to give themselves sore throats and there were cars honking and hooting outside the gate.

It was bloody morning. And it really was a bloody morning. I penned the dogs and then opened the gate for the men. But were they grateful? They were about as grateful as school kids with homework.

"You stupid cow," the foreman said. "We've been out here yelling and hooting for half a fuckin' hour."

"I got the flu," I said. "I'm a sick woman."

"Oh you're sick all right," he said. "You been 'sick' for weeks and it's the sick you find in a bottle. You want to buck your ideas up or I'll report you."

"Report your own haemorrhoids," I said, and I went to feed the dogs.

At least *they* had some food left. But it turned my guts over, dolloping it out for them, so maybe I really did have the flu. I had the sweats too and someone was driving a nine-inch nail through my skull. I went back to bed for five minutes.

Well it seemed like five minutes. And then someone knocked on my door. Now, maybe I told you, maybe I ain't, but a knock on my door is a major event, and it usually means bother. I get visitors like a super-model gets spots, and that's hardly ever, but when it happens there's trouble.

So I pulled the sleeping bag over my head and lay doggo.

But after a while the rat-a-tat turned to whump-a-thump. I thought, Simone! She's come back to 'pologise. I went to the door and squinted through one of the spyholes.

It wasn't Simone. All I could see was a tobacco-coloured eye squinting back at me and I thought, Harsh! *He's* come back to 'pologise.

So I opened the door. But it wasn't Harsh. I didn't know who it was but he looked familiar.

"Yo," he said. "Remember me?"

"No," I said, and tried to close the door.

"Keif," he said. "Yesterday."

"What about yesterday?"

"We met yesterday. With Phil Julio. You said you was looking for a personal trainer."

"Yeah?"

"So here I am. Yours for the asking."

"Wha?"

"Shit," he said. "Do you or do you not want a sodding personal trainer? Or am I getting wet in a fuckin' junk yard for sod-all?"

"I din't ask you—I asked Harsh."

"Harsh ain't available," he said. Raindrops were sliding helter-skelter down his corkscrew hair. "Do you want what's on offer or not?"

"All right," I said. "But not today. I got flu. An' I ain't had no breakfast."

"Breakfast?" he said. "It's teatime. And you've got flu like I've got lace undies."

"Teatime?" I peered past him and, too true, it was getting dark. The men were beginning to pack up and go home. I felt queasy and I didn't have the beans to keep him out no longer so he came in.

"Well, blow in my ear and call me Mary," he said, looking around. "Have you had burglars or what?"

"Burglars?" I looked round too. I couldn't think how I'd made such a mess and not noticed. Then I remembered the

51

toothbrush. "I was looking for something," I said. But the more I looked the messier it seemed and I suddenly thought about going out with Simone to the Fir Tree. I forgot the dogs, din't I? And if the dogs weren't out protecting the yard anyone could of walked in and pinched my wad.

I rushed outside into the rain. I was in a panic. My wad was mine. I didn't want to be poor again before I'd had a chance to get used to being rich. But the dogs were all snarly from being woken up too early and there, nailed to the wall, was the Puma bag—all safe and sound. I goosed it and unzipped it just to make sure.

And then I thought, who the fuck cares if someone got in last night? If the dogs were penned up they were penned with my pennies. So I hadn't been a doodle for forgetting them, had I? I'd been smart. So suck on that. Which made me pretty mellow walking back to the Static.

"Why you always so vex?" Keif said. "I never knew a girl so scratchy."

"I ain't vex," I said, 'cos I wasn't. "If you can't take the heat . . ."

"Oh I can take the heat," he said. "Question is, can you?"

"Forged in the furnace, me," I said, 'cos I was.

"You really want to get fit?" he said. "For true?"

"Yeah," I said, "but I got—"

"Bollocks," he said, "you're hung over. Don't look at me like that—'s true."

"Fuck off."

"I didn't come all this way for you to chat me down."

"Then you can bloody go away again," I said. "Why did you come?"

"Well," he said, "I like a burly girly an' they don't come burlier than you. You got potential. 'Sides, you said you'd pay."

"Now *that* bit's for true," I said. "*That* bit I believe. You're after my wedge."

"Which d'you think I am?" Keif said. "Cheap or free?"

"I don't care what you are," I said. "I told Harsh I'd pay him. Not you."

"We been there already," he said.

"Well, I know Harsh is worth a bundle," I said. "What do I know about you?" Crafty, see—stone crafty.

"Pedigree? Okay. My dad was a boxer. When he retired he trained the youth section at the Ring O'Bells gym. You heard of that, encha?"

"S'pose so," I said. Everyone's heard of that—it's where loads of London fighters hang out.

"Well, he trained me too."

"For a boxer. Big deal."

"What d'you care what for? You want to be a wrestler?"

"I *am* a fuckin' wrestler. Who the fuck you think you're talking to?" I was really narked. "I'm the fucking *London Lassassin*."

He ducked. "Too slow," he said. "Listen, stupidy. You want to get back in the ring you got to get back to basics. Basics is what it says—like what everyone has to do—from the ground up."

"You can take your basics and shove 'em up your base," I said, "from the ground up." He backed off. "Who the fuck you think you calling 'stupidy'? I ain't stupid."

I could of mashed him against the door—I was that roiled up. But I kept remembering the rent man—I took a shot and he decked me. S'pose I took another shot at Keif and instead of dodging he decked me? S'pose that's what happened? I could of mashed him. I *should* of mashed him. But my brain got in the way.

"I got a headache," I said.

"What?" he said. "I can't hear if you don't shout."

"Deaf as well as dumb," I said. And then someone else knocked on my door. Jeez, what a day.

Keif was backed up against the door. I was going to tell him not to open it, but he opened it before I could get the words out. And a good job he did, 'cos there in her long slick raincoat was Simone again. She came back. She came back. She came back.

She said, "I came to see if you'd like a drink. I didn't know you had company."

"He ain't company," I said. "He's my personal trainer. Like I said. Remember? You din't believe me. But here he is."

"We was just going out for a run," Keif said. Can you believe the nerve of the man?

"Tomorrow," I said.

"I just wanted to say I'm sorry for walking off last night," Simone said. "I thought we could have a drink and talk."

"Yeah," I said. She was back and I was thirsty.

"Run first," said Keif.

"Cock off," I said.

" 'Cos if you don't, I'm quitting," Keif said. "I mean, it's been a long, interesting association an' all that, but I got me limits—like I only work with professionals."

"Bog-dollops!" I said.

"Oh please don't start shouting again, Eva," Simone said. "I'll wait till you get back."

"I'm gonna marmelise you," I said to Keif.

"You gotta catch me first," he said, and went jogging out my door and across the yard.

"Go on," said Simone. So I went. Oh, serious fuck.

Chapter 8

Thud-thud-thud, pound-pound-pound went my feet. And hey-diddle-diddle went my heart. I thought it was going to jump out through my ribs and lie like a dying fish flopping around under my trainers. I felt sick.

"Who's the slusher?" Keif said.

"Who . . . you . . . calling . . . a slusher?" I said. I could hardly speak I was so angry. "That's my sister you're calling down."

"That's right," Keif said. "Little more pace, little more pace—we don't want no sweet old grannies hooting to pass."

I was soaked to the skin. Rain bounced off my nose and into my eyes. My feet were bruised.

"C'mon," Keif said. "We ain't hardly done a quarter of a mile yet."

Thud-thud-thud, and then more thud.

"Get a move on," said Keif. "You want to talk big in front of your sister you'll have to do better than the forty-minute mile."

Pound-pound-pound. What do they put in training shoes these days? Lead soles?

"Pick it up," said Keif. "I seen an ox with mad cow disease run better'n you."

"I . . . hate . . . running." I couldn't breathe enough air to puff.

Thud, pound, stumble.

"Okay," said Keif. "You can walk now. You done 'bout a mile and a half. All you needed was a little encouragement."

"Call . . . that . . . encouragement?"

"Walk, I said. Don't hang off the wall. Brisk walk."

"You can brisk walk down a drain and not come up."

"Atta girl!" said Keif. "Now you know what a marvel I am, what's the wages?"

I told him what the wages were and where he could stick them. But while he was laughing I thought, oh shit, now Simone's met him so I'll have to keep him. At least for a week. I wished she could of met Harsh. With Harsh as my personal trainer she would of taken me more serious. What the pooping hell would she make of this joker? Could anyone look up to me with a personal trainer like Keif?

So we haggled and the rain came down. And I didn't know what was rain and what was sweat but it didn't matter 'cos whatever it was I was drenched through to the marrow.

In the end, he said, "Okay, man, safe." And we was agreed. Spit on my hand and call me a berk if you like, but I told Simone about a personal trainer and he was the nearest thing on sale.

But when we got back to the Static Simone was gone.

"She don't hang about, your sister," Keif said, "but at least she cleared up."

She had. The Static was all neat and tidy, but I was so gut-whacked that she hadn't waited I went and locked myself in the bathroom cubicle where Keif couldn't see me. I'd went to all the trouble of hiring me a personal trainer and she couldn't stop around long enough to 'preciate it.

I washed in cold water 'cos I'd forgot to put any on to heat, and the water was as cold as my heart.

Still, when I got out Keif had found a couple of teabags and boiled some water.

"No milk," he said.

"Milk's for wimps," I said.

"No food," he said. "That for wimps too? You get out of your body what you put in. What do you eat? Chain saws? Battery acid?"

"Personal trainers," I said. I was thinking of dropping him off the payroll now Simone wasn't there.

"Serious, man," he said. "What's the plan? You get fit—is Mr. Deeds gonna let you back in?"

"Mr. Dirty Deeds ain't the only game in town."

"You got other connections?"

"I could go up North. They take wrestling more serious up North."

"Ever thought of the novelty circuit? Gladiators? Oil? Mud?"

"That ain't fighting," I said. "That's show biz."

"Sport *is* show biz," he said. "Fighting's show biz. Boxing's show biz. Ever thought of boxing? You got the physique for it."

"Nah," I said. Boxers just stand there and hit each other. They don't throw each other around and get down dirty on the mat. I like getting down on the mat. I like the pins and moves where weight and speed count. I'm good at it.

But I didn't say anything. I was too low-down blue. Mr. Deeds wouldn't let me back in, and anyway, if he did what's the point? My sister couldn't even stop around while I went out on a training run. I'd been searching for her, hoping for her, wanting her for years, but when I found her she didn't want to stick with me like I wanted to stick with her. She couldn't wait five minutes. She just upped and left me with a joke personal trainer.

"What's up?" said Keif.

"Nothing's fucking up," I said. "I need a drink."

"Finish yer tea."

"Stuff yer tea."

"My arse ain't a satchel," he said. "All what you told me to stuff this evening wouldn't fit into a warehouse."

"Listen, satchel bum," I said, "you ain't my gaoler—get off my case."

"Safe," he said, getting up. "Stew in it."

See? He didn't give a toss neither. And I was *paying* him.

At which point Simone walked back into the Static.

"Where you *been?*" I said.

"Just down the shops," she said. "I saw you didn't have anything to eat. Don't yell. You didn't think I wouldn't wait, did you?"

I should never of doubted her. She unloaded a carrier bag, and pulled out a lovely big bottle of Jamaican rum. Now that's what I call a sister.

Keif said, "You really Eva's sister—same mother, same father?"

"Same mother."

"Fer true? Her well-being your well-being an' all that?"

"Yeah."

"Well then," Keif said, "you won't object if I carry this away." And he picked up the lovely big bottle of Jamaican rum and walked out with it.

"Oy!" I yelled.

We both ran out after him but by the time we got to the door he'd vanished into the rain.

"The cheek of it!" Simone said.

I was so narked I could hardly utter.

"Did you see what he did?" Simone said. "Did you *see*? Who does he think he is?"

"Keif," I said. "He's my—"

"Personal trainer. You told me. You let him treat you like that? I'm surprised at you, Eva. You used to be able to stick up for yourself."

Ouch. I said, "Well, he's . . ."

"I mean, can't you get someone better than him?" Which gave me a problem. I couldn't talk Keif down like I wanted to 'cos then Simone'd think I couldn't afford anyone better. So I said, "Well he's very good on basic fitness and that sort of thing. I been sick recently."

"Yeah, but Eva, a black guy with no manners—or is he your boyfriend?"

"*Shit*, Simone . . ."

"Because, otherwise, why would you let him dictate to you like that?"

"I *ain't* letting him dictate," I yelled. "And 'sides, I'm thinking of letting him go."

"I should bloody well think so," Simone said. "And don't shout."

"But he *ain't* my boyfriend. He *ain't*."

"So you might fancy him or something."

"I ain't *got* a boyfriend. I ain't *interested*."

"All right, all right," said Simone. "I didn't mean you couldn't have one if you wanted one."

"I *told* you," I said. "I ain't interested."

"Don't get so worked up," Simone said. "You're better off without, believe me. It's just I couldn't stand to see that guy treat you so mean—walking off with your rum—the cheek of it."

See? She did care. She really did. She was looking out for me just like I always looked out for her.

"I bought you a toothbrush," she said. "You couldn't find yours."

I was so melted she'd remembered, I went straight off to the cubicle and scrubbed my teeth. My mouth felt cool and my teeth felt slippery. And then I noticed that the muscles in my calves and thighs felt warm and burny. So I thought, I *can* get it all back—if I work I can get hard again. If I had Simone behind me, Simone to watch me, I could do it all—be the London Lassassin again. There wasn't nothing I couldn't do if I could do it for her. I wouldn't mind the pain at all.

When I got out of the cubicle she was there, leaning her back against the counter looking at an old poster—a Deeds Promotion poster with my name on it. All the old names were on it—Harsh, Gruff, Pete, Phil and his dad—and it gave me quite a turn to see it. I don't know where she found it 'cos I thought I got rid of everything that reminded me.

I said, "Yeah, well, it's hard coming back from injury."

"I thought you said you'd been sick," she said.

"As well," I said. I didn't want to tell her what really happened.

"See, it's rough in the ring," I mumbled. "I done me back in. I got the flu later."

"Oh," she said. "Bad luck."

"Yeah," I said. "Athletes is finely tuned animals. Put your back out of whack and it can take forever healing."

"So that's why you need a personal trainer," she said. "You must've been doing really well at the wrestling if you can afford one of those."

"Top of the tree, me."

"Then why's your name at the bottom of the poster?"

"Old poster," I said. "Before I reached me full potential."

60

I wished she'd talk about something else.

"Come on," she said, like she could read my mind. "Let's go out. That idiot stole our rum so there's nothing to stay in for."

So we went out. Only this time I remembered the dogs. Simone quite liked Milo but I could see she was shit scared of Ramses and Lineker so I put her outside the gate before I let them out.

They could smell a stranger so they piled out of their pen and chased over to the gate to see her.

"Shut up," I yelled, trotting behind them. "That's my sister. She's okay."

I wanted her to stand up close to the gate so they could get a proper whiff of her and know she was welcome. But she didn't want to get too near.

It was Ramses really—some dogs have a nose for blood, some dogs can sniff out dope, some are ace with explosives—but give Ramses a tiny whiff of fear and he'll suck your veins out through your belly button. I told you Simone was too sensitive. It made Ramses want to take advantage.

"They're awfully big dogs," she said as we walked away.

"They're proper bastards," I told her proudly. "I trained them myself."

We didn't go to the Fir Tree. I couldn't remember exactly what happened last night but I could remember the landlord hadn't been polite.

"Not fit to be a publican," I said as we went past and turned left on the main road.

"Pardon?"

"Nothing. I'm starving. I ain't eaten all day and me blood sugar's taken a nose dive." As a matter of fact I suddenly couldn't remember when I ate last. Not at all.

"Simone," I said.

"What?"

"Nothing," I said. I was going to tell her I couldn't remember when I ate last, but I thought I better not. What if she thought I was a nutter? What if she didn't want a nutter for a sister?

We went into the Cat and Cowbell and I ordered a meat pie and chips to go with the beer. Simone had another of those white wine things.

"What?" said Simone.

"That drink," I said. "It's piss elegant, ennit?"

"Is it?" she said. "What you said about blood sugar . . ."

"What?"

"Well, you know an awful lot about fitness and things."

"'Course I do."

"We could go into business together," she said.

Together. She used that word again. It made me glow.

"How?" I said.

"I don't know," she said. "Open a fitness centre. You know all about whatsit, um, training, and I could manage it—look after the glamour end. You know, sunbeds and leotards."

That was a stunner. In business together. It meant she did want me around. She could see our future and it was together.

"Yeah," I said, gulping my beer. "Why not? When I retire I'll be the most famous fighter ever—we could call the place The Lassassin . . ."

"When you retire?"

"From the ring." I was eating meat pie like there was no tomorrow. How can you be that hungry without knowing? "Simone," I said, "I want to be the most famous fighter there ever was. Famouser than Haystacks, Klondyke Kate, Kendo Nagasaki. I can do it. I know I can . . ."

"Shshsh," she said, "everyone's staring."

"Let them stare," I said, "that's what being famous is all about." I turned to look at everyone who was staring at me and, oh choke on your chips, there was The Enemy. The Enemy looked at me just at the same second I looked at her so I couldn't pretend I ain't seen her.

"What?" said Simone.

"Bugger," I said. "Someone I know. Bloody politzei."

"What?" she said. "Police? Shit."

"No worries," I said. "Ex-politzei." But when I looked over again I saw that The Enemy was with Mr. Schiller and a geezer I didn't know. Well, I didn't know who he was but if I didn't know *what* he was you could fold me up, stick me in an envelope and post me to Rio.

"Scrub that," I said, "ex-politzei at the trough with real politzei."

"Let's go," Simone said. "I'm still allergic."

See, whatever else changes there's one thing never changes— it's like the colour of your eyes—you're born with it and you go to the grave with it—and that's what you think about the Law. It made me feel homey. Simone, for all her white wine thingies and fancy-speak, was still my sister.

"Finish your drink," I said, "they ain't got nothing on me." I went on shovelling meat pie into my gob and washing it down with bitter. All the same, I wanted to leave 'cos I didn't want Simone to know I'd been working for Lee-Schiller. That was a real come-down for someone like me, and I wouldn't of done it except I was on my uppers. But I didn't want Simone to know that neither.

But Simone had ants in her bloomers and she wanted to go before I'd finished my pint. Trouble was, we had to walk past politzei on our way out, and The Enemy turned round, all teeth and tits, saying, "Hello, Eva. I didn't know this was your pub."

"It ain't," I said. "Wouldn't be seen dead in here. It stinks of pork."

"Don't be so bleeding rude," she said. "I've told you a million times . . ."

"You can tell a pig by the company it keeps."

"Oh act your age, Eva," she said. "I didn't know you knew Sergeant Chapman."

"I don't," I said. "But I could smell him from across the room." I was getting a glow on—I could tell she was annoyed 'cos her jaw went rigid.

"Come on!" Simone hissed in my ear.

"I just wanted to say—no hard feelings," The Enemy said, looking at Simone, "and don't accept any three-pound notes if you happen to do any cash jobs for anyone round here."

"I wouldn't work for anyone in here," I said, "not if I was living in a cardboard box."

"Okay, okay," she said, grinding her teeth. "Only some funny money's started appearing on the patch, so be warned."

I swung away. I said, "Simone? Have I got dribble on my chin? Do I look like a retard baby?"

"No," she said. "Eva . . ."

"Simone?" The Enemy said. "Is this *the* Simone? Your Simone?"

"What of it?" I said. "Who's business is it if she is?" But I wanted to tell her. I was so proud I said, "Some of us get what we want in spite of all the blibbers trying to bring us down."

Suddenly Simone slipped her hand through my arm and said, "Look, Ms. . . . ?"

"Lee."

"Ms. Lee. It's been lovely meeting you, but I'm afraid we have to rush off to another appointment." And she turned me round and we sort of sailed out of the Cat and Cowbell.

I was so impressed I kept saying in my head, "Hey, we gotta rush off to another appointment. Another appointment." It made us sound so fancy-pants-important. I felt brilliant walking out onto the wet street with Simone's hand tucked in the crook of my arm.

"You are the business," I said. "You're fucking incredible."

"Don't you *ever* do that again," she said, snatching her hand away.

"What?" I felt like she slapped me. "What I done?"

"Don't you ever make a scene in front of the cops again," she said. "Don't you *ever* talk about me to a copper again."

"I never," I said.

"What do you call *that*, when it's at home?" she said. "You were drawing attention to us."

"I never," I said. "It's that Anna Lee—she's got her conk in everyone's business . . ."

"I don't care who she is," Simone said, backing away. "You shout and yell and insult everyone and it's like waving a flag and saying, 'I'm a wrong'un, I'm a bad'un, come and take me on.' And I don't want to be around when you're doing that 'cos it's like you're tarring me with your mucky brush too."

"I *ain't*."

"You're yelling *now*," she said. "I came to see you 'cos I thought maybe we could get together, maybe we could do something together. But you ain't changed. I thought maybe you might've changed. But you haven't."

"I *have* changed," I said. "I'm the London Lassassin. I'm famous. I got me name on posters."

But she walked away. I ran after her.

"Simone!" I said. "What do you want? I'll do anything you want."

"Yeah?"

"Yeah."

"Then stand there and count to a hundred," she said. "I'm going home."

"Wha?"

"Stand still and count," she said. "Or I'll not come back."

"But why?" I said. "*Why*, Simone?"

"'Cos it'll stop you chasing me and shouting," she said. "If you can do that I might come back. Might."

Chapter 9

Have you ever done that? Stood like sponge cake in the rain, sopping up everything the night dumps on you, counting? Just counting. And did you ever get past forty?

I kept getting screwed up around thirty-seven. I must of got to thirty-six or -seven a hundred times, but Simone didn't come back.

Then I thought, maybe she didn't mean she'd come *straight* back, maybe she meant she'd come back tomorrow. So I stood there dithering a little longer. I mean, what if she *was* coming straight back, and I wasn't there? What'd she think then?

But it's a long time to stand still doing bugger-all but counting, so in the end I went home. And I thought, it's all down to that pile of cow-flop, The Enemy. If she hadn't of been there and mouthed off about Simone everything would of been all right. Simone and I would of sat there all comfy-cosy and made plans about the fitness centre. Instead I was going home alone and I didn't even know where Simone was staying.

It's a good thing The Enemy didn't come out and see me. If she had it would of been curtains for her. I'd of strung her up by the tits and left her swinging for the crows. It was all her fault.

So I trudged home all cold and wet. My legs were aching from the running and I didn't know what to think. It was like the light went out every time Simone left. I had to make her stay. Whatever it took, I'd do it just to keep the light on in my head. But I didn't know what it took. I felt knitted and knotted. Till I got home.

I knew what to think when I got back to the yard. I was twenty yards from the gate when I met Milo trotting towards me.

"Milo!" I said. "What the fuck you doing out?"

"Herf," he said, like nothing was wrong. But it was. It had to be if Milo was out on the street instead of in the yard.

"Heel!" I said.

"Hip," he said, falling in behind me like he was taught.

"And shurrup!" I said, swiping at his snout.

The gate was swung wide open. The chain was lopped in two pieces. I could see that much by the street lamp. The yard was dark.

My torch should of been in my hand. But it wasn't. It was inside the Static. Usually I carry it with me everywhere. It's a dirty great heavy thing—a good cosh. But you don't take a cosh for a cosy-comfy drink with your sister, do you?

I walked into the dark yard. I stopped and listened. Nothing. I don't like it when it's quiet.

"Ramses!" I yelled. "Lineker!" If Milo was out on the street, where were they? I didn't want to cross the yard to the Static without them. There are too many heaps of bent metal, too many machines, too many hidey-holes.

And then I heard them—a low throaty snarl from Ramses and a sharp "Yak-yak" from Lineker.

"Here!" I yelled. "Ramses! Here!"

But they didn't come.

"Shit," I said. "Okay, Milo, it's you and me kiddo." Because

even though he's not much more than a whelp he's got good
ears and a nose to sniff out trouble. At least he could warn me.

"Come, Milo," I said. "Home."

"Herf," he said, and trotted off towards the dog pen.

"Not *your* home, stupid," I said.

He flattened his ears and trotted on. I was on me own.

"Fuck," I said, and I set off running, keeping low, sprinting
for the Static.

No one jumped out at me. No one stopped me. I reached
the Static, grabbed the tyre-iron I keep by the steps and burst
in through the door.

"*On your knees, scum*," I shouted, 'cos there's an advantage to
going in loud. But no one did doodle. And that's because there
was no one there to do doodle.

I snatched up my torch and switched it on. Then I searched.
There was no one in the kitchenette, no one in the shower-stall
or bedroom. No one there at all. And as far as I could see no
one had come inside.

"Okay," I said. "Where the fuck are you?"

I went outside, torch in one hand, tyre-iron in the other. All
I could hear was the dogs going ape over the other side of the
yard. But first I went to the dog pen.

Milo was outside looking wet and pitiful like he wanted to
get in and go to bed. I pushed him out the way. I was narked
with him.

"Stay!" I said. But when I went into the shed he followed me.

The Puma bag was still nailed to the wall. It was still full. I
let my breath out with a big hiss.

"Safe," I said. Keeping hold of your stash is hair-raising
work.

"Hip?" said Milo.

"Hip yourself," I said. I wasn't quite so narked now. But I
pulled Milo out of the shed and made him come with me. He

didn't want to, but I made him. I couldn't let him bunk off the action.

There was action. I could hear it. That creepy *rrr-argh* from Ramses said there was something going down.

At first I thought him and Lineker had someone trapped in one of the dead motors. But as I got closer I thought they'd killed him. They had something down on the ground and they were worrying the life out of it.

Let 'em, I thought—that'll teach the bugger. But then I thought, no, that'll bring the shite on my head for sure. It ain't fair, but the Law puts your dogs down if they kill or maim anyone. Even if it's his fault and they're only doing their job. You'd think a person could protect her stuff any old way, wouldn't you? You would if you had a single brain in your head. But you'd be wrong. 'Cos the Law ain't got a single brain in its head and what the Law says goes. There's natural justice and then there's the Law and, believe, the two don't even shake hands.

So I said, "Ramses, Lineker, back off." And then I shouted it, 'cos this really was the dogs' day for doing their own thing and they weren't listening.

"Stop," I yelled. "*Sit.*" And in the end they did as they was told.

Then I went forward and saw that what they was tearing at wasn't human. It was an empty padded anorak. I was quite disappointed—all me nerves going jingle-jangle for sod-all.

The bugger who'd cut my chain and broke in had been chased off and left his coat behind. He had to leave his coat—it was either that or leave his arm. The coat arm had a tattered gash right through it and the edges were stained red.

First off, I sat the dogs down and checked them out to make sure it wasn't their blood. I don't know why I bothered. None of them dogs would've won a medal for obedience that night. They were pissing me off, and that's a fact.

"You're really pissing me off," I said to Ramses, because if there's a ringleader it's him. And I clouted him to make him sit still. "You want to go back to basic training? You want that, eh?"

"Rragh!" he went, giving me the eye.

"Shurrup when I'm talking," I said. "You think you're the boss. You ain't."

His lip went up. He gave me a look at his teeth.

"R-r-r-r," he said. He was stone out of order. Lineker and Milo sat there watching. They were all wired up too. If they'd of been people they'd of been on the edge of their seats.

I tried to stare Ramses down. I couldn't lose a fight with him in front of Milo and Lineker. But Ramses kept his evil little eyes on mine. And I suddenly knew he felt the same way. He'd beaten one human already that night. He'd tasted blood. It was his night. And he wanted to prove, now and forever, that he was top dog.

"Yeah, you bastard," I snarled back at him. "You want a fight? I'll give you a fight. I want one too."

True. Absolutely fuckin' true. I did want a fight. I'd had it up to my eyeballs not knowing which way was up.

We stood there facing up to each other. He was just waiting for me to back off or turn away or drop my guard. But I didn't. Neither one of us backed off.

"Chickenshit," I said.

"R-r-r-r-ro!" he said.

"All mouth," I said. "Where's the muscle?"

When he came at me he came straight for my throat—half a ton of flying dog. But I was ready for him. I dodged and knocked him out of the air with me torch. I didn't have time to think. He was up and charging again almost before he hit the ground. He was much too quick.

I dodged again.

"Wow!" said Milo, 'cos I trod on him. The stupid fuckin' pup caught himself in my ankles, and I went arse over topside.

Sometimes it's the accident which saves you. As I toppled, Ramses missed his aim. When I landed on my back my legs flew up and hit him in the chest as he went by. The kick turned him over in mid-air. He didn't land on his feet. He went down and that gave me the split second I needed to fling myself sideways and grab for his choke-chain. I caught it under his chin and I caught some of his wattle too. First he pulled away, squirming low on the ground, dragging me a couple of yards through the mud. He was twisting his neck trying to find the angle so that he could get his jaws round my wrist. It was like catching a shark—all that raw muscle writhing on the end of my arm.

Then he changed tactics and came in on me. But I was ready for him. It was exactly what he used to do when he first met me, when I was training him—he'd pull away with all his strength and then, with no warning, lunge in.

I clenched my fist round his choke-chain and locked my elbow straight so that he ran onto my fist. I didn't give an inch.

Then it was my turn to start twisting. I kept an iron grip on his chain and his throat and rotated my arm from the shoulder. I had to roll over, but with each twist his head sank lower and lower. It took every ounce of my strength but in the end his head was down on the ground and all he could do was lie on his side.

I still had to be very very careful. If I gave him even the tiniest chance he'd be chewing on my windpipe like it was macaroni cheese. Ramses is a bitchin' bastard dog. As dogs go he's as bad as they get. That's why he's so brilliant at his job.

It's a good thing I've got a wrist like a riveter's 'cos he hadn't given up yet. He was just waiting. He could read every twitch of my grip the way I could read every twitch of him. He knew and

I knew I couldn't hold him down forever, lying flat in the mud, just by the strength of one outstretched arm. He knew and I knew I'd have to come in close to finish the job. His horrible glittering eye told me everything he was thinking. He didn't blink once.

I inched in, keeping the strangle lock on, holding his head down. And then, just as my wrist was giving up, I heaved one knee over him, reared up and sat astride. Now I could use both hands and all me weight. I had him. I had him good.

All I had to do now was wait for him to agree with me. I didn't have to hit him or nothing—that's just stupid 'cos it doesn't work. The point is he'd got to agree with me that I'm bigger and better than him. He's got to agree that I'm the boss and that I got him good.

If he was another wrestler he'd of whacked the mat. The ref would of counted a submission against him. If he'd been one of my regular opponents like the poxy Blonde Bombshell or Olga from the Volga he'd of done it in two seconds flat. But Ramses ain't them, I'm glad to say. Ramses ain't no wimp.

So we waited in the rain and mud. Both of us wet through. Both of us cold and caked with oily grunge.

And in the end he agreed. How could I tell? Well, I dunno, really. He ain't a person. But I know him and I knew it was time. So I sat up and got off of him.

As soon as I got off of Ramses, Lineker ran away. Ramses got up. He gave himself a good shake. He sprayed mud and water all over me but I said nothing. He didn't even look at me. But with no warning at all he attacked Milo. Milo should of ran away too but he didn't have Lineker's experience.

Ramses charged him, bowled him over, picked him up by the neck, slammed him down and stood over him pinning him by the throat. And I said nothing.

What did Milo do? Well he did the only sensible thing a

pup can do—he lay with his paws in the air and cried. I suppose the very same thing's true of kids everywhere, whatever sort of animal you are. If you're a kid and you're really truly up against it all you can do is wave your paws in the air and cry. That's life. I'm glad I'm not a kid no more.

And I said nothing 'cos, even though Ramses is only a beast and not a person, he's got his pride and he's got to prove himself against the next one down from him.

So I let him. It didn't last long 'cos as I say, even if Milo didn't have the brains to leg it like Lineker, he did have the brains to wimp out real quick.

Ramses gave me one snappy look. "That's you next time," said his nasty little eyes. And he gave himself another great shake and stalked off about his own business.

"Get up and shut up," I said to Milo. "You ain't hurt." But it looked as if Ramses had thrown Milo's pelvis out of whack again. He was gimpy and shivery. So I picked up the anorak with the torn sleeve and wrapped it round him.

I carried him to the Static. Milo was having a rough time lately, and I wasn't feeling too hot myself.

I lit a couple of paraffin heaters and set some water on the hob. Milo didn't give a hip or a herf so I rubbed him down and he went to sleep next to the stove. I wished I could do the same. I wished I could go and buy me a big bottle of something warming and finish the fool day. But I couldn't, could I?

Someone broke into my yard, lopped my chain and got savaged by my dogs. I couldn't bunk off.

I washed the mud away and put on dry clothes. I needed a bit of a think and I couldn't do it in sopping duds.

See, it was the dosh, wasn't it? It was those silky zillions. It had to be. Stands to reason, don't it? I mean, what twat would risk losing his arm to Ramses for engine parts and car stereos?

I was thinking and thinking, but the only people I could

think of, who knew about the Puma bag and what was in it, was the people I lifted it off. And they wasn't the sort of people I wanted to meet on a dark night with only a torch in my mitt.

They fired a freaking gun at me. You ain't forgot about *that*, have you? I ain't. And all for borrowing their scuzzy car.

I mean, it wasn't as if I knew about the zillions at the time. If I didn't know about the zillions you can't exactly accuse me of thieving them. You can't *steal* a thing if you don't know it's there, can you? I was just borrowing a car. The zillions was a bonus— a reward for all my years of effort.

So those zillions was the only thing worth losing body parts for. Am I right? I know I'm right.

Next. Well, the guys I borrowed the motor from was villains. Right? Because, one—they was robbing the petrol station, and two—now they was trying to rob me. So that's right too.

But if they got zillions in a Puma bag in the back of their motor, why was they robbing a petrol station? Answer—they was greedy, that's why. Some people never got enough. They always want more. True. Absolutely fuckin' true. I mean, do you know anyone in the whole wide world who doesn't want more than she's got? *He's* got, I mean. These villains was blokes. I know 'cos I saw 'em.

And they was clever bastards. That stands to reason too. 'Cos they didn't get caught for robbing the petrol station when most people do. I know they didn't get caught 'cos if they got caught they wouldn't be out, free to break into my yard, would they?

So I got clever bastards with shooters trying to rob me. That's serious shit.

The other serious shit was—how did they know it was me? Go on—you're so clever—tell me how they knew it was me? I didn't know them from a poke in the eye with a dead turkey, so how did they know me and where to find me?

Well, I thought and thought about that one. But the answer was staring me in the face. They knew me 'cos I was famous. I was the London Lassassin, right? They saw me fight. Hundreds of people, *thousands*, saw me fight. So I'm famous. And famous people can't protect their privacy. Famous people is public property. Fact of life. One minute everyone wants your autograph and the next minute they're coming after you with a sawn-off shooter. That's the price you gotta pay.

Chapter 10

I dreamt I was the owner of a fitness centre called Muscle-bound. I was in this poncy reception room and the customers were coming in. Simone said, "You got to pay in gold coin." I really liked the idea 'cos gold is valuable, more valuable than paper money and small change. So all the customers dug in their pockets and came out with lovely gold coins the size of those chocolate pennies kids get at Christmas.

The only trouble was we didn't have a till to put them in. So I had to eat them to keep them safe. But they was gold not chocolate and I couldn't swallow them down. So Simone gave me a plateful of tiny little burger buns—just the right size. And I thought, how dainty, ain't that just like Simone? And we put gold coins in the burger buns with lettuce and tomato, and that way I could just about choke them down. Every time I swallowed a gold coin, my teeth went chunk-chink, like a cash register. So Simone knew I'd eaten it and not cheated by putting it in my pocket. I didn't feel very well.

Stupid dream, huh? Yeah, and that's the thing about dreams—you aren't in charge of what goes on in them. You ain't, I ain't, even the Queen of England doesn't get a say about what happens when she's asleep.

Dreams make me sick. Well that one did. Just as I was choking down the last gold coin I woke up coughing and choking. Real coughs, not dream coughs. Me eyes was watering and me nose was dripping real snot.

See what I mean? Thinking gave me a headache, and it worried the life out of me so I went to bed all snarled up. And then that poxy stupid dream did the rest. Take a tip from me—if you want an easy healthy life, don't think and avoid dreams.

And then there was Keif. He came knocking on my door. Which made Milo jump up and go hip-herf, so Keif knew someone was in.

"Hey, sweetness," he said, when I opened the door.

"Who you calling 'sweetness'?" I said, and I sneezed all over him. "No one said you could call me that."

"Well," he said, "thought I'd try a little honey on you."

"Thought wrong," I said. "Save it for someone who gives a bollock." And I sneezed on him again. Milo ran outside to have a piss on the doorstep and I was glad to see he wasn't limping no more.

"I ain't running," I said. "I told you I was sick yesterday but would you believe me? You probably killed me, making me run bleeding miles."

"Kill you?" he said. "Am I a sixteen-wheel rig? *Am* I, girl? If I ain't I didn't kill you. 'Cos that's what it'd take."

I don't know why that made me laugh. It wasn't funny but it made me laugh and cough and sneeze.

"Go back to bed," Keif said. "I'll get you something fer that sickness." And off he went.

Oh yeah, I thought, I'm too sick for training so the joker can't cut another slice off my wedge, so he blows and leaves a sick woman all by herself. Typical.

I called Milo in and while I was waiting for him I noticed that some of the blokes in the yard were staring.

"What you gawping at?" I yelled.

"Got a boyfriend at last?" the foreman yelled back.

"Got bread puddin' for brains?" I shouted. I was stone narked. "That's my personal trainer, in case it's any of your business."

"Can't be her boyfriend," said another of the dildos. "He ain't got a white stick or a guide dog." And all the dildos laughed. But I didn't. I gave 'em the finger and slammed the door on the lot of them. Dirty bastards.

Why is everyone chatting back at me all of a sudden? Have I got the word "gravy" tattooed on my forehead? Maybe they can all smell it like chicken vindaloo wafting out of the Static.

All I could smell was a noseful of snot. So I went back to bed. With a couple more hours of kip maybe I'd feel fit enough to drag myself out for some medicine.

I dunno how long I dozed but I just lay there feeling shivery and gibbery and achy. And then Keif came back.

He didn't even knock. He just breezed in, saying, "Hey, Babyface. Doin'?"

"Don't you fuckin' walk in here without knocking," I said. "This ain't *your* drum."

"Brought Cousin Carmen," he said.

"She can bugger off too," I said. And then I shut up. I didn't say another dicky-bird 'cos I saw Cousin Carmen. Cousin Carmen was a tiny little woman in a big coat. You could pick her up in one hand and put her in a cupboard—she was so small.

But she had the eye.

I seen that eye before. It's like a white-wall tyre.

In chokey, once, I knew a woman called Ella Mae. No one roomed with her even though she had one of the corner units with two windows and two bunks. No one dared, and even the screws knew about the eye and they never said a word to her.

'Cos this is an eye that sees round corners. It can see through brick walls. It ain't an eye you disrespect.

They told me there was this other woman—she was three months pregnant when they banged her up and she got special privileges. They say it went to her head and she queened it over everyone including Ella Mae. They say she pushed in front of Ella Mae in the dinner queue three times running. After the third time she started to get sick. And then she started vomiting, but she didn't apologise to Ella Mae. And they say she vomited so hard that the baby came out through her mouth and that's how she lost it. They say there was blood everywhere, even coming out of her nose. She didn't die or nothing. Ella Mae didn't kill her. But she lost the baby and she was never the same after.

That's what they told me in chokey and I took one look at Ella Mae's eye and I believed.

They said Ella Mae was an obeah lady, and you don't disrespect obeah ladies unless you want to be awfully sorry. Well, Cousin Carmen had the very same eye.

So that's who Keif brought into my Static, and that's why I kept my trap shut and didn't kick him out even though he came in without knocking.

Milo went, "Hip-hip," and jumped off the bunk.

"She only got a dog to keep her warm," said Cousin Carmen. "Light the stove, boy. Why you got no light in here? Why you got boards in your windows?"

"No glass," I croaked. "Someone broke 'em. I din't have no money to fix them."

"Humph," said Cousin Carmen. "Why you pay my boy to put muscle on an' you don't pay for glass?"

I couldn't answer. I was so used to having no glass in my windows, it didn't bother me.

"Humph," said Cousin Carmen. "No light. No air. No wonder you sick."

"It ain't that," I said. "I had a dream."

"What dream?" she said.

So I told her. It was that eye, see. You think I go around telling people the fool things that happen in my sleep? You think I'm stupid? Well, I ain't. But when an obeah lady says, "What dream?" you don't think twice. All right?

"A fitness centre called Musclebound," Keif said. "Not bad. Not good but not bad."

"Wasn't talking to you," I said. I was really narked he heard.

"It ain't a dream about no fitness centre," Cousin Carmen said. "She dream she choke on gold. She wake up sick. Mebbe she wiser asleep than awake."

"Not hard," Keif said. "She poisoned herself. She stoatious all the time."

"*Ain't*," I said.

"You listen to me," Cousin Carmen said. "No more shouting loud. I gwan do something for you. You got medsin, boy?"

"I got it," Keif said.

"Heat it up," she said. "No boilin', mind. Heat slow like fe baby milk."

Talk about poison! The medicine was greeny and it had scum on top. It was sweetish like she'd put a spoonful of honey in it to hide the taste of pond slime.

"Drink it down," said Cousin Carmen. "All."

"All?" I could see Keif laughing and I didn't like it.

"All," said Cousin Carmen, and she fixed her obeah eye on me.

So I drank it down while she watched, and it was all I could do to stop myself retching. Then she smiled and her face cracked into tiny splinters. She only had two teeth.

"You tek me home now, boy," she said. And they blew out

the same way they blew in—no hellos, good-byes or by your leaves. No nothing. Blow in. Feed me poxious fluids. Blow out. If Keif had the nerve to come round again I'd marmelise him. On second thoughts, though, maybe I better not. If Keif was Cousin Carmen's Cousin Keif, she might not take too kindly to me mangling him. And I didn't want to do the smallest thing to ruffle Cousin Carmen. No way.

But I did have a little mind-movie where I head-butted Keif and he crumpled up like yesterday's paper—except that the taste in my mouth was so foul I couldn't enjoy it.

I'd just made up my mind to go and use that brand new toothbrush Simone bought me when I crashed—zonk—and went to sleep with green swamp and rat droppings on my tongue.

The next thing that happened was that I woke up and pissed pints. Gallons. I dunno what that stuff was Cousin Carmen gave me but it greased the old plumbing like you wouldn't believe. Pints, gallons, *rivers*. But I wasn't sneezing no more.

I ain't a superstitious person, but I do believe there's things those obeah ladies know which nobody else knows and if you stay on the sunny side of them you'll be all right. There's always a sting in the tail though—it's like making a pact with the devil. So, maybe I wasn't coughing and sneezing no more, but I was pissing pints and feeling as wobbly as a raw egg on a china plate.

Which is why I was sitting in front of the paraffin stove holding on to my knees when Simone came. The yard was empty and quiet and I should of let the dogs out except I was waiting for my legs.

"Eva," Simone said, "what's the matter?"

"Nothing," I said.

"Aren't you well?"

"I told you," I said. Because it's true—I been telling everyone that I had the flu but no one believed me. Well, Simone might have but that's because she's my sister. Everyone else always wants to believe the worst of you.

I was so pleased to see her the strength came back in my legs and I got up.

She said, "What's the matter? You look different."

I don't have no mirrors in the Static so I couldn't see what she was talking about.

I said, "I been thinking."

"What about?"

"What you said. Going into business together. We could call the fitness centre 'Musclebound.'"

"That's a good name," she said.

"And I been thinking—I don't want to shout no more. I just want us to be together. I don't want to stand in the rain and count to a hundred."

"Oh Eva," she said. "I didn't mean it. It's just I get so upset when people shout."

"Wasn't shouting at you."

"I know," she said. "I know."

And she did know.

"Listen," she said, "let's go out for a meal. You know, Eva, I don't understand how you can live in this place. I can't wait to get you out to somewhere decent."

She cared about me. She really did.

"I can't go out tonight," I said.

"Why?"

"Someone broke in last night. I got to stop in and take care of business."

"Who?" she said, all startled.

"Dunno," I said. "It was while we was at the Cat and Cowbell. I didn't see who. The dogs got him."

"Oh God," she said. "This is a bad place in a bad area. You've got to find something else. Fast. Was anything stolen?"

"I can look after meself," I told her. "It ain't so bad."

"But it is," she said. "Someone broke in. What happened? What got stolen?"

"Nothing," I said. "The dogs got him first. They're good dogs. You need a semi-automatic or a machete to get past Ramses and Lineker."

"But that's so awful," Simone said. "I hate to think of you out here all by yourself. Are you sure nothing was stolen?"

She was gazing at me with those dark blue eyes, and it was like I was seeing her for the first time. Like all the other times were scrambled. Like I'd been peering in through a dirty window, not seeing clear.

She said, "I want to begin again too."

I was just going to ask, "Begin what?" I was just starting to ask, because she'd had a life, she'd had a whole life without me, and I didn't know what it was. I wanted to hear the whole story. But I didn't have time to ask.

There was a crash and the door flew open.

Simone screamed.

Two blokes charged in. Two big blokes with no faces. One big bloke had a blade. One big bloke had a lump hammer. He barged towards me, hammer high.

I leaped back. I fell arse up over the paraffin heater. Paraffin spilled. Blue flame licked. I was sitting in licking blue flame.

Simone screamed again.

I couldn't look. Fire was spreading like water across the floor. I rolled.

I couldn't look at Simone. I was rolling. Slapping myself and rolling.

Simone screaming. Wait, fucking wait, girl. I can't help you now. I'm burning up.

84

I grabbed the sleeping bag off the bunk. I rolled in it. I rolled on the flame. I smothered it.

I got up.

I was alone in the Static. The two blokes were gone. Simone was gone.

Where? The blue flame licked and flickered in my brain.

And shit—the ankle of my sweat pants was alight. I slapped it out.

Fucking where . . .?

I ran out the door. I slammed it behind me. *Where? There.* Two big blokes dragging Simone across the yard. I grabbed the tyre-iron off the step. I ran.

In the dark as I ran I saw my ankle burst into flame again. One fiery sock. I ran through a puddle.

Simone was screaming, "Help me, Eva." Shrill and scary, like a little kid. "Help me, Eva."

And I'm running through toffee. I'll never get there. I can't see—there's blue flame in me eyes.

One bloke peels off the group. Stands his ground. Hammer high.

Says, "Stop right there."

I stop.

He says, "Make one move and you'll never see your sister again."

Shrill, strangled, "*Help!*" from Simone.

I swing my arm back. I sling the tyre-iron. It leaves my hand—woosh. And—*thunk*. The bloke with the hammer catches it just below his chin. It seems to wrap itself round his neck like an iron worm and drag him down.

He's on the ground. I throw myself after the tyre-iron. I land on the bloke. I grab the hammer. I hit him.

I hit him with his own hammer, and time stood still.

I hit him with his own hammer. And the hammer head disappeared inside his skull.

And time stood still. And everything shut up. Not a tick. Not a tock. Not a scream from Simone. Not nothing. Just a big empty space. And a man's head with a hammer stuck out of it.

Then the bloke with the blade said, "Jesus Christ. Shit. Fuck. What've you done?"

He dropped Simone. Dropped the blade. Staggered towards me.

He says, "You killed him. You fuckin' killed him."

He says, "You fuckin' killed him," without moving his mouth. His face is a deformed slab.

He staggers away.

I look up.

Simone is down on her knees. She's holding her head in her hands. Her shiny raincoat is splashed with oily mud.

I get up.

I go to Simone. I sit in the mud beside her. My ankle stings. I start smearing mud on it. I pack mud on the charred bottom of my sweat pants. Thick cold mud soothes the raw patches on my skin. I daub more on. I make a circular pattern in the mud with one fingertip.

I am waiting for Simone to say something.

Chapter 11

After a long time Simone got up. She went slow-slowly over to the bloke with the hammer. She knelt down beside him. She didn't do anything. She just looked.

"Oh God," she said. "God, God, God."

I said, "I din't mean it."

"What?" she said.

"I din't mean it," I said. "I had to stop him."

"Oh God," she said.

I said, "Is he?" and she said, "Oh Christ," so I knew he was. It would've been worse, I suppose, if he wasn't. Suppose he wasn't, and he got up and walked away with a hammer stuck out of his head?

Suddenly I knew we was in trouble.

I got up and went to the gate. I didn't know what time it was. I couldn't remember when the yard emptied. I didn't know how long the gate had been left open.

I shut the gate and locked it tight. There was no sign of the other bloke. Simone's little Clio stood by the kerb. And I thought, suppose I've locked the other bloke in instead of out? Then I thought, well it's his fault too. Because we was in so much trouble I didn't know what to think.

I wanted the dogs out. But I couldn't let them out. There was a dead bloke on the ground.

"Milo!" I said. Where was Milo? He'd been in the Static with me when Simone came but I didn't notice him after the blokes came.

"Simone," I said. "Where's Milo?"

But she didn't answer. She was trying to pull the dead bloke's head off.

"What you *doin'?*" I said. But she didn't answer. I went over. I thought she'd gone potty, see.

"*Don't!*" I said.

But it was a stocking the bloke had over his face. She'd turned him over and she was pulling it off.

Oh, I thought. Oh. Well, that was why the bloke's head looked so deformed. I should of understood but I was in such a panic. I didn't see what I was looking at.

Simone pulled the stocking up to his forehead, and I stared at the bloke's face. His eyes were open and he looked like he didn't understand. The stocking cut a puzzle line just above his eyebrows and he looked as if he was going to open his gob and say, "But I don't understand."

I said, "Who the fuck is he?" and she said, "Oh God."

"Do you know who he is?" I said. " 'Cos I never seen him before in my life."

She just shook her head.

"Then why?" I said. "I don't understand." 'Cos I was trying to remember the bloke who tried to shoot my head off. But I couldn't. That'd been a total fuck-up too, and I couldn't remember seeing his face. I thought he was pointing a stick at me. But it was a sawn-off shooter.

"Why?" I said again.

She looked at me then. She hardly had no face—just eyes

staring at me from under wet hair. And the bloke with the puzzle-frown seemed to be staring at me too.

"I din't mean it," I said. "I couldn't help it. It wasn't my fault." 'Cos it wasn't. I was just trying to . . . "What we going to do, Simone?" I said. "What we going to do?"

"Shut *up*," she said. "Just shut up. It's *you*. Not me. I always knew one day you'd fuck up so bad you'd never be able to fix it. Now you've done it."

"But they was taking *you*," I said. "I was trying to . . ."

"But why was they taking me?" she said. "What've you done, Eva? What the hell have you done now?"

"Nuffin,' " I said. "I ain't done nuffin'."

"Call this nothing?" she said. "You killed him, Eva. Why did you have to kill him?"

"I din't," I said. "I only hit him. I only hit him, Simone. I've hit people harder in the ring. When you're wrestling, Simone, you hit people all the time. And they don't die. No one never *dies*."

"You ain't in the ring," she said. "And even if you were you wouldn't hit them with a hammer. And shut up shouting—someone'll hear."

"Don't leave, Simone," I whispered. "Please. Don't. I can't think. I don't know what to do."

"Shut *up*," she said. "I can't think either."

So I shut up and she didn't leave.

See, we was in so much trouble I really couldn't think. I kept looking at the bloke, and I'd think, "Who are you?" And, "What we going to do?" And then I'd start asking myself where Milo was. I just couldn't seem to keep my brain in one place. It was bouncing off windows. It wouldn't stick to the subject.

Simone said, "We've got to get rid of him."

"Yeah," I said. I was so relieved she said that. I couldn't stand him staring at me no more.

"Could we bury him here?" she said.

"*No.*" That was a horrible idea.

"Why?"

"Why?" I said.

"Yeah, why?" she said. "If we bury him here we won't have to move him."

I thought about it. It was still a horrible idea.

"Um, 'cos of the dogs," I said.

"Shit," she said. "They'd dig him up."

"Yeah," I said.

"Where, then?"

"Dunno." But at the same time I said that, a picture came in my mind of something rolled in a carpet being dropped off of a bridge in the rain.

And a split second later, Simone said, "In the river." So maybe we're psychic, Simone and me. Or maybe we saw the same movie.

"How do we get him there?" Simone said, and I said, "I ain't got a carpet."

"What?" she said.

"To roll him in."

"Oh for Christ's sake!" she said.

"You got a car," I said.

"He ain't going in my car."

"Well, how, then?"

She couldn't answer that, so I opened the gate for her and she drove the Clio into the yard.

She opened the boot. I looked at the boot and I looked at the dead bloke.

"Shit," I said.

"What?"

"Big bloke, little car."

"Well, excuse me!" she said. "I don't want him in my car anyway. And you'll have to close his eyes. He's freaking me out."

In the movies, see, someone just passes a hand down the dead guy's face—sort of stroking—and the open eyes close. I didn't fancy stroking our bloke's face. Suppose it wasn't that easy? Suppose you had to press the eyelids down with your thumbs? Suppose they kept popping open again? No, I didn't fancy that at all.

Instead, I had a much worse thought.

"Simone," I said, "maybe Milo's in the Static."

"What?"

"Milo," I said. I looked at the Static. It hadn't burned down.

"What about Milo?" Simone said.

"I knocked the paraffin stove over."

"So?"

"There was burning paraffin on the floor," I said. "Milo might be trapped in there."

"So what?" she said. "We've got a dead guy here."

"So *what?*" I said. But I had to forgive her. Nothing was normal and she was very twitchy.

She said, "What about his eyes? You killed him—it's up to you to close his eyes."

"No it ain't," I said. Because in the movies the person who strokes the dead guy's eyes is usually a doctor or someone who cares about him. The killer doesn't do it. It ain't fitting.

Besides, there was Milo.

"Pull the stocking down again," I said.

"Fuck that," she said. "Where are you going?"

"Milo," I said.

"Don't leave me," she said.

"Come too," I said.

So we both went to look for Milo, and I was ever so pleased I had something else to do. Except I was wetting myself with

91

worry for Milo. I was hoping there wasn't much paraffin left in the stove, but I didn't know. It was Keif who lit it, and maybe the stupid bugger filled it first. But, see, even if there wasn't a big fire, Milo could of been overcome with the fumes.

And supposing, when I opened the Static door the whole shebang burst into flames with the fresh air?

So I went and got the big fire extinguisher from the equipment shed.

Ain't it amazing? I could deal with the idea of my home burning down but I couldn't close a dead guy's eyes. Ain't it stone peculiar how you can think clear as a bell about one thing and not about another?

If Milo was dead I could close his eyes. No problem. But it was such a grim thought—the pup I reared by hand lying all charred on the floor. Suddenly I got shaky and I could hardly hold the fire extinguisher.

"Open the door slow," I said to Simone. So she did, and I pointed the nozzle through, ready to shoot down the flames.

But there weren't no flames. There was smoke and a huge stink but there weren't no flames.

"Milo," I called.

But no one said, "Hip-herf." So I put the fire extinguisher down and picked up the torch.

I searched that Static from North to South, and from East to West, but I didn't find no half-grown pup. Then I searched again 'cos if I didn't, I'd have to go out and handle a dead bloke. And besides, where was Milo?

There was a big hole burnt in the carpet, and there was a big hole burnt in my sleeping bag, and there was scorch marks all over the place. But otherwise the Static wasn't much worse than it was before. Except Milo was missing.

"He ain't here," I said to Simone.

"I can see that," she said. "Come on, Eva."

"I gotta find him," I said.

"Bloody *hell*, Eva," she said.

"What?"

"We've got Wozzisname out there. Suppose someone comes?" She was getting twitchier and twitchier. And I couldn't blame her.

So I took the burnt sleeping bag and the fire extinguisher and we went back to Wozzisname and the Clio. And we un-zipped the sleeping bag and rolled Wozzisname onto it and zipped it up again. We did it all of a rush and I didn't think much about it, except I stuck the hammer in by his feet and the fire extinguisher between his legs. Which I thought was pretty clever 'cos it was really heavy and it'd make Wozzisname sink like a stone when we dumped him in the river.

The brilliant thing about the sleeping bag was that it was army surplus and it had a hood. So when we covered Wozzis-name's head with the hood and pulled the drawstring tight you could hardly see his face at all. It was nearly as good as a roll of carpet and I didn't have to stroke his eyes.

Problem. You got a dead bloke, a fire extinguisher and a hammer zipped up in a bag. You've got a tiny little Renault Clio to put it in. You can't put him in the back seat 'cos the Clio ain't a four-door saloon. You only got a slim sister in high heel shoes to help you. What do you do?

Shit, I nearly walked away. I nearly collected Ramses and Lineker and what was left of my chattels and walked away. I could of.

Fuck Wozzisname. Let the next ijit who walked in the yard find him. And deal with him. Let them try and lift him. And the fire extinguisher. Go on. You try it.

Borrow a bigger motor—I can hear you saying that. Shows how much you know. Shit, it's hairy enough driving round Lon-don in your own bought-and-paid-for car with a dead bloke in the back. If you ain't bought and paid for the car there's too much to go wrong.

There was only one thing legal about what we were doing, and that was the car. So I wasn't going to give up on it, was I?

Another really manky idea was to stuff Wozzisname in one of the wrecks in the yard and let him go through the crusher. Simone thought that was a good one till I showed her how the wrecks was all stripped out shells. And how easy it was to see when there was something inside them.

Besides it was sort of disgusting. I hated Wozzisname—I really truly loathed him by that time—but I still couldn't think of putting him through the crusher. Simone only said that 'cos she didn't want him in her car.

You can't blame her, you really can't. After all, I didn't want him in my yard.

In the end, when I was ready to rip the back seat out of the Clio, I noticed you could just tip it forward to make a bigger boot space. You'd of thought Simone could of told me that. It was her car. But she was hardly talking to me by then, and I had to do everything myself.

I sort of hefted Wozzisname in bit by bit and tamped him down. It wasn't very tidy. But we was ready.

Then Simone said, "Shit. What's the time?"

She looked at her watch, and I erupted my brainbox. I said, "Whaddya mean, 'What's the time?' You got a *date* or something? You ain't going *nowhere*. You *ain't*. Whaddya care what the fuckin' time is? You ain't walking out on me this time."

"What're you going to do? Kill me?" she screamed. "Stop fucking yelling, bitch. It's only half past eight. Don't you understand? It's only *half past bloody eight*. We can't dump who'sit when it's only half past eight. Not in the middle of London we can't."

And then she burst into tears. And, fuck, why not? Only half past eight, and I'd lived seven lifetimes already. I couldn't believe it. There were people outside the yard only just going out to dinner or to the pub. London was full of people out in the street, going drinking, clubbing, courting. Going every sodding where. We couldn't dump Wozzisname for hours.

I was just about to erupt my brainbox again when this voice from the gate called out, "Hey, sisters. What's all the fightin', sisters?"

Chapter 12

Simone dropped down behind the car like she'd been shot. "Who's there?" she said. "Has he seen us? Who *is* it?"

"Keif," I said. "It's sodding, poxy, twat-faced Keif. He's my . . ."

"Personal trainer," she said. "You bloody told me. You've got to get rid of him."

"What's he doing here?"

"How the hell should I know?" she hissed. "He's yours, not mine. Just get *rid* of him."

"*How?*"

"Hey, sisters," called Keif.

"Make him go *away.*"

But I didn't want to talk to him. He'd see what I done on my face. I was a whole 'nother person since he came in the afternoon with Cousin Carmen, and he'd seen what I done in me eyes. You can't whack a bloke with a hammer so hard he croaks without it shows in your eyes. Fact of life.

"Yo, Eva," Keif called. "Comin' in."

"*No!*" I yelled. I ran to the gate.

"Bugger off," I said.

"Is what I like about you, Eva," Keif said. "You know how to manners a man. How you doin'? You feeling a little better?"

96

"Better?" I was feeling one hundred and twenty-five per-cent pure crap.

"Yeah. Not coughing-sneezing no more?"

"Oh, that," I said. "Listen, meat-head, I got a bone to pick with you."

"Promises," he said. "What now?"

"Your Cousin Carmen. Her potion. What was it—piss poison?"

"Oh that," he said with a grin you could of wrapped twice round his neck. "Mebbe I should of warned you. No. The poison was all your own. Potion just call it out of you."

"Fuckin' obeah ladies," I said.

"Too true. But that's why I'm so big and strong today. Cousin Carmen don't allow no sick child round her house."

He was chatting on as if everything was normal—as if *I* was normal. Sometimes it's really useful that blokes are such insensitive buggers.

"Listen," he said, "now you a toxin-free zone, you going to invite me in?"

"Fuck off," I said. "Got things to do. Got to let the dogs out. You won't like my dogs."

"Liked the little one," he said.

"You won't like the big ones, and they won't like you. They're attack dogs."

"What you got you need attack dogs for?"

"Job," I said. "We're security guards."

"What you loading the car for?" he said. "You flittin' or what?"

"Fuckin' questions," I said. He *knew*. He was only pretending he couldn't see Wozzisname in my eyes. He *knew*, and he was toying with me.

Then Simone said, "Hello, Keith." She'd come up from behind without me hearing.

She said, "We had a bit of an accident. A fire." Oh, she's so clever when she's back in control.

"Yeah," I said. "It's your fault. You should never of lit that stupid heater."

"Come on, Eva," Simone said. "He wasn't to know."

"What happened?" Keif asked.

"Just a bit of a fire," Simone said. "As you can see we're having to dispose of some burnt things. Don't mind Eva—she's a bit shaken up."

"Oh, I don't mind Eva," he said. "Hey, girl, sorry. How bad was it? Need somewhere to stay?"

"How very kind," Simone said before I could tell him to knob off. "No, it's quite all right. If Eva needs somewhere to stay she can stay with me. We're fine, honestly."

"Okay, safe then," he said. "Bit of weight training tomorrow, Eva? You up fer weight training?"

Maybe I should've told him about the weight I'd just been lifting, but Simone said, "We'll see. She doesn't want to do too much too soon after the flu."

She was so smooth I could of spread her on bread and eaten her. I mean, she was all wet hair and hunted eyes, but her voice was smooth and classy. She was freezing Keif out. I could tell.

He said, "Ain't I seen you somewhere? I been trying to remember since I first met you. You ain't an actress or what?"

"Oh well," she said. "I've done a little modelling. But I shouldn't think you'd've seen any of that."

"What?" he said.

"Oh, you know," she said, "fizzy drinks, handbags. Nothing special."

"Hey! A model!" Keif said. "Wicked."

And I nearly agreed with him. A fuckin' model. No wonder she talked so fancy. And why not? She was pretty enough to be a film star. But I could of screamed at her for not just slapping him down. What was we *doing* boogying around, talking about modelling?

"I gotta let the dogs out," I said.

"Okay," Keif said. "Mebbe best. Saw a guy hanging round when I came. Thought you had a visitor but mebbe he's hanging round fer to steal something."

"What?" I said. "Where?"

"Over there," he said, pointing, and sure enough, in the shadows at the corner of Mandala Street, there was a lurker trying to look like a bit of wall.

"Oy!" I yelled. "Bum-drip! Yeah, *you!*"

"Eva, don't," said Simone.

"You sweet-talkin' some other guy?" said Keif. "Damn!"

"Oy!" I yelled. "Don't think I can't see you."

The shadow came unstuck from the wall but it didn't come any closer.

"Simone there?" he called. "I'm waiting for Simone."

She *did* have a date. On top of everything, Simone had a twatting date. I wheeled round to face her.

"You *said!*" I yelled.

"Shshsh," she said. "I didn't know he was coming. I *swear.*"

"You sodding *what?*" I said.

"Don't shout, Eva," she said. And then to Keif she said, "Eva doesn't like my boyfriend." Can you believe that? I didn't even know she *had* one.

"I won't be a minute," she said.

"You ain't leaving," I said.

"Don't shout. I've got to talk to him, send him away. It won't take a second."

So I had to unlock the gate to let her out, and then of course, once the gate was unlocked Keif wanted to come in.

"Soakin' out here," he said.

"Well, you can't come in," I said. "Soon as Simone comes back I'm loosing the dogs."

"Yeah, okay, but Eva, you just had the flu or what. Mebbe we should go in an' I'll make a cup of tea for you."

"Can't," I said. "Kettle's burnt."

"Least get out of the rain."

"Smoke," I said. "Bad stink. It gave me a terrible headache." Over his shoulder I could see Simone and the shadow. She was waving her arms around.

"Headache?" said Keif. "Come here, baby doll. Ain't no headache I can't cure."

He swung me round and got his hands on my neck. What a stone liberty! The *cheek* of the man!

"Woh," he said. "Rock hard."

"Oy," I said. "Knob off!" I couldn't, I really couldn't credit it. I still had a dead bloke in the yard and my joke personal trainer wanted to massage my neck. If I'd been a fainting sort of woman I'd of passed out.

"Unreal," I said.

"Told you," Keif said. "I got voodoo digits. Man, have you got a knotted neck!"

"Bog off," I said, "that's muscle tone."

"Tension."

"Muscle tone."

"Safe, sister," he said. "I'll allow good muscle. But it's knotted like a barb-wire ball."

He had big hot hands. I stood there like a horse and I didn't know what to do. I couldn't think. Those big hot hands were making me feel little and weak when I needed to be hard.

I jumped away. "Don't," I said.

"If you worry about your sister," he said, "she gone."

I looked over at the corner. No Simone.

"Where?"

"Dunno," he said. "Long gone."

I went out the gate faster than a greased torpedo. I sprinted to the corner. No Simone. I looked up Mandala Street. Just an empty market in the rain. Not hide nor hair, not sight nor sound of Simone. Just wet paper and soggy cabbage leaves blowing in the wind.

I ran down Mandala Street. "*Simone!*" I yelled.

No answer. "*Simone!*" I howled. How *could* she? How could she blow and leave me with Wozzisname all folded up in the back of her car when I didn't know what to do?

"*Simone!*"

"Hip?"

"Milo?" I said.

And there he was, crouched under a rusty barrow.

If there was a god he'd be a stand-up comedian. Look at it my way—I want Milo, I get Keif. I want Simone, I get Milo. If there was a god I'd pelt him with rotten tomatoes. Bad jokes—that's all gods is good for—bad sodding jokes.

Now I had a shivering, sopping wet pup, I had a joke personal trainer *and* I had Wozzisname to cope with. But no Simone. Was there *ever* a woman in so much trouble? I ask you. Was there? 'Cos if there was, give me her phone number and we'll start a self-help group.

Do you know what the spookiest bit was?

Milo was scared of me. Of *me*, who'd hand-reared him from a tadpole. He wouldn't come out from under the barrow.

Maybe Keif was too thick to see what I done in me eyes, but Milo wasn't. I knelt down and put my hand out to him, but he backed away and showed me his teeth. He never done that before. It wasn't aggression, it was stone fright.

I didn't press him. I stayed where I was, kneeling on the pavement. There wasn't nowhere to go anyway. I might as well sit there all night and let all the trouble in the world fall on my head. That's what it felt like. Every drop of rain was another spot of trouble. More and more trouble until I couldn't bear the weight.

"What's doin'?" said Keif.

Shit, there was no shaking that guy.

"Milo," I said. "He's under that barrow and he won't come out."

"Why?"

"Spooked."

"What of?"

"Dunno."

" 'Spect it was the fire, eh?" Keif said. "Why not move the barrow?"

"*No!*"

"Why?"

"What's the matter with you?" I said. "You move that barrow, you take away his hidey-hole. Then he's even scareder."

"So then you give him a big hug and a bone or what?"

"Fool."

"Why?"

" 'Cos I ain't got a bone and you don't hug attack dogs."

"He ain't an attack dog," Keif said. "He's a pup and he's scared."

"Boo-hoo-hoo," I said. "He's got to want to come to me."

"Pigs got to want to fly," he said. "Hey Milo baby, come to poppa."

And, oh jeez, that idiot pup crawled out from under the barrow and licked Keif's big hot hand. I felt so sick I could of laid down and died among the cabbage leaves.

"Told you," Keif said. "Have I got a way with dogs and women or what? Voodoo digits. You listen, girl, when I tell you."

He picked Milo up in his arms and marched off to the yard.

And Milo let him do it.

My guts was dry-heaving and I didn't have an ounce of fight left in me. God was a clown and I was a killer.

I got up and followed.

Chapter 13

I thought I was going crazy. I thought my head was exploding and I was going stark barking mad.

I pushed the Clio so it was backed up against the Static and no one could open the boot. I went to the pen to let the dogs out.

In the Static, Keif was making a cup of tea and warming up some soup.

And I was stone staring crazy.

I let the dogs out. They were nervous. They could smell killer on my breath. They knew. Ramses wasn't giving me an ounce of trouble tonight. He took one look at me and said to hisself, "She done it—she finally gone and done it. She's madder than me tonight." And he walked round me on tiptoe.

And Keif was warming up a pan of soup.

There was a dead bloke not three feet from the stove and Keif was warming up soup. For me.

I hit a bloke with his own hammer. I hit him so hard he croaked and Keif was making soup.

I didn't know if I was coming or going. You think I should get rid of Keif? Yeah, me too. But, like, whaddya think I am? I ain't a movie director. I can't say, "I don't want Keif in this scene," and then Keif ain't in the scene. This is real life. What am I supposed to do?

Keif wouldn't go away. He said, "Here, get this down you, girl." And he gave me a steaming mug of chicken pasta soup. What am I supposed to do?

I got Wozzisname all scrunched up in the boot of a car not three feet away and a streaming mug of soup in my mitt. What am I supposed to do?

Should I give the soup back and say, "I just fuckin' croaked a bloke so I don't deserve no chicken pasta soup?" Then should I go back out in the rain and slit my wrists with a rusty nail out of remorse? Is that what I should do?

Tell me. Go on, tell me.

I was hungry, so I ate the soup.

That's what you're supposed to do with soup. You're supposed to eat it. That's all clear and simple.

But what're you supposed to do with a dead bloke in a sleeping bag? Get old voodoo digits to magic him away? Turn girly and say, "Keif, baby, I been a bad girl. It wasn't my fault." Flutter, flutter with the old eyelashes. Swoosh-swish with the poxy stocking tops. "Keif, baby, help me out of this and all of heaven will be yours." Well, maybe Simone could of done it. But Simone fucked off.

In the movies the body rolls into the river, plop. All done and dusted. Sometimes they roll the whole car into the river, plop, glub-glub. All gone. Except Simone wouldn't allow that, for sure. Wherever Simone was.

Sometimes the car explodes. Like my head. Thwhump-whump. No car. No dead bloke.

Well, I can't do that, can I? Not in central London. Not when Simone wants her car back.

So what am I supposed to do?

"Eat your soup," Keif said. "Don't look so mollixed. You seen a guy make soup before aincha?"

So I ate the soup and three feet away Wozzisname stared out into a dark car boot 'cos I couldn't bring meself to close his eyes.

I wanted to take a pill and go to sleep, and not wake up till someone else did something about Wozzisname.

In a different movie, I'd be Ms. Big. I'd chop a wedge off of all my zillions and I'd wave it under Keif's nose. "Got a little job for you, boy," I'd say. And he'd say, "Whatever you want Ms. Wylie." And while he was out I'd find another Keif and tell him to get rid of the first Keif.

"What's up?" Keif said. "You're staring."

"What's up with *you?*" I said. "You're still here."

"Come an' sit on my knee," he said. "We'll see what's up with me."

Can you believe this? I was wrong. God ain't a clown. God's a totally crazy-insane movie director.

"Are you absolutely bonkers?" I said.

"Yeah," he said. "Sit on my knee. You don't have to like it."

"Save it for Milo," I said. "He's your little pet. I ain't."

"Workin' on that," he said. "If this was the Wild West I'd be a horse-tamer 'stead of a personal trainer."

"So why don't you go West and boil your ugly bonce?"

"Think I'm ugly, girl? I don't need to be pretty, know it?"

Milo didn't think he was ugly. Milo stuck his head on Keif's thigh and snoozed. That pup needed massive retraining.

"Serious, man," Keif said. "This place a *mess.* You can't sleep here tonight."

"I don't sleep at night," I said. "I mind this yard at night. I sleep mornings."

"True?" he said. "Ain't a good way for an athlete to live."

106

"Ain't staying forever. Simone and me, we're going into business together."

"Fer true?"

"She said. And I can stay with her. You heard."

"I heard," he said, and he just sat there with Milo kipping on his thigh and a dead bloke not three feet away.

"So why're you still here?" I said. "I'm okay."

"Sweet 'n' dandy," he said. "I see what I see."

"Who cares what you see?"

"Well, since you ask, I see someone needs lookin' after."

"See wrong. You couldn't see wronger if you tried all year."

"See a good athlete gone bad. You let yourself go, girl."

"Fuckin' did *not*," I said. "Wasn't me. Mr. Deeds let me go. All them turdy heavyweights. Barred me."

"Yeah," he said. "They told me. You a legend at that gym, girl. Eva this, Eva that. Eva a monster with three heads and the baddest mouth in South London."

"They still talk about me?"

"So I think, I gotta see this girl. 'Cos if they treat a big woman like they treat a black man then they treat a black man like a big bad woman. Like enemies, girl, like enemies. So my days is numbered too."

"I wish you'd seen me fight," I said.

"They never said you was a bad fighter," he said. "They said you was a bad woman."

"Believe. And bugger off."

"Will do," he said. "Even though you beggin' fer me to stay. First, what you got wrong with your ankle?"

What ankle? I'd forgotten the ankle but that silly sod only had to mention it and it started to sting again.

"Burnt it," I said. "In the fire. It's all right. I'll put some more mud on it."

"*Mud?*" You know what you putting on it? You putting oil and slime and dog germs. You killing yourself or what?"

"Don't you bring your Cousin Carmen back here on account of my ankle," I said. "Don't you fuckin' *dare!*"

Cousin Carmen would see through the Static wall for sure. She'd see through the metal of the Clio too. She'd see Wozzis-name with his eyes open, staring back at her. I'd rather lose my whole leg than have her coming in with her potions, lookin' through my walls.

"You ain't scared of one little old lady," Keif said, showing me teeth you could play honky-tonk on. "Come here, I'll wash that mud off for you."

"Do it myself," I said. 'Cos those big hot hands made me feel small and I didn't want them anywhere near me.

"Suit yourself. Now, don't you cry or nothin' but I goin' home." He stood up. I stood up. And there didn't seem to be enough space.

"Hip?" said Milo. He jumped awake, all shuddery again.

"Here," I said. I scooped Milo up and dumped him in Keif's arms. "Take Milo," I said. "You want someone to look after, take Milo."

That'd give him something to do with those big hot hands.

"Only for tonight, mind," I said, "while he's nervy. I want him back tomorrow. And don't you make him go all soft. My dogs gotta be hard."

"Yeah, yeah," Keif said, "you like 'em hard. I'll remember that or what."

What the hell do you do with a bloke like Keif? *What?* I never met a bloke like him before. Maybe there's blokes like Keif all over the world only I never met one before.

Maybe it's 'cos this is the first time I've been rich so I ain't used to blokes coming after me for my money. It ain't anything else. Believe. I ain't someone blokes come after. And I'm glad.

Waste of time, all that. Blokes make complete pillocks of sensible women, and who wants to waste their energy on that stuff?

Whether they want them or not women spend a huge amount of energy on blokes. Even me, who knows better. Look at how much energy I spent getting shot of Keif—and he's alive and can use his legs, if he bloody chooses to.

I washed my ankle with cold water and soap the way he told me to. And it hurt. Ain't that blokes all over? What they tell you to do doesn't hurt *them*, does it? No, it hurts *you*.

All the time, I was waiting. I was waiting for Ramses and Lineker to tell me Simone had come back. I was waiting for Lineker to go, "Yak-yak-yak," and Ramses to drown him out with, "Ro-ro-ro." Then I'd go to the gate and let Simone in. Then I'd know what to do.

I hate waiting. I sat on the bunk. I didn't have no sleeping bag to wrap myself in 'cos I'd gave that to the dead bloke.

It got to eleven o'clock and then twelve, and all I could hear was rain bouncing on the Static roof. And I couldn't think what was keeping Simone. I couldn't seem to think at all, if you must know.

Then I dreamt I put the Clio through the crusher. I dreamt the Clio went through the crusher and came out like a crumpled box except for the boot which popped open. And everyone in the crowd went, "Ooh, look at what's in that car!" Because, suddenly, the crusher was in the middle of the ring. "Boo, hiss," they all went. "Bucket Nut can't even put a car through a crusher." So I had to do it again. Only this time, although the car came out the size of a beachball, there was the dead bloke's head peering out of what was left of the window. His eyes popped open, and he said, "I demand a return match." The referee awarded me the beachball and the head as a prize and everyone started clapping.

So *my* eyes popped open, and it was dark, and at first I

109

thought the Static was leaking 'cos I was all wet and I could still hear the rain rattling on the roof. But then I knew I'd been dreaming and sweating even though it was cold and I hadn't meant to go to sleep.

I went to the Static door to call Ramses and Lineker. For once they came straightaway. I gave them each a Bow Chow biscuit but they didn't want to hang out with me. And it was all Wozzisname's fault 'cos there he was, not three feet away, freaking everyone out.

In the movies the killer shoots someone and then sticks the gun in the dead bloke's hand to make it look like he topped himself. The next thing you know the house is full of cops and medics. They deal with the body.

Why am I going on and on about the movies? Well, I'm thinking about the movies 'cos I don't have nothing else to go on. I don't. I never done anything like this before. I can't say to myself, "Well last time I croaked a bloke I did such and such, and that worked all right so I'll do it again." But there are dead blokes in the movies all the time. I can tell you that 'cos when you're in chokey there's bugger-all else to do except watch movies about dead blokes on TV.

But when push comes to shove, when you're in that situation yourself, movies is no bloody help at all. Or maybe I seen the wrong movies. In the movies I seen, dead blokes just lie in the street for someone else to pick up. Or there's somewhere to put them. They don't hang around freaking you out while you wait for your sister and even your own dogs won't talk to you.

Simone kept the Clio key in her pocket so I had to hot-wire the car. I couldn't wait no longer. I hot-wired the Clio, and Simone was going to be really pissed with me 'cos I broke one of the panels on the steering column.

Maybe I don't know what to do about dead blokes, but I do know how to borrow motors. At first I thought I could just leave the car somewhere, because you'd be surprised how long it takes for some people to notice a borrowed car in their street. Then I'd have time to collect the dogs and clear out.

But it was Simone's car and she'd want it back. She wouldn't want the politzei to come knocking on her door saying, "Got your lost motor back for you. Oh and by the way, there's a dead bloke in the boot."

No, the river was the best idea. If I could tumble Wozzis-name into the river that'd be that. I'd never have to think about him again.

At least, now, I was doing something else but think about him. At least, now, I was driving him to the river. We was going somewhere. We wasn't waiting no more.

Chapter 14

Have you been across any London bridges lately? Was there ever a time you was alone on one of them? I mean, really alone—no traffic, no nothing.

'Cos I couldn't find a buggering bridge without it had traffic on it. Even in the pouring rain. Even at three in the morning. London don't stop for nothing.

I went north over Lambeth Bridge, turned east, and then came south again across Westminster, and then east again, then north over Waterloo. And I thought I was going to keep driving north, east, south, east, north and east again till I ran out of bridges and it was daylight.

So I had to give up on bridges. Bridges is a waste of time if there's something you want to drop off of them without anyone seeing.

And another funny thing—London has the River Thames running the whole way through it. But it's bloody hard to get a car close to the water—except in places like bridges where everyone else can get close to *you*. There's always a building in the way.

I thought of driving out to the country. There's lots of dead things left lying on roads in the country. But even country peo-

MUSCLEBOUND

ple would sit up and notice if I dumped Wozzisname on the
ground with all the dead badgers and rabbits.

I got almost to Greenwich, and by that time I reckon I'd of
settled for a deep puddle or a hole in the road. But I couldn't
find one of them neither. I almost gave up and took the dead
bloke back home. I couldn't make up my mind which was
worse—having him at home or driving him around in my sister's car.

I was feeling very queer and lonely, and I didn't really know
where I was. I was squinting this way and that, not knowing
what to look for, when all of a sudden I realised I was going
through a place where there were yards like my yard—yards
with car bodies, metal and lifting gear in them. And it was
quiet.

It was quiet because there weren't no blocks of flats or shops
or high streets. Just junk yards. So I nosed around, driving
slowly in a circle. And right up close to the river I found an
empty space with a portacabin in front and nothing but a few
hulking trucks behind.

That's when the Clio ran out of petrol. I'd just noticed a sign
on the portacabin that said "Security Office." And I'd thought
—that's the first likely place I seen all night. Except for the security guard, which made it impossible. I was about to drive on
when the Clio decided to run out of petrol.

It just coughed and died. And there I was, outside a security
guard's office with a dead bloke behind me.

When the car stopped it felt as if the dead bloke had caught
up with me. When I was driving it was like he was chasing me.
Now that I stopped I sort of expected for him to sit up and tap
me on the shoulder.

I was so spooked I got out and walked away. Well, what was
I supposed to do? The Clio ran out of gas. Outside a security

113

guard's portacabin. Just like that. There's only so much a woman can stand, and I hit my limit.

I walked away. I crossed the road and started to walk back west. Then I stopped and looked round.

The Clio was sat in the middle of the road. It was in a no parking zone. There wasn't any other cars. The Clio sat all by itself in the middle of the road saying, "Oy! Look at me." I s'pose if I painted it stripy and stuck a flashing beacon on its nose it'd be more obvious. Hard to see what else you could do.

And it was Simone's car.

So I just stood there. And after a while, I calmed down a bit and saw that there was no light on in the security cabin. There was a TV aerial, but no blue flicker, so the TV wasn't on neither. There was blinds at the windows, but they weren't closed.

If I was lucky, there was no security guard in there.

Was I lucky? Well, after the night I'd been having, would you bet your mortgage on me being lucky?

Me neither. I wouldn't bet a dirty snot-rag on it.

On the other hand, there was bugger-all to guard. And there was no fence—just one of those weighted barriers which swings up when you press on the end.

So what was a security office doing there? The place was like a bloody great car park or a site big enough to build a supermarket on, only there were no cars and no building works. Just some clapped-out old trucks, standing by themselves, at the back next to the river wall.

So I bet my freedom on it.

I walked back, pressed on the end of the barrier and swung it up. Then I waited for the flashing lights, sirens and armed guards.

Nothing.

I waited some more.

More nothing.

I went back to the Clio. I released the handbrake. I pushed. I pushed and steered till the Clio rolled past the swing barrier, past the security office, and into the big empty space.

I'd of pushed the Clio straight into the Thames if I could. But I couldn't 'cos there was a chest-high concrete wall stopping me.

I was streaming sweat and rain. I was gasping for breath. But I was well off the public road and there was only a wall between me and the river. I could hear the water lapping. Across the water it was all lit up. Across the water was a big shiny glass and steel development all lit up with peach and turquoise light. But on my side of the water it was dark and windy, and the river smelled old and dirty.

I pulled myself up on the wall and looked down. Down there was loppy choppy water. Down there was a dead bloke's grave. Not far.

Not far at all, except Simone had the car keys in her pocket and I couldn't open the back of the car.

I was jumping up and down. I was whining like a dog. I wanted to howl. I wanted to roar. I wanted to pick the Clio up in one hand and hurl it as far away from me as I could.

They say rage gives you strength. Maybe it does, but it doesn't give you enough to chuck a car in the river.

And maybe you think a dead bloke should be treated with respect. He should be carried by six slow men looking sorrowful. He should have lilies and someone to cry for him.

Not this one. This one had to be dragged from the back of the car through to the front, and he had to be booted out through the door. Because he'd sort of set in a scrunched up position. He wasn't floppy no more. You couldn't fold him, unfold him or bend him round corners.

I hope I never have to hate anyone that much again. I didn't hate him that much when I hit him with his hammer. I was

115

scared, I was angry, I was panicked when I hit him. That's all it took to croak him—panic. But it took real blind rage and hatred to bury him.

Who the fuck was he to ruin my life and give me bad dreams and follow me like I was wearing him round me neck? Who the fuck was he to make me sweat, give me muscle cramp, break my back? Who the fuck asked him into my life? Who the fuck told him to manhandle my sister and put me in a stone panic? Not me. For sure, not me. It was his own sodding idea. It wasn't mine. It wasn't my fault. And now I was having to clean up after him. Poor old Eva, don't think about her—go right ahead and get yourself croaked in her yard. Go on. Leave her to pick up the pieces. By herself. As usual. Got any shit-work? Give it to poor old Eva. That's all she's good for.

I toppled Wozzisname off the concrete wall and he sploshed into the River Thames and the water ate him up.

You'll never know what a weight it was off my back, off my mind, to see him go. The only thing I was sorry about was my sleeping bag. Even with a hole burnt in it my sleeping bag was too cocking good for the likes of him. Splosh, he went. Splosh went the fire extinguisher and the hammer.

I wished I could of done it with a ton of semtex—a bloody great explosion would of suited me better. "Splosh" didn't quite express my mood.

And I wasn't done yet. Oh no. What about the car? The useless sodding car. The one with no gas in its tank. Think that's going to grow legs and walk back home by itself? Ha-turding-ha. I had to push it. I had to push and steer it out past the portacabin, out through the swing barrier, out onto the road, along the road. Push, steer, push, push, push.

So there I was, pushing, somewhere in Deptford, pushing, looking for a service station, pushing, and, knock me down with a number nine bus, the steering flaked out. It locked. I couldn't turn it no more. The creeping crappy Clio would only go in a straight line. And there aren't any straight lines in London.

Well, that finished me. What was I supposed to do? I keep asking, but no one answers. I can't keep making it up for myself. I can't. I'm all wore out.

I was finished, done, through. This time when I left the Clio in the middle of the road I didn't look back. I just walked away and kept on walking. I didn't go back.

I know it was Simone's car and she'd want it. I know it was hardly a mile from where I dumped Wozzisname. You don't have to tell me. I *know*. But it was just too hard. And I was too tired.

So I walked away. Bugger it all. I don't care if I spend the rest of me life in chokey. I can't sort it out. It's too hard.

Chapter 15

My back hurt so much I couldn't put my socks on. I couldn't bend forward, and I couldn't raise my knees high enough to get at my feet.

It's a good thing I didn't have to get up and open the door. Or it's a bad thing, 'cos the door swung open and Keif pranced in without knocking.

"Doin'?" he asked. But I'd slept so deep and dead that at first I couldn't remember what the hell I *had* been doing.

"What's the time?" I said.

"Time for your weight training," he said.

"Where's Milo?"

"I gave the puppy dog to Cousin Carmen fer to calm his nerves."

It was four in the afternoon, and usually that's a good time to get up. If you *can* get up. Me—I couldn't even shout at Keif. I took a deep breath to bawl him out for not bringing Milo home, and my back went into spasm.

"Eh, eh, honey babe," Keif said. "You hurt or what? Lay yerself down."

I could hardly even do that. It was the curse of Wozzisname. I was paralysed in a scrunched-up position with a sock in one

118

hand and all I could do was topple sideways onto the bunk just like Wozzisname toppling off the wall. He did this to me.

"What you done, woman?" Keif said.

"Wrecked me back."

"You don't want to go weight training, just say so. Some folks do anything to get out of work."

"Ooof!"

"What's that? You chattin' back or what? Just stay cool. Relax."

Have you noticed? When it's the last thing you can possibly do, people tell you to relax. Having a baby? Your whole family's just been wiped out by a nuclear cloud? Your back's in spasm? Relax. A dead bloke reached out of the river and put a hex on you? Just relax, babe. Stay cool.

Thanks a whole bloody bundle, Keif, honey babe.

"Fuck off," I said, but Keif had already gone.

It couldn't be anyone but Wozzisname. I got a back like an ox. I got more muscle in my back than most two people put together. I'm proud of my back. It never ever gave me no bother before. So what's different now? Wozzisname. That's what.

I think, now, I should of said a few words when I tipped him in the water. A few nice words, I mean. I did say a few words only they wasn't the sort of words a dead bloke wants to hear. I should of said something like what they say at funerals. Just to make sure he didn't come back and hex me. Only I don't know what they say at funerals.

I never thought about it before—but why do you think they write stuff like "Rest In Peace" on gravestones? Well, if you ask me, they don't do that 'cos they hope the dead bloke will have a nice quiet time when he's under the gravestone. No. It ain't a hope. It's an order. It means, "Stay there. Don't come crawling back to put the whammy on me, mate." *You* rest. Give *me* peace.

Or stay cool. Relax. Which is what I'll put on Keif's grave-stone. Which he'll be needing sooner than he thinks.

No. No. Don't listen. I can't talk like that no more. I can't talk like I want to do for Keif.

That's part of the curse of Wozzisname. He's taken all the fun out of saying stuff like, "I'll sodding kill you." A killer can't say that no more without she means it. Or she *might* mean it. For true. Who knows what she means anymore.

I didn't say, "I'll sodding kill you," to Wozzisname. But I did kill him. I didn't mean to. But I did. So I can't go round saying the words no more. Because, now, they're for real. They ain't pretend words no more. Wozzisname took all the pretend out of the words.

Then Simone turned up. I'd given up on her. I'd wanted her, I'd waited for her all night. She didn't come. And I thought we was back to square one—I'd have to wait another ten years before I saw her again.

She walked in and I couldn't even sit up.

"Eva," she said, "I . . . where's . . . ?"

"Shut up," I said. "Keif's around."

"Where?"

"Dunno." I couldn't even look her in the eye 'cos I was lying down.

She sat on the edge of the bunk next to me. "Why aren't you up?" she said. She smelled of scent and soap.

"I wrecked my back," I said. "Last night."

"Oh," she said. "Where . . . ?"

"Shshsh," I said.

"I was only going to ask where you put my car," she said.

"Oh," I said.

"Well?" she said.

"Don't ask," I said.

"It's important."

120

"Oh is it?" I said. "Wasn't it important last night? *Wasn't* it? Where the fuck *was* you? Doing something *important?*"

"Shshsh, yes," she said. "I've got something really awful to tell you."

"Eat it," I said. "Chew it and eat it yourself. You walked out on me." I couldn't help it. I couldn't take any more bad news. She walked off and left me when I was in more trouble than a one-legged matador in a bullring.

"What're you so umpty about?" she said. "Boyfriend gave you a hard time? Is that how you did your back in?"

"*WHAT?*" And my back spasmed so hard I nearly reared off the bunk.

"Well he was here last night and you say he's around now."

"He didn't stay. He ain't my boyfriend. He *ain't*. I got rid of him. Like you was supposed to do with yours. But you didn't. You fucked off with him. You just blew—like you always do."

"I didn't just blow," she said. "You've simply no idea what I went through last night."

"Big bloody deal," I said. "What about what *I* went through?"

"Shut *up*," she said. "We can't talk about that if your . . . personal trainer's coming back. There's something else, so shut up and listen."

"Or what?" I said. "Wotcha going to do? Walk out? Make me count to *two* hundred? Wotcha going to do, eh?" And I sort of went, "Wooof," 'cos my back knocked the breath out of me. It's really hard to fight with someone when you're lying flat and your back keeps going into spasm.

I said, "I don't want to fight with you, Simone."

"Really?" she said. "I thought that's what you did best."

She sounded so cold and sarcastic I thought she was going to walk out. There wasn't anything I could do to stop her. I couldn't even see her face. I buried my head in my arms. She didn't say anything for a while, and I thought she might've gone.

Then she said, "Oh poor Eva. Last night really knocked the stuffing out of both of us, didn't it?"

"'S okay," I said. But she started stroking my hair with her soapy hand and it made me feel better.

"Please don't let's quarrel," she said. "It was so horrible last night. So horrible. But it's going to be even worse if we quarrel. If we fight, we've let the bastards beat us. We can't let them destroy us, Eva. I know what you did, Eva. But I'm standing by you the best way I can."

She stroked my head and Wozzisname sank down in the river where he belonged.

I said, "I don't understand, Simone. I don't understand what happened. I don't understand why Wozzisname came here."

"That's what I've got to tell you," she said. "But you've got to stay calm. Please, Eva, stay calm and let me talk. Shall I get you a little drink first? For your nerves."

"Later," I said. "Don't go away." I wanted her to keep on stroking my hair. And she did. It was better than a drink.

She said, "Eva, do you remember, a couple of days ago, you went to see Ma and she was moving out so as not to pay the rent?"

"Yeah."

"But the rent man came and you had a bit of a tiz-woz and you ended up paying everything Ma owed."

"Yeah," I said. "He had a baseball bat or he'd never of got past me."

"Shshsh," she said, stroking. "It's okay. But the thing is, you had a whole pile of money, and Ma got it into her head that you'd come into a fortune. This is what I found out last night, Eva."

"How? How did you find out?"

"That guy," she said. "That guy who was hanging around. The one you thought was my boyfriend. He isn't my boyfriend. I told you, Eva, I've just come back from abroad. And I told you I'd been married. Didn't I?"

"Yeah."

"Well, I'm like you, Eva. It was a rotten marriage, and I don't want to know about guys anymore. So that guy wasn't *my* boyfriend. He was one of Ma's . . ."

"One of Ma's what?"

"Shshsh," she said, "don't get so excited. I was going to say he's one of Ma's boyfriends but I don't think she's known him long enough to call him that."

"But you said he was yours," I said. "You did."

"I know," she said. "But your trainer guy was there. We didn't want him knowing our business. Did we? Well, did we?"

"No!"

"So I said the first thing that came into my head. I wasn't exactly thinking straight."

"Me neither."

"No. I didn't want Keith knowing anything, so I just said the easiest thing. Because I didn't know why one of Ma's fellers would be looking for me, and I didn't know why he'd be looking for me at your place. It all seemed very wrong."

"But you went off with him. You fucked off and left me for him."

"Take it easy, Eva. I had to. You don't understand. He was one of the guys who was dragging me away. He was the one who put a knife to my throat. The other one . . . well, you know what happened to the other one. Both those awful guys were Ma's fellers."

"*What!*" I said. And my back kicked me in the guts again— ooof.

123

"Steady," she said. "You promised you'd stay calm. I haven't finished yet."

"What else?" I said. "*Why?*"

"For money," she said. "Why else? Ma cooked up this plan with two of her boyfriends. Oh Eva, it's so stupid, so *cruel*, I can hardly tell you. I'm so ashamed. I'm so ashamed Ma's our mother."

I wish I could of seen her face. Her voice was almost choked up with tears when she talked about being ashamed of Ma. But I was lying down and I couldn't sit up and put my arm round her.

"I'm so ashamed," she said. "I thought it was because of something *you* did. But it wasn't—it was *my* fault. You killed one of Ma's fellers and it was my fault."

"Don't cry," I said. "Don't. It wasn't your fault. I panicked."

"But I was blaming you. Afterwards. When we were trying to get rid of . . . you know . . . and I shouted at you."

"But we was both shitting ourselves. Like, it wasn't a good time for neither of us."

"But you don't see," she said. "It was Ma's plan, because she knows how you feel about me. How I feel about you. Why d'you think she suddenly told me where to find you after all these years? Why now?"

"She thinks I'm loaded?"

"Yes, that's why. She thought she could get your money through me. I told you it was stupid. I said it was cruel. She thought, if she got us back together again, we'd care about each other again and then she could use me against you. She's unbe-lievable, Eva. She's our mother. How could she cook all this up against us?"

"Don't cry, Simone," I said. "It ain't no big surprise to me. She ain't a proper ma. Never was. Never will be. She's a toad and she laid spawn in a puddle. That's us. You and me. She never thinks she got to care for us. That ain't what toads do. We got to take care of ourselves."

"But she's our mum."

"How?" I said. "How was she ever our mum? You might of thought so 'cos you was the pretty one and she was nicer to you. But when the chips is down we're both toadspawn and she ain't a proper mum."

"You're so calm, Eva," she said. "I thought you'd go apeshit."

"I ain't shocked, if that's what you mean. You're the one who's shocked."

"I expected better."

"See, that's where we're different," I said. And it was funny, because, now I knew the worst, I did feel quite calm. And there was a bit of space in my brain where I could feel sorry for Simone. If Simone had even the littlest idea that Ma loved her then Simone was very wrong and very sad. It's always sad when someone comes down from Cloud Cuckoo Land with a bump.

"But Eva," she said, "don't you get it? Those two fellers of hers—they were faking an abduction. Ma and those two fellers were going to make you pay for me. They were going to threaten my life and then sell me to you."

"You don't have to spell it out," I said. "I ain't stupid." Because the one thing Wozzisname said before I threw the tyre-iron at him was, "Make one move and you'll never see your sister again." I should of thought then, how did he know Simone was my sister? But I didn't think, did I? He knew because that was the whole point. Simone and me is sisters and we take care of each other, and that was what Ma was going to use against us.

"But it all got balled up," I said.

"What got balled up?" said Keif, blowing in like he owned the place.

Chapter 16

The Static juddered 'cos Keif's a big guy and he bounced in without knocking. Simone was so startled she leaped off the bunk.

"Why don't you *knock?*" I yelled. "You jump in like it's your house, not mine. We're having a private conversation."

"You always so please to see me," he said. "You warm this heart of mine. So what's this thing got balled up?"

"My life," I said. "When I met you."

"Ah sweetness, you say these pretty things. Now, in return, I'll mend your back."

"Later," I said. "We're talking." Because I wanted to go on talking to Simone. I wanted her to go on stroking my hair. We were so close. And she forgave me. It was like all the forgiving I'd ever need. And at last I was beginning to understand what happened last night.

"No," he said, "not later. Now. Before the damage 'come permanent. Leave it till later, we'll need Cousin Carmen."

"Shit," I said.

"Surprise at you, Eva," he said. "You an athlete, an' all. You should know these things or what."

"What you going to do?" I didn't trust him an inch.

"Embrocation. Manipulation. No aggravation."

"Voodoo fuckin' digits," I said.

"You got it," he said.

"You ain't going to make me piss Niagara Falls again?"

"What?" said Simone.

"Last time," I said. "His Cousin Carmen . . ."

"Well," she said, "you won't need *me* then, will you?"

"Don't go," I said. "Don't go, Simone. I do need you."

"Eva can't get up," Keif said. "Probably ain't had nothing to eat since last night. Nothing to drink neither. Put the kettle on, woman. I'll have two sugars in mine."

"You've got a nerve!" Simone said.

"Got a finely tuned athlete here," Keif said. "Got to look after her. Scrambled eggs is dandy. But not too much butter. Oh, and whole grain toast. None of that white rubbish."

"Are you going to let him talk to me like that?" Simone said.

But I couldn't move. I had to lie there, facedown, helpless. It was like I was a little kid—I couldn't see nothing but legs. And I had to put up with Keif and his big hands and his patter.

"Chill," he said, "relax." Like anyone could chill when a bloke pulls all the clothes off your back.

"Don't go, Simone." I was desperate.

"Be still," he said. "She ain't leaving 'cept it's to buy fresh milk and eggs. That right, Simone? You be cool. I ain't sexin' you or nothing, even though you beggin'."

"Bugger OFF!" I yelled. But it hurt to yell so I just had to lie there.

"What you done here?" he went. "Oh, whoa, heat, yeah, inflammation. What you been doin', Eva, carrying houses? Pushin' bungalows? Oh yeah, mischief in the lumbar region . . . You been dissing your lumbar region . . ."

And so on, and those big hot hands got bigger and hotter

and hotter and bigger until I thought he'd put a boiling kettle on the small of my back.

"Fuckin' ow-ow-ow!" I went. And suddenly there was a . . . well, like a flash of pink light—pouf—and . . . well, what? I don't know. I sort of dropped off the rim of the bath and went round and round and down the plug-hole.

When I woke up me eyes was watering and there was a bad smell.

"What's going on?" I said. "What a pong! Your embrocation's as foul as your flu cure."

"Your sister burnt the toast," he said. "Ain't the embrocation."

"This isn't a kitchen," Simone said. "It's more like a vagrant's campsite. What do you *eat*, Eva? There's nothing to cook with."

So she was still there. I felt ever so peaceful and maybe I dozed for a couple of minutes. But afterwards I could sit up on the bunk and eat my eggs and burnt toast.

Simone was complaining and cross. "I don't cook," she was saying. "I'm not your damn wife. Who scrambles eggs anymore?" So if Keif hadn't been there it would of been like we was real family. But Keif was strutting tall and so full of hisself he needed two Statics.

"How 'bout that, eh?" he said. "Genius or what? Am I good or am I *good?*"

"So you do a decent back rub," Simone said. "So what?"

"Ask Eva, so what. Ask her. She couldn't even lie down. Now look. What am I, Eva?"

"You're a cocky bugger," I said. "Okay, okay—you got good hands." I was too relieved to put him down.

"Told you. Din't I tell you?"

"You told us," Simone said. "What I want to know is, what's in it for you? Why're you hanging around? What're you doing here?"

"What she pay me for," he said. "She want fitness, that's what she gets. Plus a little extra 'cos she wise enough to hire pure talent."

"He's my personal trainer, Simone," I said.

"She needs me."

"There's more important things than body building," Simone said. "There's much more, isn't there, Eva?"

It was a shame. I wanted to think we was normal, that there was just her and me and a bit of argy-bargy with Keif. I didn't want to think about how I wrecked my back or about Ma and Wozzisname. Having a bad back and eating burnt toast was like a holiday from all that. I didn't want it to stop.

I said, "I got to get fit again."

"See?" said Keif. "It ain't body building. It's yer life. It's yer discipline. It's what keeps you alive and gets you out of bed in the morning. You can't rely on your body, what've you got?"

"Yeah," I said. "If I ain't fit, what am I?"

"You want me to tell you?" Simone said. And I almost thought she was going to say what I was in front of Keif. I thought she was going to say I was a killer and killers didn't deserve toast and back rubs. And what was I doing thinking about my body when I'd just tossed someone else's body in the river? I almost thought she was going to say that in front of Keif but of course she didn't. It was just me, thinking it. But it scared me.

"There's more to life than a body," Simone said. She looked hard in me eyes.

"There ain't no life at all without one," Keif said. He seemed like he wanted to sit down with Simone and argue it out. But Simone kept looking hard at me. And I was all confused—like maybe they was both talking about the dead bloke, not about me getting fit.

"Well, obviously," Simone said in her freezer voice. "But

other things matter too. Like family." She never took her eyes off me, so I said, "Yeah."

And then, 'cos she kept staring, I said, "We got to talk family business, Keif."

" 'Kay, safe," he said. But then he gave me six stretch-and-curl exercises and told me how to lie down. As if I didn't know.

Simone was fuming. I didn't know why she couldn't say, "Fuck off, Keif," like I can. If she could just say, "Bugger off," she wouldn't have to fume about it. Of course, with Keif, you can say "bugger off" till you're cross-eyed and he still don't listen. But it's better than dropping hints. I ain't much good at hints.

"Why do you put up with him?" she said when he went. "Why, Eva? He's impossible. You let him walk all over you."

"Do not!"

"Do! You fancy him, that's why. Don't tell me he's your personal trainer again. I'm sick of hearing about it. He's a joke. He's ugly, he's rude. But I think you fancy him."

"I fucking *don't*."

"Don't you shout at me, Eva. I'm sick of that too. You fancy him and he's laughing at you."

"I *don't*. He ain't."

"Why don't you get rid of him then?"

"I *am* getting rid of him. Only now I got to wait till me back's better."

"Excuses," she said. "Ask yourself why he's hanging around. He's always here."

"I'm paying him," I said. "Simone, I *don't* fancy him. I don't. I ain't interested. I *told* you."

"How can I believe what you told me? You said you were getting rid of him days ago but he's still here."

"Paid him till the end of the week," I said. Which was true.

"You're impossible too," she said. "You're made for each

other. Can't you see how dangerous he is? You've got something to hide, Eva. But he's always here. He could've overheard everything we said. He's after you for your money, Eva, and sooner or later he's going to find out something about you that'll give him a real handle on you."

"He don't know nothing," I said. "He can't. I ain't going to tell him anything, and you ain't neither."

"It isn't just us," Simone said. "It'd be all right if it was just us. Eva, you don't get it—it's Ma and her other feller."

That stopped me right where I stood. I said, "Ma knows?" But of course she knew. I knocked off her boyfriend, and her other boyfriend—the other bloke with no face—saw me do it. I was up to my chin in the slurry pit.

"Shit, Simone, what'm I going to do?"

"I don't know," Simone said. "I just don't know. Ma's drinking. When I came here she'd been drinking for hours. I'm doing the best I can, keeping her quiet, but she's on a binge and I don't know what she'll do next. You know what she wants, Eva? She only wants to give that feller a proper funeral."

"*What?*"

"Don't yell. She wants to see the body and give him a proper send-off."

"She can't." I was so upset I jumped off the bunk till my back reminded me to sit down. "You're kidding, Simone, tell me you're kidding."

"I wouldn't kid about a thing like that. She went berserk, Eva. I didn't know what to do."

"But it was her fault. She sent him."

"Try telling her that. She's acting like a grieving widow. I can't describe how disgusting it is."

"But she can't have him back," I said. "He's gone."

"Bring him back," Simone said. "I can't answer for her if she doesn't get her own way."

"I *can't*."

"He was in my car," she said. "You moved the car, right? You know where you put it, don't you?"

"But you said, 'Put him in the river.'"

"Yes, but . . ."

"So I put him in the river. All by myself. How do you think I wrecked my back?"

"Christ!" she said. "You're kidding?"

"Not."

"Just the way he was?" she said. "You didn't search him or anything?"

"No!"

"You didn't see if he had a wallet or any identification on him?"

I stared at her. I hadn't thought of any of that. All I thought about was how to get shot of him. And that was so hard, so very hard, I couldn't think about anything else.

Simone stared back at me. She was white and there was dark horseshoes under her eyes. She said, "He's in the river? And for all we know he's got papers and stuff in his pockets which'll lead him right back to us."

"I didn't think," I said. "You didn't say. Last night you just said put him in the river."

"Did I?"

"Yeah. So I did."

"Christ, Eva, what am I going to tell Ma?"

"Why tell her anything? It's her fault. You said so yourself. She's against us, Simone, always was."

"That's why I've got to keep her sweet. You don't understand. She could shop us to the police."

"She *wouldn't*," I said. "Even Ma."

"She's a dipso."

"But it was her fault. She was going to kidnap you."

"Kidnap her own daughter?" Simone said. "Who's going to believe that?"

I was in the slurry-pit all right and the shit was rising. Simone looked so tired. Sometimes when we was little and in trouble we'd hop into bed and pull the covers over our heads like a tent and pretend no one could see us. I wished we was still little, because it seems that the bigger you get, the bigger the trouble you get into.

"I *can't* get him back."

"Where did you put him?"

"I don't know."

"Whaddya mean you *don't know?*"

"Don't shout at me, Simone. It ain't my fault. I was all alone. You left me. I was just driving around and around 'cos I couldn't find anywhere quiet. I think it was sort of Greenwich or it might of been Deptford."

She stared at me like I came from Planet Weird.

"What about the tide?" she said.

"What about it?"

She buried her head in her hands. "What about my car?" she said.

"It ain't my fault," I said.

"What ain't?"

"You took the keys. You didn't leave me enough petrol. I was pushing and the steering locked. I had to walk away from it. I *had* to."

Simone is a very gentle person, always was, so she didn't scream at me or hit me or nothing. She just leaned forward till her forehead was resting on her knees. She put her arms round her knees and started rocking backwards and forwards.

"Where did you leave my car?" she said, all muffled.

"I don't know. Not exactly. I think it was sort of Deptford."

"Right next to where you dumped the . . . I mean, where you put *him?*"

"Not right next. I pushed it for ages."

"Christ," she said into her knees, rocking like an egg with blond hair. "I don't suppose," she said, in a tiny little voice, very slow, "I don't suppose you wiped your fingerprints off, did you?"

" 'Course I did," I said. Who did she think she was talking to—an amateur? I always do that. Second nature. At least I hoped like hell it was second nature, because, truth to tell, now I thought about it, I couldn't seem to remember what happened when the Clio finally conked out. I couldn't seem to remember how I got home or nothing. But Simone was so upset I couldn't bring myself to give her any more bad news.

" 'S all right," I said.

"What's all right?" She looked up at me with those hunted-haunted eyes. She needed comfort.

"You got to do what everyone does," I said. "You got to report your car missing. You got to tell the insurance. You got to act like you got your car nicked."

"Yes," she said. "Okay. That's okay."

" 'S all right. Honest. The car weren't nowhere near . . . him, Wozzisname."

"Jim," she said. "His name's . . ."

But I clamped my hands over my ears. "Don't tell me his name," I said. "Just don't. I don't want to hear it. I don't want to know nothing about him. He was dragging you away, Simone, he had a knife to your throat. I don't want to know he's got a wife and kids or a mortgage or eczema. I don't want to know none of it."

"Okay, okay," she said. "Don't get so excited."

"I'll go and see Ma," I said. "I'll sort her out."

"No!" she said. "She'll go bananas. She's bananas already.

134

You don't want to know anything about her bloke and you don't want to see her bereaved."

"But, Simone, she isn't bereaved. She scored him in a boozer or something. She never hardly knows them."

"Eva, that isn't what she says. That isn't what's happening. You don't know—it's like he's the love of her life."

"I don't believe it."

"Me neither. But you can't go round there—you're the Terminator or the Antichrist. You're an animal, Eva—she wants to have you put down."

Chapter 17

I couldn't spend another night like the last one. So when Simone went off to deal with Ma I went down Mandala Street to buy a new sleeping bag before all the shops shut. I took Lineker, and left Ramses to guard the Puma bag.

I took Lineker because I was weak and slow. I had to walk careful like an old lady. I couldn't stride out and hop over puddles. I couldn't move like meself. And if someone was going to jump me I couldn't clout them proper or do a runner.

It wasn't just Ma and her other feller I was thinking of. I hadn't forgot the blokes with their shooters. I ain't stupid. What about when my yard got broke into? What about that jacket with the torn bloody arm? You might of forgot that but *I* ain't.

Between Ramses and Lineker, Lineker is the prettier. He ain't as effective as Ramses but he's politer to take out in public. And if you must know, he don't pull like a steam train which is what Ramses does. I wasn't up to being dragged along at a hundred miles an hour. I wasn't Jumpin' Eva Flash no more. I was Crawlin' Eva Flash, and I didn't like to leave the yard in that state. I felt like a crab without a shell.

You don't think about your back till it lets you down, and

then you don't think about nothing else. It's always there, behind you, reminding you. Like it's saying, ho-ho, you thought
you had armour. You thought your muscle was your armour.
Well, girl, you took me for granted once too often. Now see
how it feels. You can have as much muscle as Mr. Universe but
it won't do you a scrap of good without a good back to back
you up.

I bought a brand-new sleeping bag in camouflage colours. It
really looked the bollocks—like an SAS guy might of slept in
one just like it, in the desert or in the jungle or on the moors.
Somewhere really truly hard. It even had a bit of mosquito net-
ting attached.

Because I kept thinking, if things got any worse, or even if
they stayed the same for too long, I might have to hit the road
or go to ground or something. Just to get out the way.

I bought an army surplus rucksack too—lightweight, with
all sorts of waterproof pockets and zips and straps. I could afford the best. No fake shit for the London Lassassin this time.
No picking up and walking away with stuff other people leave
lying around. No. It was all legal, bought-and-paid-for gear.

I bought a skinning knife with a jagged edge, and a holster
you strap on your leg to put it in.

I bought a multi-purpose tool which does everything from
bolt-cutting to pruning your roses. I bought a billy-can to heat
your tea or stew in. I bought a portable primus stove. I bought
a box of waterproof matches.

I bought a pair of strides with concealed pockets all up and
down the legs. I bought a combat jacket. I bought a waterproof
poncho which can double as a lean-to tent. I bought a new pair
of boots. I was tired of being cold and wet. What's the point in
having zillions if you're still cold and wet?

If the shop had sold Kalashnikovs I'd of bought one of them
too. I could see meself walking out from behind the Static with

a Kalashnikov in my arms, saying, "Oy, monkey-brains, what's them little sawn-off peashooters you got there? You want to cock around with me, mate?"

And the monkey-brained bastards, they'd just go, "Uh-oh—too much fire-power," and they'd back off and I wouldn't have to touch them. And I'd be safe and Simone'd be safe. And we could even sit out a siege if we had to 'cos we'd have everything we needed for survival.

The bloke in the shop said he couldn't find me a Kalashnikov but he could get me a crossbow which would stop a rhino at ten paces, and you don't need a firearms license for it. He didn't have one in stock but he could order it for me.

Ain't that the biscuit, though? "Can I order it for you, Modom?" When you ain't got the gold, it's all, "Oy you, don't touch the goods if you can't afford them." But if you flash a little of the crinkly stuff, it's all, "I'd be frigging delighted to order you one."

"Yeah, yeah, my man. Order me six and be quick about it. And while you're at it, have this little lot gift-wrapped and sent up to my penthouse with a dozen red roses and a crate of spritzer-thingies for my sister."

Oh yeah, I was feeling heaps better when I walked out of that shop. Heaps. Even my back felt oiled by that bugger's smarm. I like a bit of smarm once in a while. And this is the same bugger who wouldn't let me press my nose against the window a week ago. I wouldn't be broke again if you paid me.

I was wearing the new strides and combat jacket when I came out of the shop.

"Rrrr," said Lineker, because he didn't recognise me in new clothes.

"Shurrup, stupid," I said as I untied him. I thought I deserved a beer after spending so much dosh. I ain't used to spending dosh so it went to my head and I needed a little something to calm my nerves.

Me and Lineker set off for the Fir Tree, but did we get there? I tell you—I ain't never had a social life like this before. I can't even get a simple shlurp without someone comes along and interrupts.

This time it was a total stranger—a spotty prat who looked like a drooping weed. He was so droopy I could of tied him in a half hitch round a telegraph pole, but three things made me very leary.

First off—Lineker went, "Yerrrr-ack," and Droopy-drawers backed away the length of the leash.

Second—he was wearing a spanking new anorak.

And third—his left arm was bandaged right up to the knuckles.

"This your dog?" he said.

"What's it to you?" I said.

"Only, can I talk to you?"

"What about?"

"Listen, it's really important," he said.

I kept walking and he kept shuffling sideways the length of Lineker's leash away. All the hair on Lineker's back was up in a ridge and I was really glad I brought him along. Droopy-drawers wasn't much more than a kid, but he was wearing an anorak big enough for a bloke twice his size and he could of been hiding anything under it.

"Got to talk to you," he said.

"Well I don't got to talk to you," I said. I wished I was walking faster.

"No, look," he said. "Someone said . . . like . . . someone said you . . . like . . . someone said you was known for having it away with cars."

"Someone said wrong," I said. "Piss off."

139

"No, look, someone said you did it all the time. He said this place round here is . . . like, an elephant's graveyard for nicked motors."

"Fuck off, Droopy-drawers," I said. "You calling me a thief? *Are* you?"

"Na," he said. "I ain't calling you nothing. I do a bit of that meself."

"What?"

"Twocking."

"Hah!" I sneered at him. Twocking, in case you never heard of it, is Taking Without the Owner's Consent. And if that's what you call nicking motors it prob'ly means you make a habit of it and it prob'ly means you've been caught at it. Which made Droopy-drawers a loser.

"Dunno what you're talking about," I said.

"No, listen, be serious," he said.

"Serious?" I said. "If you think I nick things, *you* be serious. You call the cops."

"I might."

"Go on, then."

"No, look, forget it, I just want to talk to you about a red Carlton you might of . . . er . . . seen."

"Ain't seen nothing."

"Shit," he said, "I'm in serious bad trouble."

I could of said, "What trouble?" but I ain't that stupid. I just kept walking.

"No, listen," he said, "I'm so much in the shit. I wouldn't be talking to you else. Listen. That red Carlton ain't mine so I don't care you took it. It ain't mine. I was just delivering it somewhere for someone."

He was sweating. I didn't have to look at him—I could smell him. And so could Lineker. We both know the abdabs when we meet 'em, and old Droopy-drawers had the abdabs bad. Which

140

cheered me up no end. But it made me leerier too. You never
know what a droopy wossock with the abdabs is going to do.
'Specially if he might have a concealed sawn-off in his anorak.
We kept walking.

"No, wait," he said. "Me and my mate seen you."

"Seen me what?" I said. "In the ring?"

"No, listen—seen you at that garage on Jamaica Road."

"Jamaica who? Never heard of it."

"We asked around. Listen, we asked around and they all said
it had to be you. You're known for it."

"Said wrong. Now get stuffed, get knotted and get out me
way."

"And that breaker's yard . . ."

"What yard?"

"Where you hang out. They said all sorts of dodgy gear goes
in there and don't come out."

"That was you, then," I said. "Nearly lost your fuckin' hand,
din't you?"

"No, wait. I was only looking."

"Look somewhere else," I said. "I ain't seen your Carlton and
I ain't seen you. Next time me or my dogs catch you in my yard
you'll lose your arms, your legs and your droopy dick. Now piss
off while you still got something to piss with."

But he didn't. I tell you, this is the screwiest time of my life.
A year ago if I told a droopy dick to piss off he pissed off double quick. A week ago there wasn't no one to say piss off to.
Now, I'm telling more blokes to piss off than you can shake a
stick at, and they don't, none of 'em, take a blind bit of notice. I
ain't never been this popular before. Maybe that's what being
rich is all about.

"No, wait," he said. "Listen, I can't believe you're so fucking
hard-hearted. My mate and me, we're in so much trouble—

141

we're going to be killed. Listen, we'll be killed if we don't come up with that Carlton."

"Well go and look for it then," I said. "But don't look for it round me. I ain't fuckin' got it and if you look for it in my yard again you'll be dead for sure."

I shouldn't of said that. Saying that made me feel cold. It made my back kick in and my teeth ache. 'Cos we was almost at the yard when I said it and a few steps further on you could almost see the spot where Wozzisname popped his clogs.

"I'll look," Droopy-drawers said, "and you better pray God I find it, 'cos if I don't find it soon, *and* what's in it . . . no, seriously. Listen to me . . . if I don't, the last thing I'll say to the heavies who do for me . . . yeah, the last words out of my mouth will be your name."

"What's *your* name?" I said. "So's I can watch the obituaries."

"Look, who're you kidding? I ain't tellin' you my name."

That brought us slap up against the yard gate and Ramses came to say hello at a hundred miles an hour. Which put Droopy-drawers somewhere in between the rock and the hard place, 'cos even if Ramses and Lineker didn't know the name his mum gave him they knew him by another—I.N. Truder.

So when I told him to piss off again, he went. And I was ever so glad 'cos he was getting right on my hump about that sodding red Carlton. Who did he think he was—not believing me like that? Calling me a liar. He had no right to call me a liar even if I wasn't exactly telling the truth. He didn't know me, so he had no right to call me names.

On top of that, I could see Keif monging about under the streetlamp on the other side of the road and I didn't want him hearing what Droopy-drawers had to say.

I pretended not to see Keif while I unlocked the gate.

"Whotcha doin', gorgeous?" he said. "Thought I told you to rest. 'Stead you're out breakin' hearts and walking your dog."

"Gawd!" I said, acting all startled. "You spying on me?"

"Keeping an eye on my patient," he said. "Hey, girl, your sister indoors or what?"

"Why? What you want with her?"

"Why? You jealous?"

"*What you want with her?*" I wasn't playing no more.

"Easy, babe," he said. "I don't want nothing with her. I want something with you. Without her."

"Oh," I said. "What?"

"Got a problem," he said. "You the expert. Advice is what I need. Don't look at me like that, I ain't going to bite or what."

My mouth must of dropped open. Never, since the dawn of time, has a cocky bugger like Keif ever asked my advice. Cocky buggers like Keif tell you. They don't never ask.

"You gonna let me in or what?"

So I let him in and I calmed the dogs down. We went to the Static and, just to prove that I can use my own kitchen if I must, I put the kettle on.

Keif said, "Now lie down. Gotta ease that lumbar thing. No charge this time. Voodoo digits for free. Once in a lifetime offer."

So I lay down, 'cos last time helped so much. You wouldn't think a cocky bugger like him would actually be good at anything, would you? Cocky buggers, normally, are only good at telling you how good they are.

More likely it was Cousin Carmen's embrocation. I could feel the heat straightaway. It seemed to ooze right through the skin of my back all the way through my spine and settle in my guts on the other side.

"You relaxed or what?" Keif said. "Do I know how to soften 'em up or don't I know nuffin'?"

"Shut up," I said. "That's ace embrocation, though."

"Embrocation only half of it. Application's the other half."

I was so drowsy I only mumbled, "Cocky bugger," into the bunk cushion.

He said, "Got my first fight tomorrow."

I suddenly felt totally sorrowful, 'cos maybe I'd had my last fight a year ago and he was crowing about his first one.

He said, "I'm fighting Pete Carver."

"Lucky old you," I said. "Give him one from me, and make sure it hurts."

"What?" he said. "Speak up. What I want to chat about—I think they're setting me up. I dunno about this wrestling game. They show you all the moves an' stuff but they don't really tell you nothing. And all the hoopla about dressing up as a witch doctor an' chanting mumbo jumbo. They sprung that on me."

"Yeah," I said. "Mr. Deeds tried to make me wear a mask."

"What? Hide that pretty face?"

"Fuck off."

"Serious, man, my mum and dad's coming. My mum's going to go hyper if I do all that Africa crap. So I tried telling Mr. Deeds but he said . . ."

I rolled over. "He said, 'It's just a bit of fun, where's your sense of humour?'"

"Right, man. That's what he say."

"And then he said, 'He who pays the piper calls the tune. You dance to my tune or you're out.'"

"I told him my mum'd kill me if she saw me in a grass skirt with a bone through me nose."

"No shit?" I said. "I got to see this."

"So Mr. Deeds say he's invested serious cash in my training and if I don't fight I'll owe him money. So I go to my parents and say, 'Don't come an' see me fight.' And my mum say, 'What's the matter, you 'shamed of *us?*' Can't win, man, can't win."

I can't tell you how weird it was to hear this. I thought it was just me. I thought it was just me they wanted to stuff head-first in a box and say, "Do this. Don't do that. Be what we want you to be or you're out—barred." And I was jealous, 'cos he had someone to fight, and I don't just mean Pete Carver. And I was jealous 'cos his mum and dad wanted to go and see him in the ring. My ma never came and saw me. She was 'shamed of me. She never thought I might be 'shamed of her.

"Did you ask Harsh?" I said.

"Nah. But he overheard some of it. Like in the locker-room when all the guys were giving me verbals or what. He said something about goats."

"What? What did he say?"

"Oh man, what was it? Something like—'The horse that can walk but allows itself to be dragged like a goat will . . .' Dunno what he said. Dunno what he mean. Harsh ain't an oracle, and I ain't a horse or a goat."

That made me jealous too. Harsh was always saying stuff I didn't understand but I wanted him to say it to me, not Keif. I'd of worn a grass skirt if only Mr. Deeds'd let me fight again. Anything. I would. Well, maybe not anything. I wouldn't wear a mask over me face. You can't breathe in a mask. You can't see or hear proper. You can't be who you are in a mask.

And then I thought maybe Keif couldn't be Keif in a grass skirt.

So I said, "You got to be something."

"What d'you mean—I got to be something?"

"Well, like I was always the Villain. I always wore the black. And it was great. I could be as bad as I wanted."

"Oh yeah, man," Keif said. "I don't mind being something— I don't mind being the baddy. Safe. It's the insult, see."

"So why aincha a boxer like your dad? You don't have to dress up for that."

"Wanted to be a boxer," Keif said. "Like, when I was a kid, watching old fights on video. My dad had them all. And I

145

wanted to be Sugar Ray Leonard if I didn't grow too big, or Muhammad Ali if I did grow big. They had *style*."

"I wanted to be Klondyke Kate. She had style too."

"But I got a weak head. I could take any punch to the body. But you blow on my chin and I'm in sleepy-time."

"Don't you ever tell Pete Carver that," I said. "Just never tell any of those sods that or you'll be going bye-byes twice nightly."

"I ain't foolish, girl. Hey, know what? You cleared my mind."

"Eh?"

"Yeah. I ain't going to dress up like Big Chief Wogga-wogga. None of that shit. So fuck 'em. That's me last word. I'll be Muhammad Ali—white dressing gown, red satin, tassels, all the gear. And I'll dance and rap an' they won't know what hit 'em."

"They'll bar you."

"So?"

He didn't want it like I wanted it. They were giving it to him but he didn't want it enough to be scared of being barred. And I thought, if they gave it back to me, if they unbarred me I'd even mind my manners with tossers like Pete and Gruff.

"They can like it or lump it," Keif said. And maybe I'd of said the same before last night, before Wozzisname. But now, now I wanted to be who I was before Wozzisname. Before all the things which made Wozzisname happen. If I'd still been the London Lassassin, they wouldn't of happened, would they?

They wouldn't, 'cos I'd of been in training and I wouldn't of let my fitness slip, or my relaxed mental attitude. I wouldn't of caught the flu or let The Enemy fire me. See, your body is your life—when it's fit and strong it backs you up. But when it's weak it lets all sorts of bad stuff come creeping in—like flu germs and evil mojo.

Chapter 18

I was glad Simone didn't come round till later. She didn't get along with Keif, and he didn't get along with her. Which was queer because everyone likes Simone. It's me you ain't supposed to like, and a year ago I used to get paid for it. Everyone hates the Villain. They *love* hating the Villain. That's what made me so popular. But now I ain't the Villain. I'm just another bad'n. That's the curse of Wozzisname again. The minute he laid hands on Simone and I took hold of that hammer the curse came down.

It wasn't my fault. He made me do it. But I got cursed just the same. And Wozzisname got croaked. That's two of us who'll never be ourselves again. And it's all down to Ma. She tried to use Simone against me. Her own daughters. All for gelt. After I'd been kind enough to pay her poxy rent for her.

She never even asked me. She could of said, "Eva, I'm strapped for cash—give us a bit for the rent." And I'd of coughed up like a baa-lamb, 'cos I got family feeling. Well, I might of haggled with her a bit. I might of said, "Tell me where to find Simone or you can sodding gag for your rent." But she never gave me the chance. She just sent those two boyfriends round with knives and hammers, frightening the life out of Simone and turning me into a bad'n.

But she screwed up, didn't she? She was probably bladdered when she thought it up. Well she must of been bladdered. She's always bladdered. So she screwed up and she didn't get her gelt and now Simone and me are even closer together. If it wasn't for Simone I'd be a gibbering wreck by now.

But if Simone got along with Keif, she could of been there when Keif was treating me like the expert. I wished she'd seen that. He was even thinking of using my name. He wanted for his mum to sew red letters which said Muhammad Wily on the back of his white robe. Not Wylie, like my name, but said the same. Because it means crafty and he liked that. He said my name gave him the idea.

We was sociable, and I ain't used to being sociable, but I wished Simone was there to see it. I wished she could of heard how he said, "Hey, girl, respect," when he went away. See, that's exactly what he should of said. 'Cos I *am* the expert and I'm paying his wages. That deserves respect, which I don't normally get from him. It would of been even better if Simone was there to see.

I was hungry so I hotted up a tin of bacon bits and beans. Then I went out to check the fence. Even the dogs was giving me more respect. I was wearing my new combat jacket and feeling snug as a bug. It wasn't raining for a change and for a change no one was giving me any hassle. Droopy-drawers didn't come back. Maybe he found his Carlton. Maybe he didn't. Nothing to do with me—I didn't hide it. I never hide them. I always leave 'em for someone to find. I ain't a thief.

Simone didn't come till nearly eleven, and when she came she looked thin and tired. Actually she looked more and more like when she was little. She wasn't so done up. She was wearing jeans and a nice leather coat and she wasn't so painted. She was showing her frailty.

She brought a jar of coffee and some chocolate biscuits. I don't drink coffee usually 'cos of Harsh saying caffeine was poison, but Simone made some for herself so I had some too. I was practising being sociable. Maybe if she hadn't been taken away and adopted I wouldn't have to practise. We could of spent years having coffee and chocky bickies together.

She brought a bottle of Scotch too, so we had a drop of that in the coffee with lots of sugar. We was really comfy.

"Eva," she said, "we got to talk."

After that it wasn't so comfy.

"Eva," she said, "we've got a problem. It's Ma, and it's a big problem."

Tell me something new. When wasn't Ma a big problem?

"Don't start ranting and raving," Simone said, "but I've got to ask you something."

I didn't feel like ranting. We was comfy with our coffee and biscuits, and I was tired. Everything was catching up on me. I wanted to sit quiet and let my back go to sleep.

"Ask," I said. "You can ask anything, Simone, you know that."

"It's about money," she said. "Have you really got any?"

"Why?"

"Because if you don't we're in even bigger trouble than we were this morning."

"Why?" How could we be in bigger trouble? Wozzisname was croaked and in the Thames same as he was this morning. There was nothing we could do to change that.

"Have you got any?" Simone said.

"Some."

"How much?"

"Dunno. Why?"

"Ma wants it or she'll turn us in."

"*What?*"

"Don't shout," Simone said. "Shouting won't help. I've given her everything I've got but it isn't enough. I never had much—I was never a saver."

"You've gave her all your dosh?"

"I had to. She was screaming about the cops."

"How much?"

"Hundreds," she said, "everything I had."

"Oh *Simone*," I said. "How could you?"

"I *had* to, Eva. I can't get arrested. I can't. You *know* what'll happen. We'll be taken away and locked up. Just like the old days."

I stood up. "I'll get it back for you," I said. "Come on, Simone, we'll face her down. I'll get it back."

"Eva, no!" she said. "You don't understand. Her other boyfriend is involved. He's winding her up, egging her on. They're both drinking."

"Don't care how many boyfriends she's got. I can handle it."

"Please don't shout. I can't stand any more violence, Eva. I can't stand for anyone else to get hurt. What if *you* got hurt next time, Eva? How could I stand that? What if she got the cops in? What if we got taken away again?"

That stopped me. I said, "I'd rather die than be locked up again." But I was thinking, maybe if we got took away we'd be locked up together. Like the old days.

She said, "Me too. I'd rather die than be locked up again. I couldn't take that, Eva, all the shouting and bullying. I couldn't take it before and it'd be worse now. I've got a life now."

What was she talking about—bullying?

"I always protected you," I said. "I'll look after you."

"Oh Eva," she said, "how could you? You'd be in solitary. You'd be done for murder. I'd be done for accessory."

They'd chuck away the key. And I had a horrible thought—suppose they put us in separate chokeys?

I said, "How much does Ma want if your hundreds ain't enough?"

"How much have you got?"

"Dunno," I said. "I was never much good at counting, you know that."

"Show me," she said. "I'll do the counting." Which reminded me of the old days too. She always helped with the maths.

So I went out to the dogs' pen and I took the Puma bag down from the wall where I'd nailed it. I gave Ramses and Lineker a Bow Chow rusk each 'cos they'd done their best and no one had touched that bag except me.

I was nearly in tears. I was giving Ma my future. I was giving her all my personal training and the chance of a fitness centre called Musclebound.

I was choked up—that lovely crinkly stuff hadn't hardly been mine for two lousy minutes before I was forced to give it to Ma.

I carried it across the yard, walking slow with Ramses and Lineker, like a funeral procession. But first Ramses, then Lineker, peeled off and took a sprint to the fence. "Yakkety-ro-ro," they went. So I put the bag down really careful and went after them.

There was a bloke at the fence. With the street light behind him I thought it was Keif. He had the same brick shit-house build. But then I saw it wasn't.

"Where's Simone?" he said.

I said, "Move your big arse away from my fence or I'll set the dogs on you."

"*Simone!*" he yelled.

"Oh, *you're* the one," I said, "you're the tart-raking fuckin' dumb boyfriend."

151

"*Simone!*" he yelled. "Yeah, I'm the boyfriend all right. What you going to do about it—hit *me* over the head with a hammer?"

And then Simone was there. She flew over to the fence. She said, "Eva, leave this to me." She said, "Andy, go a-*way*. Just get out and leave us alone."

Andy said, "Oh no. I'm not having that. You said you'd only be a minute."

I said, "Come on. Come over my fence. Meet my dogs. That'll only take a minute."

"I don't trust you," Andy said to Simone, and, *wow*, you should of seen Simone then. She was my sister all right—never mind her fancy ways.

She beat the chain fence with both hands. She said, "You stupid, stupid bastard. You troll. You greedy, useless fucker."

He stepped back—it was like he got bitten by a butterfly.

I said, "What's a troll?"

And then Simone turned on me. "Go indoors," she said. "*Now*. Right now. Or I'm going back to Copenhagen and I'll never come back. You can all stew, kill each other, I don't care. I mean it. I've had enough."

Where the hell was Copenhagen? It sounded a long, long way away and it made me feel cold. I stepped back too. I said, "If you lay one finger on my sister again . . ."

"You'll what?" said Andy.

"Shut the fuck up, both of you," said Simone.

"I'll hang your bollocks over my door and you'll be dangling from them."

"*Eva!*" Simone said.

"I'm going," I said. "But I'm leaving the dogs." And I went, walking backwards so's I could see if he put one finger through the fence.

I didn't stop till my heel hit the Puma bag. I picked it up.

"That bastard ain't having you," I said. Instead of taking the bag to the Static I took it to the dog pen.

I know. A troll is the man-version of a trollop. It should be—there's all sorts of rude words for women but there's never enough for men when you need 'em. If Ma scores a bloke in a pub for the price of a rum and coke she's a slag, a slapper or a slusher. But when he scores her, what d'you call him? Unlucky?

I wasn't going to hand over all my gold to a troll and a trollop. No cocking way. I'm supposed to pay Ma off, keep her sweet? What for? What's she done to deserve it? And him—the troll, the slut-puller, with his slick face and hairy hands—what's he done I should pay him for? Scored a cheap shag off of my ma and tried to grab my sister. Does that deserve zillions? Well, does it?

I banged the nail into the doghouse wall and hung the bag on it. While I was doing that I had another thought, so I reached in, snatched a wad and stuffed it in my pocket. Then I went to the Static.

But before I got there I noticed that Simone was standing all alone with her back to the fence. Andy, the troll, wasn't there no more. She was just standing, small and cold, with Ramses and Lineker sitting in front of her. I almost had to laugh. She really blew me away, my sister. She could come steaming out, with nothing but a little thin jersey to protect her, and mouth off to a beefy bugger who was threatening me. But she couldn't walk past two dogs.

"Every time I move," she said, "they snarl."

"Oy, shit-heads," I said. "*Behave.*" And they stood down immediately.

"Don't shout at them," she said. "I've had it with abuse and shouting."

"If you don't shout, they don't listen."

"There's other ways," she said.

"What other ways?" I said. "*You* couldn't walk past them." I put my arm around her, 'cos she was shivering, and we went back to the Static.

I said, "Where's he gone, that Andy bastard?"

"I don't know," she said. "I don't care. Back to Ma's I suppose."

"Is he living with her?" None of them lived with her for more than a couple of days.

"He's always there," she said. "He smells a payoff."

See, blokes *can* smell gravy. No wonder I was so popular.

She said, "So what *is* the payoff, Eva? What've we got?"

"What're we buying, Simone?" See, Wylie by name, crafty by nature.

"Silence," she said. "Freedom."

"Do them things stay bought?" I said. "Or do you have to keep paying for them like the electricity? Every month, year in, year out?"

"I don't know," she said. "Ma and Andy, they want whatever we've got." She knuckled her eyes. "They aren't thinking ahead. But you're right. We've got to think ahead." Her knuckles were mauve with cold and she drew her knees up to her chin.

I made us some more coffee and she poured the Scotch in. She said, "I could go off abroad again. I don't need to do this, Eva. I'm stuck in the middle and I hate it."

"No," I said. "No!"

"Shshsh. If I left the country they'd never bother looking for me."

"Can I come too?"

"Got a passport?" she said. "You couldn't take your dogs."

"Don't go," I said. "Just don't."

She didn't say anything. She just looked at me with them dark blue eyes and brushed her hair with her fingers. The torch light picked up each strand and turned it silver-gold.

"Don't go," I said. "Promise. Please. I ain't got no one but you."

"You did all right before," she said. "Think about it. It's me that got you into this mess. If I hadn't come back Ma would never've thought of that trick."

"She'd of thought of another one," I said, but then I wondered, would she? She pickled her brain so regular it was amazing she thought up the first one. "It ain't your fault," I said. "You can't leave. I'd much rather be in a mess with you than not in a mess without you. You're the only family I've got. There ain't no one else. No one."

"Oh, Eva, don't say that." She covered her face with her hands and teardrops leaked down her wrists into her sleeves.

I couldn't bear it. I emptied my pockets onto the bunk between us.

"Look, Simone," I said. "Look. I don't know how much I got. Count it. Give it to Ma. Keep it. Just promise me you won't go."

She looked. She counted. She said, "Where did you get all this, Eva? It's over two *thousand*."

"The lottery," I said. "I bought a ticket." Well, I did, didn't I? I wasn't lying.

"How much did you win?"

"I didn't get all six numbers. Nothing like that."

"How much?"

"Dunno, I'd had a couple of beers—I ain't clear on a few beers."

Yeah, all right, I'm very nearly lying to my own sister. But see it my way—I didn't want her to leave, and Ma and the troll was too much for her already. What in hell would she think about the red Carlton and the Puma bag and Droopy-drawers who might have a sawn-off hidden under his anorak? Go on—tell

155

me what she'd do if she found out about that? She's sensitive. She'd bugger off for sure, and maybe I'd never see her again.

"Jesus Christ, Eva," she said. "You keep all this money lying around? Here? Didn't you put some in the bank?"

"Bugger banks," I said. "I ain't giving my dosh to a bank, 'cos then I have to ask permission to get it back. I ain't stupid. I know what they do. You got to pay for cheques and stuff. It's like your dosh got to pay rent for itself, when it can live here for free. They keep it and do what they like with it, but you got to say, 'Please, sir,' when you want any back. And then you pay to get it back."

"But it isn't safe."

"It was safe enough till now."

"Oh Eva," she said. "You need a manager. You do. You need . . ."

"Doesn't matter now," I said. I was looking at all that lovely lucre sitting on the bunk between us. It was like losing a friend.

She sat there all thoughtful for a minute. Then she said, "I can't take all this. It isn't right or fair. Tell you what I'll do. I'll take half. I'll tell Ma and Andy about the lottery. I'll say this is all that's left. They don't know any better, do they? You never told Ma what you won, did you?"

" 'Course not," I said. "And she wouldn't know about it now except I paid her rent. Out of the kindness of me heart."

"It isn't fair, is it?" she said. "Okay, so no one knows how much you've got. So I'll give Ma half. It has to be over a thousand."

"Why?"

"Because that'll seem like a lot."

"It fucking *is* a lot."

"Yeah, but a few hundred wasn't enough, so maybe if we give her a four figure amount it'll satisfy her."

"Shit, Simone, it's got to satisfy her. When did she ever *see* this much? She never had a pot to piss in. And you know she's only going to piss it away."

"I know. But it's got to be more than a thousand. And it can't be a round number 'cos that's too neat. She's got to think it's everything you've got. If she doesn't think that she'll keep coming back for more."

She decided on one thousand one hundred and sixty-seven pounds. I don't know why. She said it wasn't the sort of number you'd invent. She said the clincher was the sixty-seven. It was psychology, she said. If we'd made up a number under fifty Ma would suspect she was being short-changed. But a number over fifty was believable. She said one thousand one hundred and sixty-seven was a truthful sort of number. No one would make up a number like that.

And she was right—it sounded like masses more than one thousand one hundred and fifty. It even sounded like more than one thousand two hundred even though I knew it was less. Numbers are very, very weird, and very muddling.

And look at what she saved me! Did anyone ever have a sister as smart as Simone?

Chapter 19

I know what Simone was thinking about. Once, when we was six or seven, Ma won a lucky draw on one of her catalogues. A letter came which said, "You have won the chance to win fifty thousand pounds," and Ma got all excited 'cos she never won anything before. This letter said all she had to do was choose two of a dozen items and order them, and that way she'd be eligible for the Grand Prize Draw.

Ma ordered some anti-static rinse to keep her undies tangle-free and a tooth bleaching kit and she sat back and waited.

A second letter came, and it said she hadn't won the Grand Prize but she'd come so close they were going to give her a twenty-quid voucher and a set of hand towels absolutely free. She didn't have to order anything else.

Only by that time, Ma had pissed away the rent so she couldn't even afford to pay for the anti-static rinse and the tooth bleaching kit. So her catalogue company never sent her the voucher or the hand towels and she didn't even get the anti-static or the tooth bleach. She got nothing at all. And Simone said she was down the price of the stamp.

Remembering that, Simone said if Ma used to be the sort who gave up fifty thousand pounds or a twenty-quid voucher for a night out at the pub, then she'd most likely settle for what she could screw out of me now. She'd blitz it all away and then forget about it. Simone said people didn't change for the better over the years. They just stayed themselves and got worse.

Simone said the joker in the pack was Andy. She'd have to be very careful with Andy. He kept saying he was only doing what was right for Ma, but Simone thought he was calling the shots for his own advantage. Andy didn't trust Simone. That's why he followed her to the yard. He was the one she had to convince about the one thousand one hundred and sixty-seven pounds. In the long run he was a lot more dangerous than Ma.

Before she left Simone said, "So Eva, you've got to keep quiet from now on. You mustn't spend any money. You mustn't tell anyone about it. You haven't told Keif, have you? Well, don't. Don't tell anyone."

She was right, wasn't she? Andy mustn't know about the money. And the same went for Droopy-drawers.

I was glad I bought all my new gear before she told me not to spend anything. I'd of been very cold that night without a nice thick sleeping bag.

But I dreamt Wozzisname was sharing the sleeping bag with me. He wasn't upset about being dead but he had a deep dent in his head and he kept tickling me and nudging me with his elbows. Which made me really angry. I told him to fuck off and leave me alone but he said, "No way, girl, we married now." And his voice was Keif's voice.

The strangest thing of all was that when Keif turned up the next day he blew in saying, "Hey, dream girl." And I wondered if it was possible that one person could know that another person had been dreaming about his voice. It spooked me, because his cousin was an obeah lady and you never know if them things are passed down in families like brown eyes or warts.

He said, "Brought a friend." And he opened the door again. I was afraid he'd brought Cousin Carmen, but it wasn't Cousin Carmen, it was Milo.

"Herf," said Milo, and I thought his voice was deeper. He jumped on the bunk and swiped my chin with his tongue. He wasn't shivery no more.

"Oy," I said, "you ain't a lap dog."

He swiped my chin again and sneezed.

Keif said, "You make me sad, man. You been drinking again."

"Ain't," I said.

"Milo knows you're lying, man, and so do I. We both got a wicked sense of smell."

"Piss off to the rose garden then. Both of you."

"Might do," he said. "Your sister been here last night. I can smell her too."

"Keep your sodding nose out of my business," I said. I was so choked off with him I could of smeared his wicked sense of smell all over his face.

"My nose and your business don't like each other," he said. "C'mon Milo. We ain't welcome here."

"Wha'd'you mean 'we'? Milo's *my* dog. Not yours."

"You ain't fit for a puppy dog. When you guttered you mistreat him. When you with your sister she make you guttered. She no damn good for you, man. She no damn good, full stop. Then you no good for Milo."

"Don't you bad-chat my sister," I said. "Don't you *ever* do that. You don't know her. You don't know *anything*."

"I know you, man."

"You know *nothing*."

"If you say so," he said. He walked out the door. And Milo followed him.

I was so stone choked I leaped out of the sleeping bag, off the bunk and out the door before I remembered my stiff back.

I caught them up before they reached the gate.

"Oy you," I said. "You apologise. You better 'pologise right now. What you said 'bout my sister is pure shite."

"Shite ain't pure," he said, still walking.

"Fuck you," I said. "She's my *sister*. She's the only family I got left. You can't talk bad about her and walk away. You can't. She's all I got."

"Where's your shoes, girl?"

"Wha'?"

"You run round barefoot you'll catch the flu again."

Suddenly I felt cold and I looked round. All the men in the yard were staring and grinning. I hated myself for running after Keif. I stone hated myself for doing that.

I picked Milo up in my arms and went back to the Static. Milo had put on weight.

"I knew a boy at school," Keif said, following me.

"You still here?" I said.

"Rude boy," Keif said, "slack like you wouldn't believe. But he wrote poems like Bob Marley, like Gil Scott-Heron. A D.J. talk to him one time. He say, 'Write me a song, man, we'll take it to the studio.' But this boy, running around with other rude boys all the time, smokin' bush, buyin' rocks. So he say, 'Yeah man, cool. Tomorrow.' But tomorrow never come, 'cos tomorrow this kid is all fucked up and wigged out and he can't string two words together."

"Was he your brother?" I said.

"No, he ain't my brother. Just a kid at school I used to look up to. 'Cos he had talent. I used to respect talent. But talent

161

don't mean shit by itself. In fact talent's bad for you. It make you think you don't need nothing else. And you do."

"I know that," I said. "I ain't stupid."

"No? Then you worse than this kid I'm telling you about. You diss your talent *and* you diss your brains or what."

"But she's my sister."

"Okay, she your sister."

"Family's important."

"Yeah."

"So," I said.

"So?" he said.

"So, you want to go weight training?"

"No. You ain't up for that."

"Running?" I never thought I'd hear myself suggest running. Keif's got a point—a drop of Scotch in your coffee addles your brain something chronic.

"You ain't up for running neither. I'll do your back. Then we'll walk. But only if you put your shoes on. I don't want to be seen walking with no hippy girl or what."

So I lay down on my front, and after a while all I could smell was Cousin Carmen's embrocation and all I could feel was deep heat.

Keif said, "You know what I'm saying or what?"

I said, "Yeah." Well, I didn't say it, I just sort of groaned. And I thought, Eva, you're getting addicted to this.

Keif said, "You got to do one thing."

"Wha'?"

"Tell her. Tell your sister the juice is bad for you. See, mebbe she thinks athletes can drink sociable."

"They can."

"Listen to me. I'm giving you a way out. Couple of beers now and then—okay. Hard juice, out of your skull—not okay.

It fucks up muscle tone, it fucks up coordination. Then you get hurt, man. Look at you now."

He didn't know nothing. What was wrong with me was all down to Wozzisname. And where was Keif at one in the morning when I needed a drop of something to dull the ache? Where was he then? It wasn't him who kept me company in the night. It was Simone. She sat with me. And Wozzisname didn't come visiting till after she'd gone. It was when I was alone that Wozzisname climbed in my sleeping bag and gave me bad dreams.

"You tell her," Keif said, "tell her the juice fucks up your immune system. It's why you got the flu, man. You listening or what?"

'Course I was listening. What else could I do lying on my belly with him making putty of my lumbar region? What was I going to do? Tell him where he could stuff his sermon? You don't say that to a bloke with good hands.

"I hear you," I said.

"Speak up," he said. "Where's all the shouting gone? You going to shout for me tonight?"

"Tonight?"

"My fight, girl. You ain't forgot that. You're my fan club, right?"

"I ain't coming to that."

"Got to," Keif said. "You got to shout my name real loud. Lead the chorus or what. I want all the little girls shouting for Muhammad Wily, 'cos he the greatest. Right? Make Pete Carver mad for sure."

He didn't understand. I can't go to the wrestling. Not if I ain't in it. I can't shout his name. It's supposed to be *me*. Everyone's supposed to shout *my* name. Wrestling ain't his. It's mine. I ain't given it to him. I want it for myself. He didn't even want it that bad. I can't go and watch him up there in the light, in the ring, 'cos that's where *I* should be.

He didn't understand and he went drivelling on. He said, "Besides, my mum want to meet you. She say, 'Who's this little girl you seeing all the time, boy?' You got to explain about wrestling to my folks. My dad knows boxing but he don't know wrestling."

"I can't go," I said.

" 'Cos you barred?"

"Na. 'Cos . . ."

"Mr. Deeds can't bar you out of the audience. He can bar you out of his shows, he can bar you out of the gym. But he can't tell you what to do as a civilian. He got no rights to do that."

"But I ain't a civilian. I ain't no audience."

"Woh! Chill, girl," he said. "You gone all knotted. You do yourself a mischief. All my girls got to be soft."

And that was the problem. That was it. I got it. Dunno why it took me so long. I ain't soft. I'm hard. I ain't nobody's soft girl. I'm the London Lassassin—the one they call Bucket Nut. Keif was stealing my work, and he was stealing my name. He didn't really want neither, and he was expecting me to lie down on my belly and be soft about it. Fuck that, man. Fuck that. He even wanted my pup.

I rolled over. I said, "Fuck that! I ain't going. I ain't audience. I'm the London Lassassin. I ain't sitting in the dark."

His face was still all smiley. He didn't get it.

"You don't get it," I said. "I don't go to the wrestling. I *am* the wrestling. I don't watch. I fight."

"Oh man!" he said. "Wouldn't that be something? Wouldn't that make them creepos mad or what?"

"Wha?" He was stone bursting with himself. I took a deep breath and I would of blasted him into next month except Si-

164

mone come in. I was really glad she didn't see me with my shirt up round my neck and him with his hands.

She said, "Uh-oh, didn't know you were busy with your boyfriend."

So the blast came out 'cos I couldn't hold it back into my throat. They was all of them getting it wrong. "*He ain't my boyfriend,*" I said. "I ain't no soft girl. I ain't nobody's dream what'sit. I got me *own* shit. I'm the London fucking Lassassin."

"Don't you shout at me," Simone said. "If you want to shout at someone shout at loverboy here. Shout at those two guys waiting for you outside."

"Never knew a girl so popular," said Keif.

"What two guys?" I said.

"Herf?" said Milo in his new deep voice.

"Fucking shut up, all of you," I said, and I went out and slammed the door after me. I hoped it burst their eardrums.

Except I wasn't wearing any shoes. I forgot them again. But I wasn't going back for them. If you slam the door it's got to stay slammed. You can't slide back inside and say, "Oops, pardon me for breathing, but I need my sneakers."

On the other hand, barefoot ain't the way you want to meet Droopy-drawers and his fish-faced mate. Not when both of them had boots the size of canoes on their plates of meat. Only one thing to do—don't give 'em time to notice.

"Oy, you," I said. "Get away from my gate. I told you before."

"No, listen," said Droopy-drawers. "You listen. We found the car. No, listen, we found it but we didn't find what we was supposed to find in the back."

"Why the fuck am I supposed to care?" I said. "Fuck off."

"No. We ain't going nowhere," he said.

"I'll get my dogs," I said.

"If you walk away," said Fish-face through his little pouty

lips, "I'll fucking shoot you in the back. And I'll shoot your dogs. I don't care. I'm a dead man already."

I didn't have an answer ready for that one, so I stayed where I was. I couldn't see no shooter, but I could see two big coats which could of hidden two cannons for all I knew.

Droopy-drawers said, "You gotta listen. You gotta talk to us." If you put the both of them in the one anorak they still wouldn't fill it out. There was still plenty of room for a sawn-off.

I said, "Where would two droopy dildos like you get a shooter?" Which was stupid. A bloke with a sawn-off ain't a droopy dildo. He's a bloke you stop and listen to. You might even want to call him "sir."

The thing that made me uneasy was that they were more scared than me. They were sweating and shifting from foot to foot. They were twitching and looking over their shoulders.

"You waiting for someone?" I said.

"I told you we was in trouble," Droopy-drawers said. "But you wouldn't listen."

"Listen to what?" I said. "You said you lost your car. I ain't seen it. Now you lost something else. I don't even know what you lost. And you're going to shoot me in the back. What am I supposed to listen to? You call me a thief and a liar and I'm supposed to listen to that?"

"It's got to be you," Fish-face said. "There ain't two like you. There can't be."

"Two like who?" I said. "What the hell've I done to you that makes you want to shoot me in the back?"

"Look, we don't *want* to shoot you," Droopy-drawers said.

"I do," said Fish-face. "I don't care anymore."

"You really got a shooter?" I said.

"Yeah," said Fish-face. "You know we have. We nearly took you with it the other night."

"Not me," I said.

"Yeah, you," he said.

"You drove off with Mr. . . . with Uncle's motor," said Droopy-drawers. "It *was* you. We saw you. We found the motor. The window was blown out. You must of noticed."

"I'd of noticed if I'd been there," I said. "We're going round in circles, and I still don't know why you want to shoot me in the back."

Fish-face and Droopy-drawers looked at each other. You wouldn't think they had enough jazz between them to lick a stamp, let alone rob a petrol station or walk around with a sawn-off.

I suddenly knew what to do. I said, "I'm getting stone hacked off with you two. You got no right coming here calling me a liar. You two's the liars. Not me. I don't believe you got a shooter. I don't believe you. And even if you got one you ain't got the jazz to use it. So fuck off."

It was a dead simple plan. I'd tease Fish-face into showing me the shooter and then I'd take it away from him. Then I'd have it and he wouldn't, and he couldn't shoot me but I could shoot him. Except I wouldn't 'cos I didn't never want to see another dead bloke in my yard again. But he wouldn't know that.

Fish-face put his hand up to his collar to grab the toggle of his zip.

Droopy-drawers said, "No, look, don't. We're in enough shit already."

Fish-face said, "That's just the point. We can't be any worse off. And I don't like her. She's an ugly bitch."

He grabbed the toggle and pulled his zip down to the waist where it got stuck.

Droopy-drawers said, "You can't shoot her 'cos she's ugly."

"Why not?" Fish-face was wrestling with his zip. "Why the fuck not? I got a gun, ain't I?"

167

I was getting impatient. I was ready. I'd been ready since he first touched his zip.

"Look, no," said Droopy-drawers, "she ain't told us where the sports bag is."

The zip came free. It was taking forever, and we was in the open where the men in the yard and anyone passing by could see us. But half of me really truly couldn't believe that Fish-face, with his little pouty lips and his flat eyes, could possibly have anything as serious as a shooter. The other half was ready.

His zip came free. His anorak flopped open. He *did* have a sawn-off shooter. But it was stuck through his belt pointing at the ground. He grabbed the stock with his right hand.

Droopy-drawers grabbed his right hand. "No, listen, wait," he said.

Fish-face shook Droopy-drawers off and pulled the shooter out.

I stepped in. One step. Plant left foot. Whoosh-whack. I kicked the sawn-off.

"Fuckin' ow-ow-ow," I went. I was hopping on one foot.

The shooter popped up over Fish-face's head and landed in the mud behind him. He stood there like a daisy. He didn't know where it was.

Droopy-drawers picked it up.

I went, "Fuckin' give me that." I hopped at him and wrenched it out of his hand. I was hopping mad because I was hopping, and I was hopping because I hurt me foot. And I hurt me foot 'cos I kicked the barrel of a sawn-off with me own soft toes. I forgot my sodding shoes.

Why is everything so stupid?

If you read about it in the paper it'd go, "London Lassassin Disarms Armed Raider With Karate Kick." Well, it would if I was writing it. But it wasn't like that. It was stupid and feeble. "London Lassassin Breaks Toe." "Show-girl Kicks Better Than

London Lassassin. Armed Raiders Fall About In Gibbering Heap." Nothing turns out like I want it to.

Except I had the shooter in my hands. Big deal. The only thing you could say about that was it was safer for me. I couldn't take it serious—it was all too stupid. I couldn't take the shooter serious, 'cos I couldn't take Fish-face and Droopy-drawers serious. My foot hurt and I couldn't take nothing serious but that.

Chapter 20

I never had a gun in my hands before. I thought it'd be really brilliant—a big power surge or something. But when it happened it was no different to a spanner. Or a hammer. And you know what happened last time I had a hammer in my hand.

So I just stood there on one foot with this stupid sawn-off. My big toe blazed and I was getting a toothache. I almost gave the shooter back to Fish-face, but I wasn't quite that stupid.

It was silly. And I never thought I'd feel silly with a shooter in my hand. I felt so silly I almost blushed. But I ain't someone who blushes.

The silliest thing was Fish-face and Droopy-drawers backing away from me like I was the Terminator himself. I looked round, but no one in the yard seemed to have noticed. There was three people by the yard gate waving a shooter around at half past four in the afternoon and no one noticed. I began to have a weird feeling that it wasn't really happening. Or that it was only happening in my head.

But Fish-face and Droopy-drawers thought it was happening for real. They backed away and they was so scared they was nearly holding hands.

So I limped after them, barefoot in the muck. When we got to the pavement they turned to run. And then they stopped. They stopped because a big gold-coloured BMW crept up very slow and braked just outside the gate. The back door opened and a bloke got out.

He was short and wide. He was wearing a big black coat and hat and he looked like he'd just come from a funeral. He stood for a moment staring at us. And then he stepped forward. He slapped Fish-face once on the cheek with his big black glove.

The bloke said, "You won't mind if I send these foolish boys home, will you?"

I said, "I never asked them here in the first place. You can send them to Kingdom Come for all I care."

"I doubt if that will be necessary," he said.

There was me with the shooter, there was him with the BMW, and in between there was Fish-face and Droopy-drawers with their eyes flicking like pinballs. They didn't know which of us to be scareder of. They was practically wetting theirselves.

"Go home," he said. He didn't shout or nothing. He said, "Go home," quiet and polite. He jerked his chin and the two pillocks took off like a pair of bunnies. I wished I could of done that—just jerk my chin. I'd been telling pillocks to piss off for days, and I didn't know all it took was a chin.

"They tell me your name is Eva," he said. "A pretty name. I am Gregoriou, but you may call me Greg. The English have no talent for foreign sounding names. Yes, Greg will do nicely. Eva and Greg. Greg and Eva. It sounds friendly, yes? Shall we be friendly, Eva?"

All the time he was spouting this crap he was looking from my face to the shooter and from the shooter back to my face. I wasn't pointing it at him. It was hanging by its trigger guard from the index finger of my right hand. But he was paying it a lot of attention. And for the first time I began to take it serious too.

He said, "Those two boys mislaid an item of my property. And now I see they have lost the weapon with which they were attempting to recover it. What should I do with boys like that, Eva?"

"Spank 'em," I said. "How should I know? Just keep them off of my patch."

"I'll certainly do that," he said. "But, sadly, I can't vouch for your privacy in perpetuity. You see, foolish as they are, those boys have managed to convince me that you found the property they so carelessly mislaid."

"Bollocks," I said. "Are you calling me a thief and a liar too? Are you? 'Cos I've had it up to here with prats calling me names."

"Please," he said. "There's no need to raise your voice."

"Why not? I don't give a shit who you are. You talk like a sodding BBC newsreader, but the message is the same. You're calling me a liar and you got no right."

"Nothing so crude," he said. "A BBC newsreader? Thank you. Elocution, standard English usage, yes, I'm proud of that."

See, if I'd been listening to him on the radio I'd never think he had a care in the world. But on the radio I wouldn't see those eyes watching the shooter, would I? I shifted it in my hand, taking a firmer grip, and watched his eyes watching my hands.

He said, "Aren't you in the least curious about what it is I've mislaid?"

"You could of mislaid an egg, for all I care," I said. "I know what you lost. Your 'boys' told me."

"An egg," he said, "yes. A nest egg. A lot of money."

"Do I look like I've got a lot of money?" I said.

172

"A lot of what?" said Simone. She picked her way out of the yard, all dainty. I wished I'd seen her coming. I didn't want her hearing any of this.

"Sorry to interrupt," Simone said. "You were gone so long I didn't think you were coming back."

"Introduce me to your beautiful friend," said Greg.

"Fuck off," I said.

"I'm Simone," Simone said. "Eva's sister."

"Sister?" said Greg. "Remarkable."

Things were going downhill at ninety miles an hour. If his eyes'd been hands he'd of been stroking Simone's tits, but she didn't seem to notice.

"And you?" she said.

"Forgive me," he said. "Gregoriou. It's a pleasure to meet you, Simone. I'm sure I've seen your face before, though."

He wasn't looking at her face. I passed the sawn-off from my right hand to my left and back—just to make him concentrate.

"What's that?" said Simone, seeing the shooter for the first time. "Eva, what're you doing?"

"It's a complicated situation," Greg said. "I'm here to recover an item of property. As a matter of fact, the gun, too, is my property. Or rather, I'm responsible for it."

"I hate guns," said Simone. "Eva, give it back to Gregoriou."

"No," I said. "He's calling me a thief and a liar."

"You misunderstand," said Greg. "Can't we talk about this in a civilised manner?"

"No we fucking can't," I said.

"Of course we can," said Simone. And she reached across me and plucked the sawn-off out of my hands.

"Horrible thing," Simone said.

"Then may I relieve you of it?" Greg said, holding out his big black glove. And Simone just handed it to him. Just like

173

that. What the cocking hell was she thinking of? She just handed it to him like it was a dead rat and he was ever so kindly going to take care of it for her.

"*Simone!*" I said.

"Don't shout," she said. "It isn't yours. It belongs to this gentleman."

"Gentleman, my *arse!*"

"*Eva*, please. What on earth do you want a gun for anyway?"

"Thank you so much," said Greg.

So now *he* had the shooter. So now I really truly took it serious.

"Honestly, Eva," Simone said, "what were you thinking of—waving a gun around in public? It isn't legal. Suppose someone saw it and reported you? We'd have the police round here in no time. Think of the trouble we'd be in."

"Your sister's quite right," said Greg. "Guns are dangerous, not least to those who handle them." He turned round and put the shooter on the back seat of the BMW.

"Gone," he said to Simone. "I'm so sorry you were anxious."

"Not at all," she said. Jeez, how could a sister of mine sound so toffee-nosed? I was sweating buckets. But I had to admit she sort of cut the shooter down to size. I'd rather I had it than Greg had it, but she made sure he wasn't going to use it. For now.

Even so, I was so pissed off I couldn't hardly speak. Whose side was she on, anyway?

"Whose fuckin' side are you on?" I said.

"Yours, Eva," she said, and then she turned on Greg. "You mustn't call my sister a thief or a liar. She isn't. That's quite wrong."

"I take it you know all about each other's business?" Greg said.

"Of course I do," Simone said. But she didn't. And she

didn't know what she was getting into. She thought Greg was a "gentleman." She heard him talk like a BBC newsreader and she thought he was a "gentleman." He wasn't. He was a thug and a baboon. She just ain't knocked around with low-life enough lately to recognise one when she sees one.

I said, "She don't know nothing. There ain't anything to know. I ain't seen your sports bag. And neither has she. We ain't seen it 'cos it ain't here to be seen."

"What sports bag?"

"See?" I said. "We don't neither of us know fuck-all."

"Let me tell you a little story," Greg said to Simone. "I am something of a financier. I invest money, sometimes quite a lot of money, in other people's enterprises. A few nights ago I was called to the bedside of a sick relative. The call was urgent and it came just as I was about to deliver a large amount of cash to a business associate. But family comes first, so I delegated. I asked two young employees to make the delivery. A simple matter. I placed two items, two bags, in the back of a car and told the boys to deliver the car to an address which I had the foresight to write down. I did not tell them what was in the bags. They are not the brightest boys and I thought too much information might confuse them. I told them not to look in the bags but simply to drive to a prearranged address, leave the car and return.

"Simple as the task was, they failed to complete it. I believe that Eva knows why."

"Well I fucking don't," I said. I didn't want him to say any more. He was telling his story to Simone, not to me. And she was lapping it up, all wide-eyed, like a little kid.

"What happened?" she said to me.

"How the hell should I know?" I said. "I wasn't there. That's where he's wrong. That's where his little story fucks up.

He wasn't there neither. He only knows what Droopy-drawers and Fish-face told him, and they told him bollocks."

Greg said, "Do you know the story of Pandora's box?"

"Yes," said Simone.

"No," I said. "And I don't fucking want to. First it was bags and now it's boxes. Make your poxy mind up."

"Pandora's bags, then," he said, smiling at Simone. And she smiled right back at him. Two ever so clever clogs sharing a joke. Only the joke was me. Right?

Wrong. I said, "I don't give a stuff about Dora's bags. I don't give a stuff about Dora, and I don't give a stuff about you. I ain't seen Dora's bags, I ain't seen your bags and I fuckin' wish I ain't seen you."

Greg said, "Bags, boxes. Never mind. My point is that there is only trouble inside. Those two boys, being boys, found a sawn-off shotgun. Having found it they didn't look any further. They found trouble and made trouble with that gun. Enough. It is the other bag which concerns me now."

"Concern yourself in someone else's yard."

He ignored me. Again. He said, "Simone, you've already proved yourself to be as sensible as you're beautiful. Perhaps you can persuade your sister . . . how can I put this without causing a seismic response . . . ? The bag and its contents will bring nothing but trouble, they will do everyone, except me, much more harm than good. They *must* be returned to me."

Simone was looking at him like he was God Almighty—all huge eyes and respect. It made me feel like a tractor tyre with the inner tube overinflated. Something was going to explode in my guts.

I said, "I . . . you . . ."

"Eva," Simone said. "Calm down and stand still."

And suddenly I remembered standing in the rain counting to a hundred. "One, two, three," I said.

Simone said, "Okay, Eva, it's okay."

"Six, seven," I said.

"Pardon?" said Greg.

"Please," said Simone, "she's getting upset. We need a little time. I'll sort this out. I don't understand it, but I'll sort it out. Everything you've said is news to me. I want you to believe that."

"Oddly enough," Greg said, "I think I do. Shall I explain further?"

"Yes," said Simone.

"*NO!*" I shouted. Because suddenly I remembered Keif in the Static with Milo and I didn't know how long it'd take him to come out and join the party. Everything was falling on my head.

I barged Greg out of my path and I walked away, straight out the gate and up the road.

He could shoot me in the back for all I cared. He could mash me with his BMW and leave me in the gutter.

I felt like he'd done it already—telling Simone them things. And her looking at him like he was God Greg, and believing him. Why? If she believed him she wouldn't believe me— about the lottery and stuff. But she *shouldn't* believe him and not me. I mean she shouldn't *want* to believe him. I mean, she's my sister and I wouldn't lie to her. That's what she should believe. That's what I believe about her. I mean, why can't she be the same? How can she stand there, with me, beside me, and give him my shooter? How can she stand there with me and look at him like he's God Greg?

I don't know if she called out to stop me. And I don't care. I mean, why would she bother? Why would she bother with hulking great Godzilla when she could stand there nattering to God? Who'd want Godzilla when she'd got God? Who? No one. That's who.

So I don't know if she called out my name, and I kept on walking. And I counted my footsteps, one, two, three, like she was there telling me to. And when I got the numbers muddled up I started again from one. And I thought maybe if I could get to one hundred without jumbling any of it up, maybe if I could do that, everything'd turn out all right. But counting ain't my game. So in the end I did it for the rhythm.

Chapter 21

I was climbing up some stairs and a woman said, "You don't want to come up these steps without no shoes on."

"Eh?" I said, and I stopped. I was climbing up the stairs to Ma's flat and it was like climbing up an elephant's arse.

"You'll give yourself an 'orrible disease," the woman said. "What you want to come out without your shoes anyway?"

"Lost 'em," I said. But it wasn't shoes I'd lost. It was time. "What's the time?" I said.

"'Bout six," she said, and went on down.

I hate that. Not knowing what the time is or where it went. Or what I did in the time. Or what I was doing now. At Ma's block. When Ma was the last person on earth I wanted to see.

Habit. I was there out of habit. See, I used to come here regular when Ma was the only family I had and I thought one day I'd meet Simone.

Only now it was all different. Ma wasn't family no more, and Simone was back. And Wozzisname was one of Ma's boyfriends. Had been. Used to be. Except, now, he was at the bottom of the Thames. He wasn't smooching with Ma no more. He was smooching with a fire extinguisher and his own lump hammer. And he wasn't hot for Ma no more. He was water

179

temperature, and the water in the Thames is cold, cold water at this time of year.

So I couldn't see Ma, could I?

But it was her fault. She sent Wozzisname and Andy. And now she was screwing all my dosh out of me. She had no right to be angry about Wozzisname. I had more right to be angry than she did.

I climbed on up the stairs. Maybe I could screw a pair of socks out of her. I can't wear her shoes—me feet's too big—but a pair of stretch socks is better than nothing.

I banged on her door but she didn't come. It was freezing out on her walkway, and my bruised toe was throbbing. She wasn't there to open the door. Typical. I paid her rent and I gave her one thousand one hundred and sixty-seven pounds, and you'd think that'd be enough to buy a pair of stretch socks. But was it? Nothing's what I got from Ma, as per usual.

The next-door-woman came out. She said, "Who's that making all the racket? Oh, hello, duck, it's you."

I seen her before. One time, when Ma was out, she lent me a kitchen spatula to pop Ma's lock so's I could get in.

"No use knocking," she said. "Your mum's gone. Din't she tell you?"

"But I paid her back rent," I said. "I thought she stayed."

"Oh no," she said. "She's gone. A young bloke turned up with a van and moved all her bits and pieces."

"But where?"

"Don't ask me," the next-door-woman said. "We wasn't on speaking terms—she always left her telly on too bleeding loud. All hours. Day and night. Never turned it down when I asked. Paper thin walls. I couldn't get no sleep and the kids couldn't get no sleep. Now there's a young couple in there and all they do is fight. That keeps us awake too. But at least they go out and don't leave the telly on."

Fuckin' hell! My ma just upped and scarpered even after I paid her rent. And she didn't say where she was going. Can you credit it? She didn't even tell her own daughter who'd paid her lousy stinking rent. And that was before Wozzisname, so she had no excuse.

So now I couldn't find her to give her a piece of my mind. And it was after six so I had to go back to the yard to lock up and let the dogs out. Only I didn't want to go back to the yard 'cos I didn't know what I'd find there. And I was tired and cold already.

The only car I could borrow was a little green Yugo, so I crammed myself in that and drove home. There wasn't nowhere else to go.

One good thing though—my back was easier. Now all I had to do was get old voodoo digits to work on my foot.

I didn't expect to find Simone when I got back to the yard and I wasn't disappointed. I shouldn't of left her with God Greg. I shouldn't of done that. But she gave him my shooter and so I couldn't shut him up. I don't know what he told her. I didn't want him to tell her anything but I couldn't shut him up so I left, 'cos I couldn't bear to see her believing him and not me.

Now she'd walk out on me for sure. I was protecting her from trouble—from Fish-face and Droopy-drawers—but she ends up talking to God Greg who's much worse. Only she can't see it. He talks toffee-nosed like she does, so she thinks he's better than me. Only he isn't. He's a jumped-up baboon. And now he's a jumped-up baboon with a sawn-off shooter. And he's after my dosh. Join the queue, God Greg, take your turn. If Simone's got anything to do with it you'll get one thousand one hundred and sixty-seven pounds too.

I locked up and let Ramses and Lineker out. Then I went to the Static. I wasn't expecting to find Keif there either, but he

181

was. He was lying on my bunk, on my sleeping bag, with Milo curled up under one arm. They was both snoozing, and Milo didn't even lift an ear when I came in. That was bad, very bad. Milo's in training to be a watchdog but he doesn't wake up when someone comes in on him unexpected.

And that's Keif's fault. Keif turns everyone into candy floss.

But not me. Oh no. I banged the kettle down on the stove, *ker-rash*.

"Herf," went Milo.

"Wha?" went Keif.

"Who told you you could fart around on my bed?"

"Me?" said Keif. "I never fart in a lady's bed."

"Herf?" went Milo. He jumped off the bunk and asked to be let out. I opened the door for him. He could take his chances with Ramses and Lineker tonight and if they toughed him up it was his own silly fault—letting Keif turn him into a candy-floss attack dog.

Keif was rubbing the sleep out of his eyes. "Where you been, girl?" he said.

"Out walking," I said. "One of us remembered my training, and it wasn't my personal trainer. No—my personal trainer earns his corn kipping. You're out. Fired. Fucking hop it."

"What's the time?" he said. He was grinning at me and stretching like stretching was better than sex. "What you so bitter 'n' twisted for? Had another fight with your sister?"

I fired him. And if he took a blind bit of notice you can put a stick in my hand and wheel me out in front of a symphony orchestra—they'll pay me more heed.

He looked at his watch. "Jesus!" he said. "I'm going to be late. Me first and last fight and I'm going to be late or what. Get yer boots on, girl, let's go. C'mon."

I pulled my new skinning knife out of its holster and lobbed it at him. "Here," I said, "take me knife and scrape yer balls out of yer ears. I told you—I ain't coming."

"You are," he said. "I got it all worked out. Hey, nice knife, sugar-puss. New? Lookin' good. Everything going to be all right. You look like a soldier of fortune and when you step in that ring we going to boogy the arse off those tossers."

"We?" My gob fell open like bomb-bay doors.

"C'mon. Why not 'we'? You were right on the money. It's in your blood. It ain't in mine."

Suddenly my brain went turbo-charged. I could see it—the whole story.

I said, "You need me in the ring too. Right? 'Cos they're going to cream you, aren't they? They're setting you up, right? So you're going to need a mercenary, right? To come in and sort it. So I come in and save your arse."

"I dunno about saving my arse," Keif said. "I dunno 'bout that."

"Dogs of War," I said. "Man, we could be a tag team."

"Hold it, hold it!" Keif said. "This ain't a career move."

"Why not?"

"'Cos I ain't planning to stick around in the wrestling game after tonight."

"Why not?" I said. "It's a fuckin' *brilliant* game."

"I just want to get through tonight without no injury. Just come in with a bang and go out with a bang, and leave it. I don't want to be nobody's patsy or what."

See, he hadn't never been in the ring, under the lights, with the crowd going nuclear.

"You'll change," I said.

"I won't," he said. "I just want to know if you're on—for one night only."

"Yeah," I said. "I'm on."

"Then we gotta go, man. I don't want to be late."

"You better be late," I said.

"Why?"

"Why? You've changed your costume. You ain't going to be who they want you to be. You don't want to hang around backstage fighting about that. You got to make an entrance—you can't give 'em time to stand you down. 'Cos they will. Mr. Deeds will. He'll say, 'Do it my way or fuck off.' "

"Shit."

"And then there's me. If they see me they'll smell a rat straight off."

"So?"

"So ring Mr. Deeds. Say you're on your way but your car broke down. You'll be there, but you'll be late."

"I ain't got a car. I was going to go to my folks' place. We was all going to go together."

"I got a car," I said.

"Safe," he said. "Where's the phone?"

"Mandala Street," I said.

While he was gone I went to the shower cubicle and doused down. I even washed my hair. And I brushed my teeth till my gums burned. It's a ritual, see. Before a fight, you get clean and ready. You don't want nothing wrong or messy. So even if you got to wash in cold water, you do it. But I didn't mind. I was tingling. I ain't tingled like that since a year ago.

I put on my new combat jacket and my new zippy strides which tucked into my old wrestling boots.

But underneath the new gear I wore the black. I pulled on my black leotard and black leggings.

They were a bit tighter than they had been but they still fitted well enough. So if you're the genius who invented lycra, I want to say, "Thanks a lot," from the bottom of my heart.

For once, I wished I could look in a mirror. Because I felt like the real thing—I felt like a mercenary. I was dressed like a soldier of fortune, and that's a sort of assassin, isn't it? So it ain't like I wasn't me. I was still the London Lassassin but I had soldiers' clothes on top. And everything felt okay.

I danced on my toes and that felt good too—even the toe I bruised. My toes tingled like the rest of me.

"I'm back," I said, out loud. "Look out, Pete Carver. You won't know what hit you."

But he would know. 'Cos it was going to be me who hit him and I'd make sure he knew it was me. And I'd make sure Mr. Deeds knew. And Gruff. And Phil Julio. And Harsh. And all the other wankers who thought I couldn't hack it.

"Hey, be cool, baby-cakes," Keif said when he came back. "Mind that lumbar region. You ain't fightin', remember. You just makin' an appearance."

A lot *he* knew. I don't wash my hair in cold water just to make an appearance. No way.

"Where we going?" I said.

"Ladywell Baths," he said. "Know it?"

Know it? Of course I know it. It's the scene of one of me best triumphs. I was a bleeding star at the Ladywell Baths.

"Yeah, I know it," I said.

"Good," he said, " 'cos I ain't got a map."

But I don't need a map. I know every one of the venues where Deeds Promotions ever put a fight on. I could find 'em blindfold.

I gave Keif the keys and told him to lock the gate because I didn't want him hanging over my shoulder when I started up the little green Yugo. It had to be the Yugo 'cos I knew where it was, and I knew it still had half a tank of gas. I wished it was a Roller or a Bentley or a Merc—something grand, something fitting. But it was a little green Yugo.

Keif and me ain't little green people, though, so it was a bit like fitting a pint of cream in a toothpaste tube.

I didn't care about that. What I cared about was when we pulled away from the yard I saw a big gold BMW coming in the opposite direction—God Greg's flash wheels. I couldn't see through the tinted windows, so I didn't know if Simone was in there or not.

I didn't stop, but the sight of those flash wheels brought me down for a moment—made me remember all the stuff I hadn't thought about since Keif said, "When you step in that ring."

And I was sad 'cos I wished Simone was with us. She's only little so she could of squeezed into the back seat.

I said, "I wish Simone was here."

And for a change Keif said nothing. I wondered if he was getting butterflies.

"You nervous?" I said.

"Nah," he said. "Yeah. Nah. Shit."

"Whatever you do," I said, "even if you fuck up something awful—do it like you mean it."

"Eh?"

"Like, don't dither. Don't look unsure. If you screw up, don't be a joke—be a joker. The crowd won't mind that. But they'll eat you alive if you fart around half-hearted."

"Cheers," he said. "You really ease my mind."

"Same goes for Pete Carver. He'll do what you let him do."

"Great," Keif said, "now I feel peachy about every little thing, or what."

We drove on. Keif still wasn't mouthing off and that worried me.

I said, "This Muhammad character."

"What?"

"What did he do?"

"Float like a butterfly, sting like a bee," Keif said. "No one laid a glove on him till he got old and slow. He just dance around going, 'I'm so pretty . . .' What you laughing at?"

"You ain't going to stand in the ring going 'I'm so pretty'?"

"Yeah," he said. "That's just what I'm going to do."

"You going to do it like you mean it?"

"That the hard part."

"You won't get away with it 'less you mean it."

"Why you laughing?"

"'Cos you're dithering."

"That's funny?"

"Yeah. You're so bleeding cocksure in private. You got to be the same in the ring."

"I wonder how he did it," Keif said. "I never thought about it before. Guy gets up in the ring, in front of all them people, TV, film cameras and shit. And he say, 'I'm so pretty.' He wasn't born in England, *that* for sure."

"Was he pretty?"

"When he was young."

"Well that's it, then. Being pretty's the hard part. Saying so's a piece of cake."

"Yeah, but the guy was such a showman—he'd of said it even if he looked like your dog, Ramses. And they'd of all believed him."

"See?"

"See what?"

"You got to mean it." I couldn't think of anything else to say to make him feel brave so we didn't talk for the rest of the drive.

When we got to the Ladywell Baths Keif sat in the car like he didn't want to get out. Me, I'd of been out, up those steps and into the dressing room faster than a buttered pig. But he sat there stone moody.

He said, "Nah, Muhammad Ali definitely didn't go to school in Brixton."

Nerves, see. Who'd of thought it—cocksure Keif with a case

of the collywobbles. I could of fallen over laughing, but there was one last thing he had to do for me. He had to go to the box office and buy me a ticket. I couldn't mong around in the foyer with the crowd and the ushers and bouncers 'cos I'd be recognised. I couldn't go in till the house lights went down for the second half.

Chapter 22

I've got a routine—it's what I always do in the dressing room before I go on. But I didn't have no dressing room 'cos I wasn't supposed to be there. I had to find somewhere else close by.

I dumped the Yugo a couple of streets away from the Lady-well Baths and walked back.

Round the back and sides of the building there's emergency exits and stage doors and stuff. It's a big old place, but if you put your ear to one of the doors and listen careful you can hear the sound of the crowd when something exciting happens. You can hear this muffled roar. You can't hear the details but you can hear enough to know there's lots and lots of people having a fine old time and going ape.

It made my heart bounce. I was in the dark and cold and they was all in the heat and light. But I was going in. I was. No matter Mr. Deeds said, "You're barred." No matter them heavy-weights said I was a loser. No matter Harsh wouldn't help me. This time I was going in—back where I belong.

But I couldn't hang around getting cold and stiff. I crossed the road and went into the pub opposite. I ordered a pint of bitter.

You think I'm going to get shellacked. You think I ain't got

189

the spine to make my comeback without a snort of Dutch courage? Do you? Eh? Well, you think wrong. Mr. Deeds is wrong, Gruff's wrong, Pete Carver's wrong, Phil's wrong, Harsh is wrong, Ma's wrong, The Enemy's wrong. And *you're* wrong. You're all fucking wrong.

I took one mouthful, just to wet my whistle. Then I left the glass on the bar and went to the ladies' bog. So there! You don't know me at all, do you?

The ladies' bog was empty, but I wouldn't of cared if it wasn't. I took off my combat jacket and hung it on the hand-drier. I started stretching. It's my routine—like Harsh taught me in the days when he used to tell me useful things. Starting from the feet up. Lean into the wall for your Achilles tendons and calves, squat down for your groin, three positions. Then up for your quads. I was specially careful with my back—I spent a lot of time on stretch and contraction exercises. And it felt okay. Not one hundred percent, but okay. I went all the way up from my feet to my head and neck. And then I went back down from my neck to my feet.

Then I washed my face, hands and armpits with the pub's scented soap. When I was ready I put my jacket back on and combed my hair. I checked the mirror.

"Lookin' bad," I said. 'Cos I am the Villain, and it's my job to look bad and mean.

I went back into the bar. The saloon bar window overlooked the front of the Ladywell Baths. There were people, mainly men, out on the steps smoking fags and drinking beer. It was the interval. They were all togged up against the cold but they looked like they was having a good time.

I pressed my nose against the window and watched and waited. I was waiting for them to go inside. Then I'd know the second half was beginning.

The time came. The blokes tossed back the last of their beer.

They trod on their fag-ends. The women collected the kids who were playing on the steps. They straggled inside. My breath was coming so hot and fast it fogged the window.

Just as I was turning to leave I saw someone I knew running up the steps. Simone? With a bloke? At least I thought it was Simone. I hoped it was Simone. But by the time I'd wiped the fog off the window she'd disappeared inside.

That'd be the cherry on my hot fudge sundae if she was there to see my comeback. That'd be what I always dreamt of—her in the crowd, me in the ring and everyone going ooh-ah and shouting my name. That'd show her who to look up to, and it wouldn't be God Greg. It'd be me, Eva Wylie, the London Las-sassin.

I couldn't wait no longer. I left the pub and raced across the road, up the steps and into the Ladywell Baths.

Oh *yeah*—it was a sight for sore eyes. I walked into the hall, and there below me was the ring shining like the moon reflected in a dark pond. See, in the Ladywell Baths you got the audience on all four sides of the ring. So when you're in the ring, fight-ing, you're slap-bang in the middle.

Harsh was on—like I might of expected, 'cos Mr. Deeds al-ways puts him on first thing after the interval. It's when the crowd is filtering back from the bar, and only the purists are taking any notice. Harsh is very pure. He's what they call a wrestler's wrestler. He's strong, he's graceful and he's got all the clever moves. He used to be my hero, but when I went to him for help he told me to use a toothbrush. So he ain't my hero no more.

And he ain't the crowd's hero neither. I used to think they was all twatocks for not 'preciating him, but now I see it's his own silly fault. He don't do nothing for them—he don't make it exciting. It's like he's doing it all for a video called *Wrestling— How To Do It Right*. It's a boring video.

I was sitting at the back and I could hardly watch him. He made me feel sad and I was too twitchy to feel sad. You got to be able to sit still to enjoy feeling sad, and I couldn't sit still. I wanted Harsh off. I never thought I'd want that, but it's true. I wanted Harsh gone, out the way, so that Keif could come in.

It was Harsh's last fight in England so they gave him his full time and his win. The MC announced he was retiring. The crowd clapped, Harsh bowed. And then he just walked away, so that was that. Nobody really cared, and that was his own silly fault too, 'cos he didn't seem to care much either. Well, what d'you expect from a guy who thinks more about a sodding toothbrush than a fighter?

Then the MC announced that there was a change to the printed programme. My heart was in my mouth. What if Keif and Mr. Deeds had a row, and Mr. Deeds barred Keif? And suddenly I knew it didn't fucking matter—whoever came on next, Keif or not, was going to get *me* in his face. It didn't matter. I should of done it months ago.

The MC said, "Next up is a great South London favourite, local boy, twice heavyweight champion, Pete 'Carve 'em' Carver."

Big roar from the crowd.

The MC said, "Pete's got a new opponent tonight—all the way from Trinidad and Tobago—you don't know him yet, but you will—put your hands together for . . . er . . . *Muhammad Wily.*"

The crowd clapped a bit, but not much—they was saving the skin on their palms for Pete.

I was expecting some music—every fighter's got to have a signature tune, like mine was "Satisfaction." But there wasn't any music. Instead the roving spotlight picked up Keif coming through the stage door, wearing a white satin dressing gown. He was sort of bopping. He seemed to be saying something, but you couldn't hear what it was. Silly fart.

I cupped my hands round my mouth and bellowed, "LOUDER! SPEAK UP."

He looked my way but he was dazzled by the spot. People started laughing and that seemed to gee him up.

He took a huge, deep breath and went, "Hey, boom, b-b-boom, bibbley-bee-bibbley bee, bah-bibbley bee." He was giving himself a beat, and some of the audience closest to him started to clap in time. That geed him up more. I could see him start to grin.

He bopped down the aisle, going, "Bibbley-bee, Muhammad Wil-ee—Muhammad Wily—that who I *am*—come in like a lion—won't go out like no *lamb*—bah-boom-bah—I'm the great*est*, the lat*est*, the pretty-*est*—if you don't b'lieve I the fitt*est*—you better be wearin' yer bulletproof *vest*—yeah, yer bulletproof vest."

Some of the little kids got out of their seats and followed Keif down the aisle, going, "Bah-boom," and clapping their hands. And that was good. It made other people look and laugh.

By the time Keif got to ringside he'd run out of things to say, so he went, "Bah-boombastic—I fantastic—got arms like elastic." But he couldn't think of anything to rhyme with elastic, so he climbed into the ring and bounced and bopped.

It wasn't a bad entrance for a bloke with no music.

The MC was looking quite surprised. He went, "Boom-boom—ladies and gentlemen—Muhammad, er, Wily—boom-boom." And some of the people in the front row yelled, "Boom-boom" back at him. Keif was looking shell-shocked, but he was laughing too.

It was all drowned out when Pete's music came on. Pete don't like no one else snatching his headlines, so I could just see him making the bloke on the sound desk turn his music up real loud.

He kept everyone waiting a minute, till they was all clapping to *his* music, and then he came hurtling out of the stage door and down the aisle with his red and yellow striped cape streaming out behind. Everyone roared.

I got to admit he looked good. He doesn't do nothing fancy—all he does is grab you by the throat and say, "Look at *me!*" And you do. You can't help yourself.

Of course I hate his guts. He's got big enough guts to hate. He ain't a heavyweight—he's an overweight. And he's a lot older than Keif. But no one was looking at Keif. They was all looking at Pete, which was what Pete wanted.

"Ladies and gentlemen," the MC shouted. "I give you . . . Pete 'Carve 'em' *Carver!*"

Pete vaulted into the ring. He brushed Keif out the way and took a circuit, stopping here and there to lean out over the ropes and talk to his fans.

Keif just stood there like a dog with no bone. Soppy bugger—he should of nicked the microphone out of the MC's hand and done another rap. That's what I'd of done. I wouldn't of just stood there and let Pete take advantage.

Keif was wearing red boots and under his dressing-gown he had on white satin boxer's shorts with red go-fast stripes down the seams. He looked good when he took his robe off, but he should of made a big production out of it.

When Pete took off his cape he waved it like a banner and flung it so it sailed out of the ring to one of the bouncers. That's the way to do it, little Keifee—look and learn, boy, look and learn.

And when they did that palaver about meeting in the middle with the referee, Pete bellied up to Keif, already doing that gut-barging stuff the crowd loves. So the ref was giving his falls,

194

submissions, knock-out, fair-fight speech while Pete was pushing Keif back towards his corner.

I had to laugh. You could see as clear as day who was top dog. Pete was Ramses and Keif wasn't even Lineker—he was Milo and he didn't have enough smarts to run away.

Well, he did, sort of. When the fight began Keif was for sure using his feet. He was dancing out of arm's reach in a circle around Pete. And you could see he wished he had his boxing gloves on, 'cos he kept his hands up and every now and then he'd touch his knuckles together.

But that ain't wrestling. The crowd started in—shouting for action. Pete was keeping himself low, shuffling, arms swinging wide, reaching for contact. But Keif dodged in and out and showed how fast he was. Which was pretty fast, I got to admit. Fast, but no fun.

I got up from my seat in the back row and started down towards the ring. I was taking it easy, just a row at a time. I didn't want anyone to see me coming. Yet.

The crowd was getting frustrated. No one goes out on a freezing night and pays good money for a ticket to see one big guy dance around another big guy who can't catch him.

The front rows were beginning to chant, "Yellow, yellow," at Keif.

Pete picked it up. He started to act like he was frustrated too. He lunged at Keif, missed, lunged, missed. Then he stood in the middle of the ring shaking his head like an old bull.

"Yellow," he shouted. "I smell yellow. Wha' do I smell?"

"YELLER," the crowd shouted back. "*Carve* 'im, Pete!"

Poor old Keif looked banjaxed, so I knew that this was the setup. Keif was probably only doing what they'd told him to do backstage. He was just there to prick-tease the crowd, get them really angry with the coward, and then take his punishment. Over and over again.

Poor Keifee-baby. You could see he didn't know what to do, and it made him look small.

But next time Pete charged he almost caught Keif by swinging his arm out so wide that Keif had to spin away into the ropes. And this time Keif turned the spin into a funny little boogy step and hip hula.

"Float like a butterfly, sting like a *bee*," he called. "You got arms like an ape, but you can't catch *me*." Which made some of the crowd laugh. They was still chanting, "Yeller, yeller," but they was laughing too.

Which *really* made Pete mad. Because, for sure, it wasn't part of the setup for Keif to be the comic. Comics is in a class of their own. Comics can break all the rules and get away with it. You can't punish a comic without turning the crowd against you.

And the last thing Pete wanted was for the crowd to turn against him. He had to stop Keif from making 'em laugh again.

So I moved down to the fifth row fast. Things were going to hot up and I wanted to be in the strike zone.

Pete charged in for real. He caught Keif dodging away. He caught him, one-armed, round the waist, and flipped him. Keif landed on his back like a beetle.

The crowd went into overdrive.

Pete dropped on Keif, belly first. Keif scrambled.

Whoomp, went Pete's belly on the canvas. Keif rolled and got up.

"Ha-ha-ha," went the crowd.

Pete got up slowly, like his knees ached. Keif boogied round him. And that's where he made his mistake. He was clowning and he didn't think he had to watch Pete real careful. Pete was old and fat and his knees ached, right?

Not right enough. Pete bent over to catch his breath. He held his belly like he was hurt. He clasped his hands. He waited till Keif skipped close. He straightened, brought his clasped hands up to Keif's throat and grabbed him in a strangle. All in one quick twitch.

Pete's thumbs dug in under Keif's chin forcing his head back. Keif's hands jerked up to Pete's wrists. Wrong again, Keifee-baby.

Pete belly-barged Keif all the way across the ring to the ropes and kept pushing till the ropes bulged out. Then he freed one hand, and toppled him over the top rope.

He let go of Keif's throat as he went over backwards, and then grabbed his feet to stop him falling into the front row.

Next he snatched the second rope down and hooked it up round Keif's feet. He left Keif dangling from his knees, upside down. Keif's heels were forced back against his thighs by the second rope, and there was nothing he could do but hang there like a bat looking mega-stupid. The crowd howled.

I got up and strode forward. Heads turned. Someone said, "Oy, ain't that old Bucket Nut?"

"Less of the old," I shouted back.

I was on my way. I was nearly there when I got pushed aside by a little whirlwind in a pink frock. A woman with a bright red handbag shoved past.

"Keif," she said. "You come down from there, boy."

"Aagh?" said Keif.

"You get down from there right now," she said. "This no place for you."

"Ha-ha-ha," went the crowd.

"Sit down, Mum," said Keif.

"Why you let them say you coming from Trinidad and Tobago?" she said. "You know you born in the Elephant and Castle."

"Sit *down*, Mum!"

"Ha-ha-HA," went the crowd.

197

"Yeah," said Pete, leaning over the ropes. "SIT DOWN, MUMMY."

"HA-HA-HA," went the crowd.

"Don't you talk to me like that," Keif's mum said.

"Yeah," I yelled up at Pete. "Don't you talk to Keif's mum like that."

"I sit down when I *want* to sit down," she said.

"Shit," said Pete. "Eva! What you fuckin' doin' here?"

"*Language*, boy!" said Keif's mum.

"Don't worry, missus," I said. I could see the bouncers closing in.

I hauled myself up on the ropes.

"That's Bucket Nut!" said the people in front. "Where you been, Bucket Nut?"

"Maternity leave," some joker said.

"Ha-ha-ha."

"Fuck off out of here," Pete said.

He tried to knock me off the edge of the stage, but I scurried sideways like a crab till I got behind the corner post.

"Too slow," I yelled. "What you been doing, Pete? Eating dumplings, getting wrinkly?"

"You going to fight Bucket Nut?" someone yelled up. "You going to fight her, Pete?"

"He ain't going to fight me," I called back, swinging out of Pete's reach behind the post. "He's too old. He's too fat."

Out the corner of me eye I could see one of the bouncers helping Keif untangle himself. The other bouncer was creeping up on me. There was too much to watch and I was watching it all. You can keep your crack, cocaine and heroin. Adrenaline's my drug of choice. It's the best rush in the bleeding world. Bar none.

The ref came trotting over. "Bloody hell, Eva Wylie!" he

said. "You can't come in the ring, Eva. I can't allow you in my ring."

"Tell her," said Pete. "Just fuck off, you silly bitch, you ain't wanted here."

"You going to carve her, Pete?" yelled one of Pete's fans.

The bouncer crouched, ready. I faked left. The bouncer sprang. Pete stuck his arm out. I faked left and swung right, out of reach. I ran along the edge of the staging, hanging on to the top rope for support.

"He'll never fight me," I yelled to the fan. "He ain't even got the goolies to chuck me out."

"Oooh, Pete," went the fan. "Show her. *Carve* her, Pete!"

Pete sent off a wild haymaker. I swung back taking the rope with me. Pete stumbled forward.

Behind him I saw Keif climbing back in the ring.

"Bit more reach, Pete," I said. "You ain't really trying."

The spring of the rope boinged me back towards him.

"Try again, Pete," I called, "Arms too short? You know what they say—short arms, short dick." I was talking up. Everyone could hear.

"Oooh," went the front rows.

Pete hauled the top rope towards him. I jumped down off the stage.

Keif lolloped across the ring and gave Pete a mighty shove in the back. Pete fell into the rope. The rope sagged. Keif picked up Pete's ankles and tipped him out of the ring.

"Aaahgh," went the front row, leaping up and scattering— except for one fat bloke who wasn't quick enough.

Phlump, went Pete as he landed on the fat bloke's lap.

"Ow," went the fat bloke, "get *off*!"

Quick as lightning, I leapt back on the stage. I somersaulted over the top rope.

I was in the ring.

I was back, under the lights, in front of the crowd.

It was *mine*.

I took a lap of honour.

"Bucket Nut!" yelled the crowd.

"Okay, okay," said the ref, "joke over. You'll have to go, Eva, we got a fight on here."

"Not without *me*," I said. I took another lap.

Everyone with two legs was standing up. Everyone with a mouth was shouting.

"You all right?" I said to Keif. But I didn't care.

"It ain't exactly Queensberry rules," Keif said.

"No rules," I said. I could hardly hear him. He was hardly there. I was watching Pete lumber over to the MC's table.

"Please, Eva," said the ref, "be sensible."

The MC stood up. "Ladies and gentlemen," he said into his microphone. "As you can see, there's been a ring invasion. If you'll all calm down for a minute, while we deal with the intruder, the fight between Pete Carver and, er, Muhammad, er, Wily will resume without delay."

I ran over to the MC's side of the ring.

"There's been an invasion all right," I yelled. "But I ain't no intruder. I'm the London Lassassin. How you gonner 'deal' with me? Eh? Eh?"

He covered the mike with his hand. "Bloody hell, Eva. Get down. You're barred, you know that. Get the hell out of here."

"Make me," I yelled, at him, at Pete, at everyone. "Come up here and make me."

"Go on, Pete," yelled the fans, "*make* her."

"Oh for Christ's sake, Pete," said the MC with his hand shielding the mike. "They think this is a bloody stunt."

"Well it ain't," Pete said. "Get Mr. Deeds in here. He'll sort her out."

"Go on," I yelled. "Run to Daddy Deeds."

"Yellow," called Keif. "I smell yellow. What do I smell? I smell a yeller feller."

"*Yeller,*" screamed the crowd.

"You'll live to regret this," the MC said.

But Pete was already climbing into the ring.

Chapter 23

I danced back, taking Keif with me. Pete climbed through the ropes.

I took the centre of the ring. I unzipped my combat jacket.

"Hoo-eee," went the crowd, "take 'em off, Bucket Nut. Dum-dum-dee-dum, dum, *dum!*"

"Dirty buggers," I said. I flung the combat jacket at the ref.

"Eva?" said Keif.

"Out me way," I said.

"You asked for it," said Pete. "Now you're gonner get it."

He came in fast and low. He got those long arms round my waist and heaved me up off the canvas. He was going for the quick throw out of the ring—the quick spectacular throw.

I could tell by the way he was changing his grip, he wanted to get me above his head. He wanted to do the helicopter.

"Over here," yelled some wag in the crowd. "Chuck her to me. I'll catch her."

I let Pete swing me sideways. But that's all.

I flipped one knee up and clumped him on the ear.

I twisted, heaved the other leg up. I locked my ankles round his neck.

He still had me by the waist. I let myself hang by the waist and ankles. I twisted sideways and bit his knee.

"Shit!" he said.

I chomped harder, and that was as far as the helicopter got.

He went for the pile-driver instead. He wanted to crash me down head first.

I hung on. I wrapped my arms round his legs and hung on by ankles, teeth and arms. If I was going down, he was coming too.

"Oy ref," yelled the front rows. "She's biting. Cheat, dirty cheat."

Pete's sweat smelled of old shoes. The hair on his legs pricked my arms. His knee tasted like old burger meat.

I ain't never fought a man before. It's different. Believe.

I ain't never fought anyone who didn't shave her legs.

Biting a hairy knee *ain't* something you want to try regular.

"Ooooh," went the crowd.

"Take it easy," said the ref. I didn't know who he was talking to 'cos I could only see his shoes.

"Ow!" went Pete.

"Yum," I went.

Keif's red boots danced past.

Pete jolted me up and down. I thought he was going to shake my teeth out and leave 'em like tent pegs in his knee.

I couldn't see what Keif was up to—but suddenly Pete staggered and started tipping over backwards.

He let go of me just before he hit the canvas. I let go too. I took my weight on my hands and went into a forward roll away from him.

When I got up it looked like Keif was sitting on Pete's head.

"Two against one," someone called from the stalls. "It ain't fair."

"Way to *go*, Keifee-baby," I yelled.

203

But Pete flung his legs up, clamped his knees round Keif's ears and hauled Keif over onto the deck.

They was both arse up. I bit Pete's bum.

"*Fuck!*" went Pete.

"Oy!" went the ref.

"Dirty cheat!" went the crowd.

Pete rolled onto his back to save his bum. I jumped and landed, both knees first, on his belly.

"Ooff!" he went.

He hit out. I dodged sideways. His fist hit me on the right shoulder and knocked me over backwards.

"Yeah, Pete," yelled the crowd. "Give her some."

If he'd hit my face he'd of knocked my head off. It ain't like being hit by a woman—when someone Pete's size hits you, you stay hit.

He knocked me over backwards.

"Carve her, Pete," went Pete's fans.

Keif took a flying leap and landed where I'd just been.

"Wooof!" went Pete. He sat up, locked one arm round Keif's neck and forced him down so his ear was grinding into the canvas. He caught one of Keif's flailing arms and twisted it hard.

Keif tried to roll with the twist, but Pete got to his knees, then his feet, twisting hard.

"Bastard," he said, when he wasn't panting. "Bastards."

I got up a bit slow, holding my shoulder.

"Wotcha going to do now, Bucket Nut?" someone yelled. "Had enough?"

"I had enough of *you*," I yelled back, rubbing my shoulder.

Pete was stood over Keif. Keif was pounding on the canvas with his free hand. Pete looked like he was trying to wrench Keif's arm out of its socket. He stepped on Keif's face.

I lowered me left shoulder and charged him in the small of

the back. Wham! I jarred into him. He tripped over Keif, staggered a couple of yards and sprawled into the ropes just above the MC's table.

"Give me the mike!" he yelled. He snatched the mike out of the MC's hands.

"*Rumble,*" he bawled into it. "Rumble, rumble, rumble!"

"Yeah, rumble," screamed the crowd.

"Oy, hold it," said the ref. "Why wasn't I told?"

"Fuck off," said Pete. "We don't need you anymore—if we ever did." He threw the microphone back at the MC and spun round to face me.

"You're dead," he said, pointing his fat finger at me. "You're a dead bitch."

"Dead," shouted the front rows. "Dead bitch."

I bit Pete's finger. Well, that's what a bitch is supposed to do, ain't it? If he wants me to behave like a lady he should stop treating me like a bitch. Besides, it's rude to point.

I crunched. Then I ducked. I knew what was coming.

Of *course* I knew what was coming. And of *course* I ducked. Just not quite quick enough.

Pete's fist hit my forehead. THUNK. I swear my feet left the floor. The last thing I remember hearing was some woman in the front saying, "You asked for that, Bucket Nut."

The next thing I knew I was staring up at the lights. My dinner was hitting the back of my throat and I had a headache like a steel spike between my eyes.

But no one was taking any notice. It was like there was a disco going on in the ring. Feet, feet, feet everywhere.

I lay there, and all I could think was that Wozzisname had come back with the hammer and done for me like I done for him. Which was only fair. And I thought that everyone I knew had come to dance on my grave.

I was punchy, see. I wasn't thinking right.

LIZA CODY

I closed my eyes and swallowed my dinner back down.

When I opened my eyes again I knew what was happening—Pete had called for a rumble, and a rumble was what he got.

A rumble is when everyone gets in the ring and mixes it. It's what a promoter does when he's run out of ideas and he wants something special to wind up the crowd in the last twenty minutes.

It looked like Mr. Deeds had got a rumble he hadn't planned. There was Keif and Pete, Phil, the Wolverines, Steve Stinger, Rotten Johnny, Iron Ian, Force Four—all of them—and Gruff. All dancing to a tune I couldn't hear.

It was all wrong. There's rules to rumbles. Sort of. If you go out over the top rope you're eliminated. It goes on till there's only two left, and then those two bash it out. Women don't take part. I wasn't taking part. I was flat on my back.

I turned my head. Slowly. All I could see was feet, feet, feet. Rushing past, dancing, hopping, bopping, shuffling. It didn't look like a rumble. It looked like a punch-up.

A rumble's fun, but a punch-up ain't pretty. Anyone in a pub can have a punch-up, but only wrestlers can rumble proper.

I sat up. Then I lay down again. I wasn't ready.

The blokes was spoiling my comeback. I dragged myself over to the corner post. All the noise was beginning to filter into my brain, and it hurt.

The crowd was at lift-off point. They was in the aisles. They was at ringside. The bouncers couldn't keep them back. It wasn't a proper rumble but the crowd didn't know. They was all screaming their lungs out.

The MC was going, "Please will everyone resume their seats. Will you *please* sit down." But no one was listening.

In the ring, it looked like everyone with a grudge was doing something about it. And it looked like a war between the weights. 'Cos the heavyweights are the stars, see. They get the

206

best of whatever's going—the most money, more promotion, the biggest dressing rooms. So the little guys resent them.

In the ring it looked like the little guys was all ganged up against the heavyweights.

That made me feel better. I didn't want to see a punch-up with no point. But there's definitely a point to beating seven bells out of the blokes who've been lording it over you for years and taking the best of everything.

I wished I didn't feel so woozy. I didn't know if I was part of the crowd or part of the punch-up. I couldn't seem to focus. I'd start watching Phil head-charge a Force Four guy and then my eyes would cross and I wasn't watching no more.

I decided I wasn't part of anything. I couldn't fight and I couldn't watch. So I rolled out of the ring. I stood leaning against the platform with my legs wobbling and my guts turning cartwheels.

And then the little lady with the red handbag and the pink frock said, "You got to get my Keif out of there. You started this."

I'd forgotten all about her. She had a sweet face but it was all squeezed tight with worry. I stared at her in amazement till my eyes crossed. I looked back in the ring.

Keif was getting up off the mat. His nose was streaming blood. He seemed to be having a good time.

"It's only a nosebleed," I mumbled.

"He can't take a big punch," she said. And then the crowd surged into us and she disappeared.

"Hey Bucket Nut," some bloke said, "aincha going back in?"

Someone else said, "Pete shouldn't of hit a woman."

And someone else said, "That ain't a woman—that's Bucket Nut."

"Ha-ha-ha."

"Gotta get Keif," I mumbled. "Give me a bunk-up."

A bloke clasped his hands for me to step on and a couple of others gave me a boost and I crawled back under the bottom rope.

I only had one thought in my head. I thought, "They want me in here. They bloody *want* me in the ring."

Then I stood up and looked for Keif. I stepped over Iron Ian. Bodies everywhere. Naked flesh and wrestling trunks writhing like a tankful of toads.

I grabbed the back of Keif's boxer shorts. He spun round, fists up.

"Doing, babe?" he said. "Yee-ouch!"

Gruff whacked into his midriff and heaved him up on his toad shoulder.

"No dogs, no women," Gruff panted, "and no fuckin' nig-nogs."

He was bent from the weight of Keif on his shoulders. He was trying to edge past me to throw Keif out of the ring. The spotlights made his toad-eye glitter.

I didn't even think about it. I planted my left foot and booted him, hard as I could, in the wedding bells.

"Ding dong," I mumbled. I kicked so hard I expected to see his dirty bits pop out of his mouth. But they didn't. He jack-knifed. Keif crashed to the floor.

"Yee-ouch!" screamed the crowd.

"C'mon," I said to Keif. "Your mum wants you and I ain't feeling too good."

"Wha?" he said.

I leaned down to help him up off the canvas. I shouldn't of done that—my brain took a ride on the roundabout and my guts took a ride on the swings. I puked up on the back of Gruff's head, and I couldn't remember why he was kneeling down.

I'm not quite sure what happened then, but the next clear thing was Keif saying, "Where's your car, Eva?"

"Somewhere in Deptford," I said. We was outside in the street.

"Deptford?" he said. "What you talking about?"

Then I remembered. He wasn't talking about the Clio. He was talking about the Yugo.

"Where's my jacket?" I said. "I don't want to lose it. It's new."

"Here," said Keif's mum. We were outside the Ladywell Baths and there were three police cars parked by the steps, blue lights flashing.

As I put my jacket on I noticed how cold it was.

A tall white guy said, "How many fingers am I holding up?"

"Three," I said.

"What's your date of birth?" said the tall white guy.

"How're you going to know if she gets it wrong?" Keif said. "None of us knows when her birthday is."

"What's your date of birth?" the white guy said again. He was asking quite polite, so I told him.

"See?" he said. "Doesn't matter about us knowing when her birthday is. What we're looking for are signs of confusion."

"I ain't confused," I said.

"Then you've got a harder head than Keith," he said. "That was an almighty punch you took. Keith wouldn't have known when tea-time was."

"Are you Keif's dad?" I said. "What's the politzei doing here?"

"The hall manager call them." Keif's mum made a disap-proving kiss sound with her teeth and lips. "About time: There were little children in that riot."

"I got to go," I said. I didn't want to talk to no politzei.

209

"Keith, you take her to get her head x-rayed," Keif's mum said.

"No," I said. "I'm all right now." There was a lump the size of Pete Carver's fist on my forehead but I was feeling a lot better.

"Not sick no more?" Keif said.

"Oh," I said, remembering. "Did I really throw up in the ring?"

Keif started laughing.

"Stupid boy," Keif's mum said.

"That's a sign of concussion too," Keif's dad said. "Take her to casualty."

But people were beginning to stream out of the Ladywell Baths and there were a couple of uniforms among them.

"Bye," I said and I took off round the corner before anyone got a chance to recognise me and call out in front of the cops.

I was feeling quite clearheaded, but I couldn't find the Yugo. Maybe someone nicked it—I don't know. I was too tired to look for it careful. I borrowed an old Saab instead. I was just driving off when Keif tapped on the window.

"This ain't your car," he said.

"Is now," I said.

"Don't let Mum see you," he said.

"I'm only borrowing it."

"She'll still whack the crap out of you," he said. "That's the only time she ever whacked me—when I was fifteen and I nicked a car with a couple of mates."

"Ain't nicking," I said. "Borrowing."

"Move over, precious," he said, "I'm taking you to casualty. My folks say you should get an X ray."

"You didn't find me," I said. I wound the window up and drove away.

A Saab is a good solid car with a good solid heater so I

warmed up in no time. And as I warmed up, my heart warmed up too. I was remembering the way the crowd called my name when I got in the ring, and the heat of the spotlights on my skin. I was remembering how I barrelled into Pete Carver and knocked him across the ring. And how the crowd went "Ooh-aah" when they saw that. I'm still big and tough. I'm still the London Lassassin. And I can take an "almighty punch." Keif's dad said so, and he should know—he used to be a boxer.

I'm big enough for this life. I can take whatever "almighty" crap it throws at me.

And the crowd remembered me. "Where you been, Bucket Nut?" they said. They hadn't forgotten me. They wanted me there—they helped me climb back into the ring. You don't need a heater when you got memories like that.

And I'd given the crowd a few memories that night as well. Let Mr. Deeds stuff that in his trousers and sit on it. I wished I'd seen him but you can't have everything. Anyway, give him a sniff of trouble and he always goes missing.

But I was tired and I had a headache. I took all the good memories and stored them at the back of my mind. Tomorrow, when I was feeling better, I'd take them out and look at them one by one.

Meanwhile, driving was a bit of a problem because for some reason I wasn't seeing the traffic lights till it was nearly too late. Take a tip from me—if you ever borrow a motor and you want to get home without trouble from the politzei, drive perfect. Not too fast, not too slow. Obey all the traffic signs and stop at red lights. And don't forget to wipe the car down afterwards. Leave it as you'd like to find it. It's a favour to the owner. And also you don't want to leave traces of yourself for politzei to find. Politzei ain't a very forgiving bunch of boobies. So don't help them catch you. Okay?

Chapter 24

"Don't give me no aggravation," I said to the dogs. "I ain't in the mood." I was unlocking the gate and Ramses and Lineker came bounding up to say hello.

"Where's Milo?" I said. But Milo came trotting over, so it looked like he'd survived an evening without human protection.

All I wanted was a cup of hot sweet tea and a lie-down. A comeback is a tiring event. I wanted a cup of tea to settle my guts, and an aspirin for my noddle. I didn't want no trouble. I'd had enough of that to last a lifetime. And I was sore all over.

I made a mug of tea, but the milk was sour so I had to drink it without. I couldn't find an aspirin for love or money. It wasn't the kind of homecoming I'd imagined. I bet Keif's mum cooked him a nice hot dinner, and Cousin Carmen rubbed him down with a gallon of her magic embrocation. That'd be the perfect way to come down after a fight.

Because you do come down. At first, when you're still on a high, you don't feel anything but excited. Then, gradually, all your aches and pains come along, knocking at your door.

A fighter always has aches and pains—what else would you expect? But I went into this fight with more than my fair share. Count 'em—I had a bruised toe, a singed ankle and a dodgy back before I ever climbed into that ring. But did that stop me? No, it did not. And what's more, when I climbed into that ring, I didn't feel anything but the champagne fizz in my veins.

The same goes for all my worries and troubles. When I'm the London Lassassin it's like I walk out of my own skin. I put on another one when I put on the black costume. And every time I put it on, it's brand-new and it fits me better than my real skin fits me. All my worries and troubles are in my old skin and I leave them outside the ring.

But after a fight, when it's all over and the spotlights are turned off and the crowd goes home, I have to stop being the London Lassassin. I have to be plain old Eva Wylie again and put up with all her aches and pains and worries.

And who cares about plain old Eva Wylie? No one. That's who. But a whole crowd cares about the London Lassassin. A whole crowd boos and shouts and spits. That's what I call being noticed.

"Oh yeah," I said to Milo. "They noticed me tonight. You should of been there."

"Herf," said Milo, waking up and twitching his ears.

"So who needs milk in their tea, or hot water, or an aspirin?" I asked him. "Aspirin's for wimps."

Milo yawned.

I lay down on my bunk and pulled the sleeping bag up round my neck. I don't know if it was the bang on the head, but I kept dozing off and then waking up with my heart beating too fast. It was like the bang on the head was fighting it out with the adrenaline rush from being the London Lassassin.

It was confusing. Sometimes I'd wake up with a start and think I was going to be late for the Ladywell Baths. And then I'd doze off again only to jump up thinking Wozzisname was outside scratching on my door. That was the worst. I'd done

213

everything I could to get rid off Wozzisname but he was still hanging around in dark corners, dead and undead.

Next time I woke up, I realised it was Milo scratching at the door, wanting to be let out. So I went out with him. It was dark and damp, but it was the sort of dark and damp I was used to. Walking around with the dogs made my head feel more normal.

It was after midnight. I was tired and sore. I wanted to sleep but I didn't want to lie in the dark with Wozzisname waiting for me to nod off. 'Cos that's how it seemed. It seemed he was just waiting for me to let me guard down so that he could rise up out of the river and point his undead finger at me.

"You never even knew me," he was saying. "But you won't never forget me. You put me in the river, but you can't get rid of me that easy."

"Bugger off," I said. "You brought it on yourself. You and Ma." But I knew he wouldn't listen. No one listens.

The other person who never listens is Anna Lee, The Enemy. She turned up in her white Peugeot and tooted on her horn till I went to the gate.

I'd never admit it to her, but I was quite pleased to have a real live human being to talk to that night. Not that she's quite human—with her poker-straight posture and her poker-straight life. No one that organised is quite human.

"What you doing up so late?" I said. "Couldn't you find another poor sod to do your dirty work for you? You should be all tucked up in your bed by now."

I was a bit pleased to see her, but I wasn't going to let her in. I never invite politzei into my home. We talked through the gate.

"I came by earlier," she said. "Where were you?"

"What's it to you?" Bloody typical—she always starts with a question.

"I just wanted to talk to you," she said. "What on earth happened? There's a huge lump on your forehead. How did you get hurt?"

"Questions, questions, questions," I said. "You don't *never* have a conversation like a normal person. Everything you say, *everything*, is a sodding interrogation."

"Force of habit," she said. "It's what I do for a living. Sorry if it upsets you."

"Well, blow me down and feed me buttercups!" I said.

"What?"

"You said 'sorry.' You *never* 'pologise."

"It's the end of a long day. I must be weakening." She leaned against the gatepost, which made her look less like a cop and more like a human being. "Oh hell," she said, "now I'm going to upset you again."

"Takes more than you to upset me."

"No it doesn't," she said, "but never mind. Try and believe I'm not out to get you. Just for once, believe I'm trying to help."

"Help what?"

"You. It's about counterfeit money. Bent money. I told you about it the other night at the Cat and Cowbell."

"So?" I didn't care what she said. As long as she kept her hooter out of my hollyhocks.

"Some of the local traders came to see me and Mr. Schiller about a scattering of bad notes which have turned up in the last few days—John from the burger bar, Mr. Hanif, Value Mart . . . They've all taken fake twenties and fifties. Bad notes, but good bad notes—you couldn't tell from a casual glance. But they all came up dodgy under a detector light."

"So what?" I said.

"The police haven't seen any of this batch before. They want to see more. They want to know where it's coming from."

I said nothing. There was a heavy, low feeling starting to creep from my guts to my heart.

215

"Eva," she said, "it's coming from you. I've interviewed all the traders. You are the only common factor."

"Who're you calling common?" I said, but my heart wasn't in it. I was beginning to feel too blue to talk back.

"Where did you get it, Eva?"

"Why ask me?" I said. "I don't know what you're talking about." But I knew. I knew if I looked inside that Puma bag again I wouldn't see my future, my fortune. I'd see a load of crappy paper. I should of known it was too good to be true.

She said, "Who gave it to you, Eva? Who've you been working for?"

"I been working for you," I said. "Maybe it came from you like the rest of the shite you give me." All that lovely dosh was turning to dung, right before my eyes.

I wished she'd go away. I wanted to be alone again. I wanted The Enemy to get stroppy and flounce off, but she never does what I want her to do.

"Who else?" she said. "Has anyone else paid you this week?"

"None of your business," I said.

"That's a new jacket," she said. "New boots. Where did you get the money, Eva? You haven't had any new clothes as long as I've known you."

See what I mean? She's always, *always*, got that sharp snout in my business. It's a copper's snout.

"You don't know anything," I said. "You think you do, but you don't. I'm back in the ring now."

"That's terrific, Eva," she said. Like she wanted me to think she was really pleased. Fat chance. "So the money came from fighting. Were you paid in cash? Or did someone cash a cheque for you? You haven't got a bank account, have you?"

I should never of worked for her. You shouldn't never ever give politzei a line on you. Once they've got a line they never leave it alone. The only thing to do is to keep your lip zipped—don't give them nothing.

"Piss off," I said. "I don't work for you no more. I don't have to talk to you." I began to walk away. I'd had enough.

"Okay," she said. "But think about it. Passing counterfeit money's a serious offence, Eva. It's not like boosting the odd motor. It isn't slap-on-the-wrist time if you get caught. It's serious time—years, Eva, you could be locked up for *years*."

What about Wozzisname? How much serious time would I get for him if anyone found out? How important was passing a few bent notes compared with that?

"Shove it," I said. "You got no right coming round here threatening me. You ain't welcome here."

"I'm not threatening you," she said. "I haven't told anyone about this except Mr. Schiller. Honestly, I don't want to see you in trouble. But if I do nothing I'm colluding. Then I'm in trouble too."

"Life's tough," I said. "Buy a crash helmet."

"I'm not the one with an ostrich egg on her forehead. You need a crash helmet more than I do."

I stared at her. There are some people in this world who never bring good news. They just ain't capable of it. The Enemy was one.

"I'll give you twenty-four hours," she said. "Talk to me or talk to Mr. Schiller. After that it gets official. Think about it, Eva."

Dung and depression, bollocks and blues. That's all I ever get. People. They do nothing but bring you down. It's my comeback, right? Did anyone pat me on the back and say, "Nice one, Eva"? I must of had my fingers in my ears if they did, 'cos I never heard 'em. No. What I get is people bringing me down.

I get threats and abuse and bollocks and blues. I might as well pack up and leave town—find someone without a detector light and buy a ticket to some place where they'll take dogs and you don't need a passport, where I can get lost and start again. Is there somewhere like that? Where it ain't a crime to be big and speak your mind. Where I can do what I'm good at without everyone bars me and brings me down and gives me a headache.

"Have you got an aspirin?" I said to The Enemy.

"Yes," she said. She rummaged in her bag and gave me a card of pills. Maybe she does have a bit of a human heart after all.

She said, "Do think about it, Eva. I'll stop by tomorrow."

"Don't bother," I said. "I won't be here." And I went away to where I couldn't hear her voice no more.

Why is it—when you've got a million things to think about and they're all stacked up like traffic in a jam on the motorway—you can't think at all? How come your brain just coughs and stalls?

My brain went walkies except for thinking about the aspirins. It was like I had a bass drum between my ears, and I couldn't think of nothing but swallowing a handful of aspirins as quick as possible. After that I couldn't think of nothing but making another mug of strong sweet tea. And after that I must of nodded off again because there was nothing at all.

When I woke up there was half a mug of cold tea beside me and Milo was whining to be let out. I was sore from head to toe. I wanted a deep, piping hot bath and a pile of fluffy towels. I wanted a long slow rubdown with a gallon of Cousin Carmen's embrocation. I wanted a double helping of pasta and meatball sauce or a pepperoni pizza. Most of all I wanted Simone to talk to.

Was it her I saw running up the steps to the Ladywell Baths? I hoped it was. She should of seen me up there under the lights. If she didn't see that she'd never know what I really am—what I made of meself since she got took away. It was crucial, and she had to see it to understand it. I wanted her to understand.

I was so gut-whacked when she cringed to God Greg and handed him my shooter, but she was still my sister and she was the only person I could talk to about the money. She was the only one I could trust.

I couldn't keep the money no more. It was bent. I had a little twitch about that. Maybe it wasn't bent. Maybe The Enemy only said it was bent so she could get her sticky fingers on it. I spent half a minute hoping that was true. But I couldn't believe it. The Enemy's a stuck-up nosy cow, but it's no use complaining 'cos she's too straight and then not believing her when she says the dosh is bent.

Besides, God Greg more or less said so himself when he was droning on about how it'd do me more harm than good.

But the main reason I believed The Enemy was telling the truth was 'cos it felt like the truth. I can't be a squillionaire—I ain't born to that kind of luck. Some are and some ain't. I ain't. What I got I sweated for. Nobody ever gave me nothing for free. And it's no use thinking they ever will. Some gets stuff given to them. Not me. I got to grab.

Those squillions was just too good to be true, and I should of known they was dung. They was handed to me on a plate and I should of known it was a plateful of poop. It had to be, 'cos it couldn't be anything else if it was handed to me.

I put on my shoes and jacket and went out into the dark. It was mizzling rain. The dogs came trotting over smelling of wet fur.

We went on another tour of the yard together, and I must say they was behaving like gentlemen. Dogs and people is much more alike than they think. With dogs you got to show 'em how to behave and you got to make them pay attention. You got to prove you're the boss. Which I did a couple of nights ago with Ramses, because you can't only prove it once. You got to keep on proving it or they take advantage. It's the same with people, only people are stupider. They don't learn so quick.

Our last stop was at the dog shed. I went in and took the Puma bag off of the wall. I wanted to say good-bye to it. And if you think I'm soft you're wrong. I wasn't saying good-bye to a lousy bagful of paper—I was saying good-bye to all the things I would of done with it if it wasn't bent. I was saying good-bye to a fitness centre called Musclebound, and if that ain't worth a lump in the throat I don't know what is.

I took it indoors and laid it on the bunk. Then I filled the kettle. There was still some of Simone's coffee left so I made a mug of that with lots of sugar. I wished I still had some of her whisky to keep the cold out but we finished it all last night.

I spread the money out on the floor and looked at it while I drank my coffee. How could anything so pretty as that be dung? And how could anything so beautiful be so unlucky? Because, when you think about it, that dung brought me nothing but a cartload of trouble. Even when I thought it was the real thing it was only pretend, and it put the whammy on me. I would never of met Wozzisname but for all that pretend dosh, and I was hexed for sure afterwards.

If it wasn't for that pretend dosh Simone wouldn't have gone off with God Greg.

You won't believe the next bit—I suddenly wished I was dead. I don't hardly believe it neither, but it's true. I wished, when Pete Carver hit me between the eyes, I wish I died.

See, if I could of died right then and there, I'd of died a rich woman. Don't laugh—it's true. 'Cos The Enemy wouldn't of told me the dosh was dung. I was rich till she told me that.

If I'd died in the ring I would of died winning. And Simone would of been there and she'd of seen me die a winner. Like she thought I was rich 'cos I'd won the lottery.

Suddenly I had this horrible thought about Simone. What would she think when she found out I hadn't won the lottery? What'd she think when she knew that the one thousand one hundred and sixty-seven quid was all fake? Well, all except for the seven pounds.

She'd know I lied to her. She'd know God Greg told her true. What would she do if she knew her sister lied to her and a jumped-up baboon told her true?

No. I couldn't tell her. I couldn't ask her to help me with what to do about the money unless I told her where it came from. I couldn't do that. I only just got her back.

I had to get rid of it just the same as I got rid of Wozzis-name—on my own. So I thought, why not take it to the same place near Greenwich and dump it in the river? I mean, if Wozzisname wanted it so bad, why not give it to him?

But I was so sore, and I didn't know if I could find that place again—I only found it by accident the first time.

Then I thought about all the other greedy bastards who tried to take it off me. There was Ma and Andy. There was Droopy-drawers and Fish-face. There was God Greg and The Enemy. The politzei wanted it too. And Keif—you don't think he'd of asked to be my personal trainer without I paid him, do you? Wake *up*.

I started to feel bad about paying Keif in bent notes. But then I thought, well, he was a joke personal trainer so he ought to expect joke money. Except Keif *did* have good hands for real, and he *was* the one who suggested my comeback. And he was there with me when it happened.

But it couldn't be helped. Feeling bad about Keif was a waste of time when there was so much to decide.

If only I could sell it back to God Greg for straight money. Except he couldn't have much straight money if he had to make pretend money, could he? And anyway, how could I sell it to him without Simone finding out?

I finished my coffee, and then I packed up every last gorgeous, evil note in the Puma bag. I zipped it up. I put on my coat and went out.

"Milo," I called.

"Herf?" went Milo and trotted out of the shadows, one ear up, one ear flat.

"Shurrup," I said. "How the hell am I s'posed to think with you herfing all the time? I never knew such a talky dog."

"Herf?" he said.

"Guard dogs don't 'herf,'" I said. "Why ain't you learned nothing from Ramses? He don't speak till it counts and then he frightens the life out of you. That's how it is with guard dogs."

"Her—"

"Shurrup." I snapped his lead on. His training had taken a dive over the last few days.

"Hip," he said sadly.

"Heel," I said. I thought he'd forgot everything but he fell in and trotted to the gate on my left-hand side. He didn't try to gallop away or pull or nothing.

"Maybe you ain't attack material," I said. "Like I ain't stinking-rich material."

"Herf?"

"What'm I going to do with you?" I was trying to unlock the gate but he kept jumping up to lick my hand.

"We run a lean clean machine here," I said. "We ain't got no room for passengers. *Sit.*" He sat with his mouth open and his tongue out.

"You're so bloody big," I said. "I thought you was going to be me best dog ever. But you're soft."

I locked the gate behind us and we started along the road.

"I could give you to Simone," I said, "except she's scared of dogs."

"Herf?"

"Or Keif," I said. "He likes you. God knows why—you're such a woejous article. Trouble is, you're too bloody big to be a pet."

"Herf."

"And you're too gobby, and you eat too much."

I had Milo on my left, and I had the Puma bag in my right hand, and I didn't know what to do with neither of them.

I named Milo after the greatest wrestler that ever lived in the whole history of the universe—Milo of Croton—but he turned out soft. I bet Milo of Croton didn't go into any of his fights nattering and chattering and licking people's hands.

We were walking along, up one street and down another, while I tried to think what to do. It was raining steady now and we was the only living souls out on the streets.

"Okay, Milo," I said, "you're so gobby—talk to me. Tell me what to do."

But, just to be contrary, Milo gave me a sniffy look with both ears flat, and stopped to lift his leg on the rear wheel of a car. He didn't say nothing at all.

But, paint me purple and hang me on the hall wall, the car he chose to piss on was a red Carlton. It wasn't *the* red Carlton 'cos it had all its windows intact, and Carltons are common cars. But I was so struck by the fact it was a red Carlton I thought it was that old mojo working again.

"Milo," I said, "you're a genius."

"Herf," said Milo, grinning at me.

Chapter 25

Usually I hate Sundays. The men don't come to the yard so there's none of that lovely banging and crashing to fall asleep to. It's silent and lonely and when you can't sleep all you can do is lie there and think there's nobody around who cares if you live or die. But this Sunday I had business of my own and I didn't want no one turning up for work and finding me at it.

So it was late, nearly eleven in the morning, before I had a wash and tumbled into my new sleeping bag. And then I was so butchered I didn't hear the silence. I just crashed straight into sleep without even stopping to ask its name.

I dreamed Wozzisname was running away from me, down a long straight road carrying a Puma bag. I almost caught him but he turned round and said, "You can't even catch crabs." Then he went down a storm drain headfirst and I didn't want to go in after him. But someone in the audience said, "Aincha going to go back in, Bucket Nut?" So I had to dive in 'cos there was a big crowd of people watching and I had to prove I wasn't yellow. But I was scared I wouldn't be able to breathe.

I don't remember what happened next, and anyway, who

cares? Dreams are rubbish. It's the real things which count—like real money. You can keep all the pretend stuff. I don't want it no more.

I should of slept for seven days solid. Anyone who went to bed feeling like me deserved a really good kip. But I must of been too uncomfortable. So I got up after only five hours.

It wasn't enough, but I needed aspirin more than I needed sleep so I got up and went out.

It's a good job I did, because I found Simone waiting at the gate and it looked like she'd been waiting ages.

"Why didn't you come in?" I said.

"It's your bloody dogs," she said. "They don't like me."

See, it was Sunday and the dogs have the yard to themselves on a Sunday.

"Don't take it personal," I said. "They're trained that way."

"Well it's a nuisance," she said. "I've been standing here in the cold for hours."

"I'm going out for an aspirin and breakfast."

"Breakfast?" she said. "I can see you might need something for your head. You look like the Elephant Man. I hope you aren't expecting your boyfriend. You don't want him to see you looking like that."

"*Simone*," I said. "Give it a *rest*. You know I ain't . . ."

"Don't yell," she said.

But I wasn't yelling, honest. You can't have a headache like mine and yell—it ain't humanly possible. I let myself out of the yard.

"Simone," I said, "last night."

"Yeah?"

"At the old Ladywell Baths. Were you there? I thought I saw you go in."

"Yes," she said. "I went. Your . . . er, personal trainer said he was taking you. But, Eva, there's something we have to talk about. Seriously."

I can't tell you how chuffed I was. She was there. She saw me.

I said, "And? What did you think? Wasn't it brilliant?"

"Brilliant," she said, "but, Eva . . ."

"It was mind-blowing," I said. She was *there*. She saw. She thought it was brilliant.

"Take it easy, Eva," she said. "Calm down."

We was walking up Mandala Street to Hanif's shop. Well, she was walking—I was practically dancing. She *saw*. She thought I was brilliant.

All the same, when we got to Hanif's I stopped. I didn't want to go in 'cos Mr. Hanif was one of the people who'd complained about the bent money—as if he didn't have enough of the straight stuff. Mr. Hanif must be mega-loaded—his is the only shop round here which is open all hours, and he won't give you nothing on tick.

So I handed Simone a straight five-pound note and she went in. She bought me a bottle of the aspirin you can dissolve in water, which was great 'cos I hate taking pills. She bought bananas, bread, baked beans and bacon too.

Then we went to the Fir Tree so I could have a meat pie and chips for my breakfast, and some of the dissolving aspirin for my head.

She said, "Eva, we've got to talk."

"No," I said, "not if it's about that ponce, Greg." I was happy. I *was*. I wanted to talk about last night at the Ladywell Baths. "I said everything I had to say yesterday."

"Yes, but, Eva, that isn't all," she said. "You weren't straight with me. You said you won that money on the lottery."

See what I mean? The big bring-down.

226

"Are you calling me a liar?" I said.

"He showed me," she said. "I still had some of what we were going to give Ma. He *showed* me it was his."

"How?" I said. "Why didn't you give it all to Ma?"

"You think I was stealing it?" she said. "Shit." She got up.

"Don't go," I said.

"I'm not going," she said. "I need a drink. You don't trust me, Eva."

"I do," I said. I was amazed she thought I didn't.

She went to the bar and came back with a white wine whatsit for her and a rum and coke for me.

"I *do* trust you," I said, when she put the drinks on our table. "Why wouldn't I?"

"Don't get so excited," she said. "I thought maybe you thought I was keeping that money for myself."

"I wouldn't mind," I said. "You deserve it more than Ma."

"I wouldn't take your money."

"I never said you would. I said you deserved it more than Ma."

"Shshsh," she said. "I told you I was going to do the best I could. And when I went to Ma's place I saw there was no point giving it to her all at once. She was already bloated so I only gave her a little. And I gave Andy some. I want them to be sober so they remember. There's no point if they forget. If they forget, they'll keep asking for more."

"There ain't any more."

"I know. That's what we were going to tell them."

"That's the *truth*," I said. "There ain't any more."

"But, Eva," she said, "there has to be. Greg said . . ."

"Greg," I said, "that jumped-up baboon and his big black gloves."

"Eva, *hush*."

227

"No," I said. "It ain't right. You believe him and you don't believe me."

"He *showed* me, Eva," she said. "He's got this thing like a pen torch. When you shine it on bank notes you can tell whether they're all right or all wrong. The money he lost was wrong. And, Eva, the money you gave me for Ma was wrong too. You didn't win it on the lottery, did you?"

"I wouldn't lie to you," I said. I swigged the rum and coke down in one swallow. It was very hot in the Fir Tree. "Why would I lie to you?"

"I don't know, Eva," she said. "But it's a very dangerous thing to do. I think Greg is a very dangerous man."

"So why did you give him my shooter?"

"Don't be so childish, Eva. It wasn't yours. What were you going to do? Shoot him? Haven't you had enough violence?"

"Yeah," I said. It was very hot and my head began to feel numb and weird.

"Don't let's quarrel," Simone said. "I hate fighting. Please, Eva, all you have to do is give that sports bag back to Greg and he'll never bother us again."

"What sports bag?" I said. "Why won't you believe me? I ain't got his sodding sports bag."

"I wash my hands of this," she said. She drank her drink down. "You can't be helped, can you? I try and try, but you just won't let me help you." She got up.

"Where you going?"

"What do you care?"

"Please, Simone." I got up too. "I *swear*, I swear I ain't got his sports bag. I swear I ain't got his bent dosh."

She stared at me. She was doing her eyes different today, and they looked like an Eastern queen's eyes. I was glad I could look into eyes as pretty as that and tell the truth. Sort of.

She said, "Then where did you get the money you gave me for Ma and Andy?"

"Me head's feeling funny," I said, 'cos it was.

"I'll get us another drink," she said. "But you've got to tell me, Eva."

She went to the bar. While she was ordering the drinks I held my head in my hands and tried to remember what I thought of to tell her last night. I made up a good story last night. Well, I thought it was good at four in the morning and I had to get it right. I had to, or she'd go away and leave me.

"Well?" she said when she got back.

I gulped down half my rum to make me feel better. "I bought a lottery ticket," I said.

"That won't do," she said. "The lottery doesn't pay out in counterfeit money."

"But I did," I said. "I bought the ticket. But I didn't cash it in." The rum was helping me remember. I took another gulp.

"See, Simone, I ain't got much. I ain't had so many fights lately. Anyway, I had this lottery ticket and I almost forgot about it 'cos I wasn't feeling lucky and I didn't think I'd win. And then, see, I was broke one time, so I sold it to a bloke in a pub for a drink."

"You sold it for a drink?" she said. "And it was a winning number?"

"Numbers ain't my thing," I said. "You know that."

"I know," she said. "Then what happened?"

"Well, it was only a few days ago. Last week."

"What?" she said. "What happened last week?"

This was the tricky bit. I slurped a little more rum down.

"In the market."

"What market?"

"This one, here. Mandala Street," I said, 'cos she had to

believe me. "This woman come up to me in Mandala Street market and she said she'd been looking for me everywhere. She said my ticket came up and she and her old man won loads of dosh. She said she wanted to give me some."

"You're kidding," Simone said. "No one'd do that."

See? I told you it was tricky.

"She did," I said.

"Oh, come *on*," she said. "No one gives away money. *No one.*"

"She said it was unlucky not to. She wanted me to pick her another number. She said I wouldn't be lucky again unless I won some money. So she gave me some of the money I would of won if I'd kept the ticket and not sold it to her old man for a drink. See?"

"Not really," she said. She looked totally flummoxed. I finished my drink.

"She thought you were lucky?" Simone said. "And she wanted you to pick more numbers for her?"

"She gave me this form and a pen and I picked six more numbers."

"And then she gave you over two thousand pounds? That's unbelievable, Eva."

I wanted to say it was true but my tongue turned to felt underlay and it stuck to the roof of my mouth.

"How much was the ticket worth?" Simone said.

"Dunno," I said. I was tired. I was tired of telling stories to someone I loved. I wanted to stop. I wanted us to go back to where we was talking about the Ladywell Baths.

"It must've been worth a fortune," Simone said. "If she gave you over two thousand pounds it must've been worth over a million. Oh poor Eva. Think how much you lost."

I was feeling quite sorry for myself too. 'Cos, when you

think about it, last night, I did lose a million. I lost squillions last night. Some of it *was* for true.

"They do that sometimes in casinos," she said. "If they've had a good night at the tables, they tip some to the croupier and the doorman. For luck."

She sipped her drink. "So who was the bloke, Eva?"

"Wha' bloke?"

"The bloke you sold your ticket to?"

"Dunno." I took another big swig. It was so hot.

"You must know," she said. "You gave him a fortune and he tipped you peanuts."

"Didn't."

"Well his wife did," she said. "She gave you a little tip, Eva, a little drink. And she tipped you in bad money."

"Lousy bastard," I said. "Lousy, mean bugger."

"So who was it?"

"Dunno," I said. "But I'll give him what for if I see him again."

"Describe him, Eva," she said. "I've got to tell Greg something."

Greg. That brought me up short. I tried to gather my wits, but I was feeling so sorry for myself and I'd almost got angry with the mean bastard who tipped me bad money. When there wasn't one, except bloody Greg.

"Bleedin' Greg," I said. "He's as bad as The Enemy. 'Who, what, when, how much?' Questions, questions. That's all God Greg and the politzei do. Ask fuckin' stupid questions."

"What enemy?" Simone said. "You haven't been talking to the police, Eva?"

"Never talk to politzei," I said. "Don't never do that."

"Shshsh," she said. "Keep your voice down. What enemy?"

"Anna fuckin' Lee, The Enemy. You saw her in the Cat 'n'

Cowbell the night you made me count to a hundred in the rain."

"Shshsh!"

"Don't shshsh me," I said. "You did. An' now she wants to know how much and who and where. An' she's gave me twenty-four hours to tell her. An', Simone, I got to go away 'cos I can't tell her nothing more than I told you and God Greg. 'Cos no one believes me. Tha's why."

"I believe you," she said. "But please talk quiet."

"Can I come and stay with you, Simone?" I wanted to tell her about The Enemy and the way she never, ever lets a person alone. But Simone was having a coughing fit.

"I don't even know where you live," I said. "I don't know where Ma lives anymore. An', Simone, every twatting sod in the universe knows where *I* live. And they keep coming round with hammers an' shooters an' shit. An' questions, Simone, questions. All the time."

I was so glad to be talking for true, I couldn't hardly stop myself.

"I jus' want a few fights an' a bit of peace," I said, 'cos that's true. "An' you. Did'ja know I was lookin' for you all these years, Simone, and sodding Ma wouldn't never say where you was. And now, Simone, *now* I can't even find *her* and she sends round Wozzisname, and now, Simone, *now*, I'm a . . ."

"Sssh, Eva, shshsh. Please. You're upset. Don't be so upset."

She knew me so well—I was a bleeding misery and no one else cared.

She got me another rum to cheer me up.

"Don't be upset, Eva. Don't worry," she said. "I'm here now." And that was true too. There she was looking at me with her Eastern princess eyes and stroking my hand.

"You really saw me fight last night?"

"I did, Eva," she said. "Of course I did. You didn't think I'd miss that, did you? Are you all right—feeling better?"

"Yeah. I was good, wasn't I?"

"You were wonderful," she said.

"You was proud of me, wasn't you?"

"'Course I was," she said. "Bursting with it. There now, it's all okay."

"Yeah," I said. 'Cos it was.

"I'm here," she said. "We're together. So don't get uptight anymore. What you told me, about the lottery ticket—Eva, are you listening?"

"Yeah."

"Is that all true? Because I've got to tell Greg something, and I've got to convince him it's true or he'll keep coming after you."

"We could go away," I said. "Why tell him anything, Simone? Why did you go off with him?"

"'Cos he had a gun."

"But you *gave* him the gun. I had it, but you gave it to him."

"It was his gun, Eva." She sighed. "Eva, he's a big, dangerous man. It doesn't matter if he's got a gun or not. Even when you had the gun, *he* was calling the shots. Can't you see that? Big dangerous men always win."

"They fuckin' don't," I said. "You saw what I done last night. Pete an' Gruff's big blokes too."

"That's your answer to everything, Eva," she said. "Kick 'em in the balls."

"Too right."

"But it doesn't change anything. They pick themselves up off the floor and they're still big dangerous men. Only now they're big, dangerous and angry."

"*And* they've got blue balls. And they think twice before messing with me next time."

"So they think twice," Simone said. "Congratulations. Usually they don't think at all."

She was so bitter. I didn't like it.

"Why're you so bitter?" I said.

"I'm not bitter," she said. "Just tired. I can't kick big dangerous men in the balls. I don't want to make them angry. The only thing big men are good for is protecting you from other big men. When big men get angry they hurt you, Eva. I don't want to be hurt."

"No one's going to hurt you," I said. "You got me."

"Yeah," she said. "And you go round making big dangerous men angry."

"Well, they fuckin' make *me* angry."

"Don't I know it!" she said. "What am I supposed to do? I wish you hadn't sold that ticket, Eva."

"What ticket?"

"The lottery ticket. I wish I had so much money I could call the shots and have a bit of power. Then I wouldn't have to keep on and on *placating* them."

"Wha?"

"Big dangerous men," she said. "Doing what they want—being what they want me to be."

"Don't," I said.

"Oh yeah, right," she said.

"You're a model," I said. "Aincha got it all?"

"Eva, there are girls, fourteen, thirteen years old, doing what I'm doing now. You don't understand. You *can't* understand. They're all doing—*being*—what the big blokes want them to be."

"So, let them."

"Blokes like young flesh. Young skin. You lose your place

in the pecking order. Then you've got to do more of what the big blokes want—you've got to do what you're told, what the young ones won't do. So you've got to find a big dangerous guy to protect you from the others. You've got to, Eva."

"I don't," I said. "You don't. You got me."

She sighed. She said, "Or scratch enough money together so you don't need any of them. I wish you hadn't told me, Eva."

"Wha?"

"About the lottery ticket. We nearly had it, Eva, we were *that* close, and missing by an inch is worse than missing by a mile. Are you listening?"

"Yeah."

"You're going to sleep on me," she said. "Well I suppose it's better than shouting."

"Not sleepy," I said. But she was right. I dunno why. I put my achy head down on my arms for a second—just to ease it, and when I woke up it was much worse.

"Go home, Eva," said the landlord. "I'm not running a rest home for drunken wrestlers."

"Where's Simone?" I said. "Where's my sister?"

"That's never your sister," he said.

"*Is.*"

"Who'd've thought it—sweet kid like that," he said. "She left half an hour ago. She probably couldn't stand the snoring."

"Wasn't snoring."

"No?" he said. "We've got a generator in the basement—it must've been the generator making all that racket."

He seemed to be in a good mood so I asked him for a glass of water. I dissolved six of the tablets and drank the water. It almost made me throw up.

Then I went home. I didn't want to go home 'cos of all

the scuzz-bags who could find me there—but the landlord wouldn't let me stay in the Fir Tree and I didn't have nowhere else to go. Simone didn't tell me where she lived—well, she couldn't, could she? I went to sleep before she could, and she's too nice to wake me up. She knows I need my rest. She came to see me at the Ladywell Baths last night and she saw all what I'd went through. So she knew.

Thinking about it cheered me up. Till I got home and found that bastard Andy waiting for me. I didn't even get a chance to take the chain off the gate, so when he came up behind me and grabbed the collar of my jacket I didn't have nothing to hit him with except the shopping bag. You can't do much damage with a loaf of bread and half a pound of streaky bacon.

"Ow!" he went. "You always got to hit people, don'cha? I only want to know where Simone is." Which was exactly what I wanted to know too. And it made me see red, white and blue. 'Cos I'm Simone's sister so I got a right, but he's less than nothing and it's none of his diseased, rotting business.

"You," I said. "You want hitting, you do. I'm so fuckin' sick of you. You've took everything I got and now you want my sister too."

"You can't fob me off with a lousy two hundred quid," he said. "You killed a man. If it wasn't for Simone I'd've gone to the police. I'm not playing silly buggers anymore. I've got to see Simone. She didn't come home last night, and her mother ain't seen her. So she's got to be here."

"Listen to me, fart-face," I said, "you go back to that greedy old bag you're humping, and you tell her to squeeze stones 'cos she'll get more out of them than she will out of me. I'm dry. You hear me. Dry. Cleaned out. Bled white."

With every word I took a pace forward. I was so blazing

236

hot I was shaking my bread and bananas in his face. And he was walking backwards.

"She said there was no reasoning with you," he said.

"Then that's the one true word she spoke," I said. "You can flush the rest down the crapper. She's a poxy, lying, greedy cow and I hope she dies hurting. I hope you do too."

Suddenly, I knew, if I had a hammer in my hand, I could of hit him too. I could. I was so burning crazy mad I could of hit him just like I hit Wozzisname. They say it's easier the second time. But if they say that, they never done it themselves. 'Cos the frightening thing is how easy it was the first time. Just wallop . . . and down he went. Just wallop, and then nothing. Forever.

But when you're blazing, when you're seeing sparks, when your guts is clenched like a hot steel fist—and that fist is beating on your own insides trying to get out—what do you do? For Christ's sake, someone, tell me that. What the hell do you do? No one's ever, *ever* been able to tell me that.

I lobbed my shopping bag over the gate into the yard. I went up after it. I wasn't fit for dainty work like putting keys into padlocks. I went up the gate like I go up the ropes and post in the ring. Take the high ground—go for the flying slam.

I turned and there was dirty Andy, on the pavement—just waiting for me to slam down on him. He looked up at me with his mouth open.

He said, "You're insane. You really are." And he swung round and walked away.

He walked away and left me balanced on top of the frigging gate. Ramses, Lineker and Milo was going apeshit too. Leaping at the gate and the fence barking their fool heads off.

"*Shut up*," I bellowed, so loud it hurt my throat. "Just shut up, all of you."

And they did. But it was like there was still barking and snarling going on in me head. Which I s'pose is what they mean by "barking mad."

"Just shut the fuck up," I screamed. "All of you." And the dogs stared at me like I was crazy. And Andy looked round at me just once and hurried away up Mandala Street.

So I jumped down off the gate and ran after him. I wanted to boot his sorry arse all the way to Ma's place. Then I'd boot *her* sorry arse all the way to hell and back.

But by the time I got to the corner of Mandala Street I was out of breath and I was feeling like I wanted to puke. And I remembered I didn't know where Ma lived anymore.

I looked round the corner and saw Andy, still walking away, and I thought—that's where you're going, you dirty troll. You're off to see the trollop.

So I followed.

And it started to rain. Andy pulled his collar up round his ears and stuck his hands in his pockets. I did the same. That's what it's like when you're following someone—you do what they do. And it sucks. It really does. 'Specially if the stupid wossock you're following goes to the wrong place.

Chapter 26

I could of told him. I could of said, "Andy, you stupid wossock, Ma don't live here no more. She moved out, bag and baggage, days ago." But I didn't, 'cos I didn't want him to know I was following him.

He'd been there before—he knew about the useless lifts—and he went straight to the stairs. I didn't follow because I didn't want to meet him when he left. Which he would as soon as he found out Ma wasn't there. I stood in the courtyard in the pouring rain.

Then I thought, supposing Ma didn't leave the block. Suppose all she did was move from one flat into another in the same block?

So I kept my eyes on the outside walkways to see what floor Andy was on when he came out of the stairwell. But when I saw him again he was on Ma's walkway, on the fifth floor. Then he disappeared just about where Ma's door was. And I thought, what if Ma got her neighbour to lie to me? I could see that happening. I could just hear her saying, "You know that bleeding daughter of mine? Well, if she ever comes round here looking for me, tell her I moved out. I don't want to talk to her no more 'cos she's always on at me to tell her where her sister is. I can't be bothered with her 'cos I'm off to the pub." The neighbour woman might do it 'cos Ma could make her life a misery with all her noise and the walls being paper-thin.

I was thinking about this and what to do about it when Andy came out of the stairwell, walking straight towards me. I only just got behind a rubbish skip in time, but I don't know how he didn't see me. It was raining and getting dark, but even so . . .

He was so close I could see the worry lines between his eyes. His shoulders was hunched and his hands was rammed in his pockets. He was a big guy.

The funny thing was, though, he didn't look like a boozer. All the times I seen him before, I was too hopping mad to look at him proper. He was just this big, nasty thing between me and the light. Now, when I had a chance to look at him, I was surprised. 'Cos he looked too clean and classy to go for a scrubber like Ma. Her fellers usually look like they got bad breath. And if you make a mistake and get too close to one of them you find out it ain't just the way they look.

So I thought, I bet he's going home to his wife. 'Cos nine times out of ten, Ma's fellers are married, although you wouldn't think any decent woman would ever marry them. Ma meets blokes who're out on the razzle, and usually she only meets them the once.

Right, I thought, I'll find out where the wife and kiddies live. Then if he gives me any more aggravation I'll be able to hit him with something heavier than a loaf of bread and a bunch of bananas. I'll tell him if he doesn't stop coming round to my house I'll go round to his. So his missus can whack him with one of her saucepans and save me the bother. Which is what any decent missus would do if she found out her hubby was snogging around with Ma.

I thought I might do it anyway. After all, he ruined my life, didn't he? He was the one who put the knife to Simone's throat the night he and Wozzisname tried to grab her. If he hadn't done that, I'd never of panicked and Wozzisname wouldn't be at the bottom of the Thames with a fire extinguisher between his legs. If he ruined my life it was only fair if I ruined his.

I was thinking so hard I almost caught up with him. Which wasn't the idea at all. I had to crouch down and tie my shoelace or he'd of felt my breath on the back of his crummy neck, and then I'd of had to dot him right then and there instead of finding out where he lived and letting his missus do it for me.

So on he goes without turning round. And on I go behind him. And he knows where he's going but I don't. Which is a right piss-off. I don't like being led around like a dog.

I was just wondering if dogs like being led around like dogs when he turned into a service alley behind some shops. Halfway along he turned again and ran up an iron stairway which looked like a fire escape. He banged on the door at the top.

I was too close so I ducked down behind some rubbish bins. And I thought, he lives above a shop—maybe he owns a shop. If he owns a shop he's got dosh of his own, so why . . . ?

And then I heard a woman say, "She ain't here. She ain't been here. Bleeding sling yer hook, an' leave me in peace."

And I sat down in the wet—I was so gob-smacked. 'Cos that wasn't his missus, that was my ma.

I got it all the wrong way round. His missus lived in Ma's old flat and Ma lived above a shop. That's how they met—when she was moving out and he was moving in. They must of met the same day I had my run-in with the poxy rent man and the rent man clattered me with his frigging baseball bat. If I wasn't so aeriated from being clattered, maybe I'd of met him too.

I could just see it—her running round like a headless

chicken plucking up all that slaggy underwear from where it fell off of her walkway, and him seeing her and thinking, "Yahoo— any woman wearing tart-rags like this must be a pushover." So they go out for a drink together, and as soon as she gets bladdered—which would only be a couple of rum and cokes later—she'd say, "Yeah, me daughter's loaded. She's got a wedge the size of a pound of cheese an' she paid off all me back rent."

And then they'd cook up their greedy little game to grab my wedge off of me. Using Simone. Ma knew Simone was the most important thing in the world to me because I'd told her so over and over again for years and years.

Is that a lesson? Or it is a lesson? If you want something really bad—and I mean really, truly want it, like I wanted to see Simone again—don't never tell anyone. 'Cos if you tell anyone they'll use it against you. Even your ma. Especially your ma. If you tell people what you want, what you ache for, you're giving them power over you. First, they use the power by denying you. And then they use the power by saying you can have what you want but only if you pay through the nose for it, for the rest of your sorry life.

Keep it to yourself, I say. Don't you tell no one what you want. Don't give your ma the power to say no or yes or gimme all your dosh. If you don't do that, you'll be better off than me. You won't find yourself sitting in the wet behind a load of garbage bins with tears in your eyes and a splitting headache.

I hardly saw Andy when he came past again, and he didn't see me at all. I waited till he went round the corner before I got up and blew my nose on my T-shirt.

Then I crossed the alley and went up the iron steps to Ma's door.

Bang-bang-bang I went, with the heel of my hand against the cracked paint-work. I could hear music and gunshots from the telly inside.

242

Then, "Wha?" from behind the door. I banged again.

"Go 'way," Ma said. "I told you. Go 'way."

"It's me," I said.

Silence, except for more gunshots.

"Open the fucking door," I said, "or I'll kick it in." But, truth to tell, I was too tired and headachy to kick a paper bag.

"You would too," she said from behind the door. "You'd leave me with no bleeding door."

"Believe," I said.

So she opened the door, and there she stood in a lime green camisole thing with only half her makeup on.

"Wha'choo want?" she said.

"Talk," I said.

"I'm going out," she said. "Go 'way."

Then she remembered, and her face went all saggy.

"Oooh," she squealed. "You're a murderer, you are. Go 'way. Get away from me." And she ran off down a dark tight passage, through a door which she slammed behind her.

I went after her. I opened the door she went through and found her in her tiny grim bedroom, standing there with a wire coat-hanger in her hand.

"You going to hit me with that?" I said.

She used to hit us with wire coat-hangers when we was kids if she caught us playing in her bedroom.

"I got a right to defend myself," she said.

"Don't be so bleeding stupid," I said. I took the coat-hanger out of her hand and bent it in half. Like I should of done when I was little.

"You're a killer," she said. She sat down on the stool in front of her dressing table.

All her things were still in boxes except for a couple of frocks rumpled up in a heap on the bed. I sat down on the bed.

She turned her back on me and stared at me in the mirror.

"Look at you," she said. "You're just an ugly great killer. I always said you'd turn out bad. I always said that. I said, 'That one'll turn out bad.'"

"Well, you wasn't wrong," I said. "With a little help from you. How could you, Ma, how could you?"

"Don't look at me like that," she said. "*I* ain't killed anyone. You didn't need no help from me. You started out bad and you went on from there. You was even born the wrong way round and you ain't changed. I said, you ain't changed. So don't you look at me like that 'cos it ain't my fault."

I dunno how I was looking at her. She was sitting there with her back to me. All I could see was her wobbly white shoulders cut into squares by lime green straps. Except when I looked in the mirror, when I could see that blood red gash of a mouth jabbering.

She was talking to me through a mirror and she couldn't even do that proper. She got distracted by her own face and she started to paint her second eye.

"But why, Ma?" I said. "Why?"

"Why what?" she said. "And that's another thing—I've told you and told you but you don't never listen—don't bleeding call me Ma. People look at me funny when you call me Ma. I'm still a young woman."

"What'm I s'posed to call you? What does Simone call you?"

"Simone?" The red gash went still for a moment. "Simone don't hardly call me nothing. That other woman brought her up. Anyway it don't matter with Simone. Simone takes after me."

"Never!" I said. "She couldn't be more different."

"Simone's pretty," she said. "She takes after me. I could of done them things Simone's done if I wasn't lumbered with kids. Kids ruin yer figure."

She always does this to me. It's always her and her stuff. Always, always, always. She won't look me in the eye and talk about my stuff.

"So that makes it all right?" I said. "I ruined your figure, so it's all right to ruin my life."

"You ain't got a life to ruin," she said. "Look at you."

"I got a life, but you ain't interested. You never saw me fight. Not even once. You never even came to my home. Not once. No. But you sent Wozzisname and Andy the minute you thought I had a bit of dosh."

For a moment it looked like she was too interested in her mascara brush to bother to answer. Then she said, "Your home? What home? You'd of taken a hammer to me like you did to poor Jim. I always said you was a bad'n."

"It was his hammer," I said. "He brought it. He was going to use it on me and Simone."

"Don't be so fucking stupid," she said. "Jim wouldn't hurt a fly. It's you. You get everything upside down. It's just like you. You was born the wrong way round and you've taken everything the wrong way round ever since."

"Why did you send him?" I said. "If you wanted money, why didn't you ask?"

"Ask you?" she said. "Don't make me laugh. Anyway, I never sent him. It wasn't my fault. Don't you shout at me."

She always does this. Always. "Who'm I supposed to shout at?" I shouted. "You're supposed to be my ma."

"Shut up," she shrieked. "I said shut up. That was ages ago. You're grown up. What d'you need to call me Ma for now?"

'Cos she *is* my ma. Why couldn't she act like my ma? I could of picked her up by her jelly neck and shaken her till her blusher dropped off. Except she was my ma. If I didn't remember that I'd be as bad as her.

245

"It ain't my fault," she said. "You always blame me for everything and it ain't my fault. Now look what you done."

"What?"

"You made me eyes run," she said. "Now I'm going to have to do them all over again. You made me eyes run."

I had my thumb in my mouth. I did. And I was biting it so hard I almost bit it off.

"I'm going out," she said. "I ain't got time. I'm going out."

I said, "You got time to send Wozzisname and that scrubber-lover round to screw dosh out of your own daughter."

"Don't blame me," she said. "You want someone to blame, blame your toffee-nosed sister."

"You're evil," I said. "You're an evil slobbering lying old cow."

"I ain't old," she shouted. "I ain't. You're always blaming me. Something goes wrong—wha'd'you do?—you come round blaming me. How did you find me anyway? Simone wasn't supposed to tell you. No one was supposed to tell you."

"Simone doesn't do what you tell her," I said.

"No," she said. "You're both of you against me."

"Simone doesn't have to tell me where you live, you dribbling old tart. All I got to do is follow one of your sick tart-raking fellers."

"Wha'?"

"Andy," I shouted. "I followed Andy. Would you tell your own daughter your address? Like fuck you would! No, I got to follow your latest shag."

"You're so bleeding stupid," Ma squealed. "Andy ain't mine. He's Simone's."

"You take me for a retard, don't you?" I said. "You think Simone and me don't talk. You think she don't tell me about you. You kept us apart all these years. Well, it didn't work, Ma. We're family, Simone and me. You ain't 'cos you blew your chance."

She jumped up then and turned to face me. Her face was all twisted with spite. She said, "What's she been telling you? It's all lies. Where is she anyway? She was going to give me some money. I been waiting for her to come and help me out. She said she'd pay the rent, and now I got to go out, and me face ain't finished."

I snatched a coat-hanger off the bed.

"Don't hit me, don't hit me," she screeched. "It ain't my fault."

I had to twist it with both hands to stop me from twisting her wobbly white neck.

And then, bam-bam-bam, someone knocked on the door.

"Oh my god," Ma snivelled. "I ain't even dressed yet."

I came here to have it out with her. Once and for all. But I'm so low on her list of what's important I come below mascara, frocks and doors. There's a dead bloke at the bottom of the Thames, and one daughter's disappeared with a big dangerous man with a shooter, and her other daughter's clawing at the ceiling. But does she care?

"Get the door," she said. "Don't just stand there."

She always does it to me. Always. She makes me feel smaller than the breadcrumb you wouldn't bother to throw to the ducks. I don't matter. Even the ducks wouldn't miss me.

"You're like a big ox," she said, "a big dumb ox. Don't just stand there. Get the bleeding door."

She was struggling into a short black frock.

"Zip me up," she said. "Fucking zip me up, can't you."

Bam-bam-bam went the door knocker.

I said, "But Ma . . ."

"Don't call me that," she said. "I *told* you. Don't call me that. I got company."

She's my ma. She's my sodding sodden mother. And I can't

make it to the first bend in the road with her. She don't want to know.

She pushed past me and went to the door.

"You always," I said, "you always, always . . ."

She opened the door and a voice said, "Get a move on, we're missing valuable drinking time."

The voice was so familiar I rushed into the little kitchen to see who it was.

It was just another bloke. No one I knew. Just another one of Ma's fellers. I didn't know him. I just knew the whole crappy scene like I knew my own hand. I knew the knock at the back door. I knew the voice in the kitchen or in the hall or on the walkway.

"Nearly ready," said Ma. "Hang on."

"Don't," I said. "You got to talk to me."

"Who's this?" the bloke said.

"No one," Ma said. "She just turned up."

"If you ain't ready," he said, "I'm off."

"Wait for me, darlin'."

"I'm her daughter," I said. "She's my ma."

"Bloody hell," the bloke said.

"She's lying," Ma said. "She's lying. She's always making trouble." She kicked me hard on the shin.

"You got to talk to me," I said. "Or I'll walk out the door, and if I do, I'm never coming back."

"I *wish!*" she said. She had her arms up her back trying to pull the zip. "Wait for me, darlin', I'll be ready in a sec."

"Well, get your skates on," the bloke said. "I'm thirsty."

"Comin' darlin'," she said in that horrible little-girly voice.

I couldn't stand that girly voice. I hated the bastards who made her talk that way.

So I pushed the bloke backwards out the door. I pushed him

backwards down the iron steps. I did what Pete Carver did to Keif—I gut-barged him all the way down to the alley.

"She's my ma," I said. "She ain't your cheap shag. She's my ma an' she's nearly forty years old."

"Oy!" Ma shrieked from the top of the stairs. "Don't listen to her. I told you, don't listen. She's lying."

"Bloody'ell," the bloke said, pushing me off. "I didn't come here for no trouble."

"You all right, darlin'?" Ma squealed. She clattered down behind us. "Don't listen to her—she's mad. We'll have a few drinks. We'll have a good time. Don't worry about her—she's crazy."

"Ma!" I yelled. And I started kicking the rubbish bins to make her look at me. To make her listen. To make her stop home and pay attention.

And I went on kicking them long after she'd gone. I went on kicking them till I heard the cop car come.

Then I ran away.

Chapter 27

Maybe Keif's mum was right. Maybe I should of got my head x-rayed. I ran as far as I could. But my head was hurting so bad and all them aspirins made me feel so sick I had to stop and spew up in the gutter. I puked till my guts ached almost as much as my head.

After that I felt better and I walked the rest of the way. At the Fir Tree I stopped. I needed a drink, so I poked my head through the door. But the beer fumes and the cigarettes and the juke box made me feel pukey again.

And then I thought, I ain't never going to have another drink again. Never. Ma drinks. I don't want to do nothing Ma does. Nothing at all. Zero. I'll do the opposite. She drinks. I don't. I don't want nothing from her, and whoever she is I want to be the opposite. I don't even want her to be my ma no more.

And one day she'll regret it. One day she'll be old and wrinkly and she'll say, "I'll go round and see how that daughter of mine's doing." And she'll turn up at my back door. And the servants'll come to me and say, "Hey, there's this old bag at the door who says she's your mother." And I'll say, "What?

I ain't got no mother. I'm self-made, me. She must be lying." Then she'll regret it all right. You'll see if she don't.

So I didn't go into the Fir Tree.

Besides, I'm an athlete, and athletes got to look after themselves. I'm the London Lassassin, the one they call Bucket Nut. They love me. They say, "Hey, Bucket Nut, where you been?" And they give me a boost back into the ring.

I didn't see there was trouble till I got down the end of Mandala Street. Just as I was turning the corner I caught an eyeful of cop cars and blue flashing lights. It looked like the politzei were having a rave. In my yard. I jumped back.

And then someone poked me in the spine with something hard. A BBC newsreader voice said, "This is a sawn-off shotgun. Do not move. Just do as I say."

So I stood like a stone.

He said, "Your sister is in the car. Will you come with me—no noise, no trouble?"

"You've got Simone?" I said.

"Yes. She's waiting. Will you come sensibly?"

"Okay," I said.

He turned me, and we walked slowly all the way back up Mandala Street—me in front, him behind.

His big gold BMW was parked off the main road.

He said, "Open the door, slowly, and get in."

I opened the door.

"You look terrible," Simone said. She was there, she really was—in her shiny black raincoat and high-heeled boots.

She said, "Greg, put that silly gun down. Don't you hold a gun to my sister's back."

"She's unreliable," Greg said. "I had to make sure she didn't storm off and do something we'd all regret." He stowed the shooter under the front seat.

"Simone," I said, "that git, Andy, he ain't your boyfriend, is he?"

"Who on earth told you that?" she said.

"Ma."

"Who's Andy?" said Greg.

"A friend of my mother's," Simone said. "Eva, don't go talking to Ma. It's futile."

"What's futile?"

"Futile," said Greg, "is useless. It's worthless, vain, abortive, unproductive and nugatory."

"Isn't he amazing?" said Simone.

I said, "Simone, it was such a fuck-up."

"That too," said Greg.

"Poor Eva," said Simone.

"She lies all the time," I said. "*All* the time. She said Andy was your boyfriend and then she told her feller I wasn't her daughter. She said Wozzisname wouldn't hurt a fly."

"Who is . . . ?"

"Another friend of my mother's," Simone said. She took my hand and squeezed it. "You and I know different."

"Differently," said Greg.

"Thanks, Greg," said Simone. "We don't want to talk about that now, do we, Eva?" She squeezed my hand tight and flicked her eyes towards Greg and back to me.

"No," I said. "I've had it with all that. I've had it with Ma." I sat back in the warm car and rested my head against Simone's shoulder. We had our secrets, Simone and me. We was family.

Greg said, "Eva, even as we speak the police are raiding your yard."

"Stupid bastards," I said. It was wonderful. The politzei was crawling all over my home and they didn't know. They didn't know that home was here in a warm car with Simone.

"Why?" said Greg. "Why are the police raiding your yard, Eva?"

"Search me."

"Who called them?"

"Dunno."

Simone squeezed my hand again. She said, "Eva, you know what you were telling me in the pub?"

"Wha?"

"About the lottery ticket and the people who gave you Greg's money."

"What about it?"

"Don't get sleepy on me again, Eva," she said. "You said there was a detective woman asking questions about it."

"The Enemy," I said. "Once a copper, always a copper."

"What did you tell her?"

I couldn't remember, and, even worse, I couldn't remember exactly what I told Simone about the lottery ticket. And that could be a lot of bother because I was sitting in a car with God Greg.

I sat up straight. "Ramses and Lineker," I said. "Milo. What they done to my dogs?"

"Never mind the dogs," God Greg said. "What did you tell the detective?"

"They ain't your dogs," I said. "They're mine—and I mind."

"Where are you going?" Simone said, hanging on to my hand.

"The dogs," I said. "I ain't letting no bastard politzei take my dogs off me." I was struggling to get out of the car but she was holding me back.

Greg reached under the front seat, grabbed the sawn-off and stuck it up my nose.

"I beg your pardon, Simone," he said. "We tried it your way. Now we'll try it mine."

"Greg—*don't!*"

"What did you tell the detective?"

"Nothing." My head was back. My neck was stretched. I had a shooter rammed up my nose and it hurt.

"Don't, Greg," said Simone. "Eva, tell him. For Christ's sake, tell him what you told the detective."

"Nuffin," I said. "I don't never say nuffin to her." Well, I don't, do I? I couldn't of. It's against my religion, ain't it?

"It's my religion," I said.

"What?"

"It's like a religion," Simone said. "She wouldn't tell. Honest, Greg."

"Honestly," said Greg.

"Thank you, sweetheart," said Simone.

I can't tell you what I'd of done if there wasn't a shooter up me nose. *Sweetheart?*

"Greg, she's spent half her life in custody," Simone said. "She hates the police. You can believe her, honest*ly* you can."

"But she drinks too much," Greg said. "She isn't in control of her faculties. She runs amok—we saw that last night."

"That's wrestling," Simone said. "That's theatre, Greg. You said so yourself."

"I don't think she knows the difference."

"Fuck off," I said. "What I don't know about wrestling you can stuff under your fingernail and scratch your bumhole with."

"And she'd never do anything to hurt me, Greg," Simone said. "Would you, Eva? She'd never do anything to hurt me. If I told her that talking about you to the cops would hurt me, she'd go to her grave with her mouth shut. She would. Wouldn't you, Eva. *Wouldn't* you?"

She was trying so hard it almost made me want to bawl. And she was squeezing my hand so hard with her long finger-nails—that almost made me want to bawl too.

I said, "I'd never let you down. You know that."

"I know," she said. "Greg? Please, Greg."

He lowered the shooter. "I want to be sure," he said. "A lot depends on it."

"I know," she said. "I'll go with her. I promise, Greg. I promise, your name'll never come up."

"Go where?" I said. The shooter was lying across his knees and I was wondering if I'd have time to grab it and shoot his underpants before he blew my nose off.

"To the yard," she said. "You'll have to talk to the police, Eva, and you'll have to tell them the exact same story you told me."

"Identical, Simone," Greg said. "Exact same is a tautology. She'll have to tell the police a story *identical* to the one she told you."

"You're incredible, Greg."

"Thank you. And she must remember it so that she can re-peat it again and again in every detail."

"That's why," I said. "They're on to you like piss on a lamp-post if you forget. That's why you never say nothin'."

"This time's different," Simone said. "This time we *want* you to tell them what you told me. And, Eva, it's going to be okay, because you can always say you'd had a little too much to drink so you can't remember clearly."

"I'll remember to sew The Enemy's mouth shut with a rusty needle," I said. "Dobbing me in like that. She said she'd give me twenty-four hours. You can't never trust a copper."

"Why did she, Eva?" Simone said.

"Dunno."

"How did she know to come to you in the first place?"

255

"Dunno." I was trying to remember. "Oh yeah." Remembering's a lot easier when you don't have a shooter up your hooter.

"Local traders, she said. She was working for some local traders who were all upset 'cos someone gave them bad dosh. She said my name kept coming up."

"Ah," said Greg. "Now I understand."

"You see?" said Simone. "I told you. My sister would never knowingly do anything to harm you. She didn't know the money was wrong or she'd never have spent it."

"I got to eat," I said.

"And you will," said Greg. "I can safely say that if you tell your story correctly, and are believed, I'll make sure you eat well from now on."

"Oh Greg," Simone said, "you're so kind." Her fingers were digging into mine. So I kept my lip buttoned.

"I understand about bad families," Greg said. "It's no disgrace provided you make the effort later."

"Like you did," Simone said, before I could tell him how much he understood about *my* family.

"Come on, Eva," she said. "Let's get this over with."

She dragged me out of the car. We didn't speak till we got round the corner and God Greg couldn't see us no more.

Then she said, "This is the last time, Eva. I'm moving heaven and earth to drag your arse out of the fire and all you do is aggravate. You talk loud and show me up."

"What about you?" I said. "Wha'choo calling that piece of crap-smear 'sweetheart' for? When he had a shooter up me nose. You called him sweetheart. I *heard* you."

"I *told* you," she said. "That's what you call a guy with a gun, you stupid cow."

"*I* don't," I said.

"No, *you* get your head blown off."

"I'll blow his fuckin' head off."

"Shut *up*," she screamed. "Shut up shouting. Shut up with all this horrible talk. I'm sick of it. It's all you do."

"Ain't."

"Is."

"I'll talk nice," I said. "Pardon me language—nice*ly*. I'll talk to the police nice*ly*. And you can talk nice to fuckin' God Greg—at visiting hours. Won't that be nice*ly*?"

"You do that and I'll never speak to you again," she said. "I swear to God, Eva—if you ruin this for me I'll never see you again. Ever. I got a chance now."

"What chance?"

"Security, Eva. Can't you understand? He's got money and power."

"Bad money."

"Oh that," she said. "That's just a deal. Something he was doing for someone else."

"Bollocks, Simone. Bad money. Bad man."

"No, Eva," she said. "He could look after me. He'll look after you too. You heard him. All you have to do is talk sweet to the coppers. Just this once. He said he'd set me up in business, Eva. Think of it. My own business."

"Not yours," I said. "His."

"In my own name," she said. "In my own right. I won't have to scrape and scramble ever again."

"Only to him," I said. "Only to God Greg."

"He isn't so bad," she said. "I've met worse. Please, Eva, please. Don't do it for him. Do it for me."

"What?"

"Oh Christ!" she said. "Tell them. Tell the police the story about the lottery ticket and the woman in Mandala Street market. The way you told me."

"Oh that," I said.

"Wasn't it true? I believed you."

" 'Course it's true," I said. "I wouldn't lie to you."

"Then you will?"

"Will you be there?" I said. I didn't want to let her go.

"I suppose so," she said. "I told Greg I would. But, Eva, don't get me into any more trouble. I don't like the police either—so please, please, talk quiet."

We walked round the corner together, into all the crawling cops and blue flashing lights. I was too wrung dry to do anything else. Anyway, even if Simone wasn't beside me, I'd of had to go in. 'Cos of the dogs. They're *my* dogs, see, and I brought Milo up since he was a pup.

Chapter 28

There's laws about dogs. There's sodding laws about every sodding thing on earth, and they're wrapped around you so tight you're like a fly trapped in a wire-wool pad.

Can you believe this one? You ain't allowed to leave an unmuzzled, unrestrained guard dog alone in the place he's guarding. In case he hurts the pillock who breaks in. Which is what he's supposed to do. What's he there for, I ask you? How's he supposed to guard if he's wearing a muzzle? You might as well train a goldfish to guard a yard.

"Shshsh," said Simone. "Eva didn't know. She'll get muzzles in the morning. She only left the yard on urgent family business. She's always here otherwise. She's never left the dogs alone before, officer. Never."

The politzei was really annoyed about the dogs, so I guess they put up a good fight. Didn't I tell you—Ramses and Lineker are the meanest bastard dogs in South London, and Milo's learning. I was proud of them.

"Shsh, Eva," Simone said. "Eva's in total control of the dogs. They'll be much more trouble if you take them away."

The dogs were in a politzei van. I couldn't see them but I could hear them.

"It's all right, Eva," Simone whispered to me. "You'll get your dogs back. Stay calm."

Oh, she was a class act all right. I was so stone tired all I could do was sit back and admire her.

But the dogs was only the first stick they hit me with. The second one was stolen cars. Laugh if you like, but this didn't have nothing to do with me. Besides I ain't a thief. I don't thieve motors. I only borrow them. And I don't never bring them to the yard. Well, hardly ever. No, I park 'em, all neat and tidy, with a load of other parked cars where whoever wants 'em can find 'em again.

So I was clean. I was laundry fresh about stolen motors in the yard. See, even with wrecks, you got to have papers and proper records. And the politzei couldn't get the wrecks and the records to match. So they started to look at the secondhand motors with reconditioned engines. Then they tried to find the yard owner. But, surprise, surprise, they couldn't. So they got the foreman and the manager out of bed and brought them to the yard. And they got me.

And, surprise, surprise, none of us knew diddly-piddly. I swear I *really* don't know diddly. Honest. What they get up to in the daytime ain't none of my business. I don't even see it, do I? I'm asleep. I'm the security guard so I work at night, don't I? How'm I supposed to know?

"Take it easy, Eva," Simone said. "Don't get so excited."

But I couldn't help it. They was crawling all over everything like maggots. They was even in my Static with their maggot fingers in all my things.

They had their maggoty noses in all my cupboards, even in my bunk. They said they was looking for car stereos and speakers.

"What's the point?" I said. "I ain't got electricity. You can't run a CD player off a torch battery."

But the maggot detective didn't say nothing. He just went on turning over all my bits and pieces with his creepy-crawly hands.

Then he faced me and said, "Turn out your pockets."

"What for?" I said. "You think I'm hiding a reconditioned engine in me pocket? Or a Kalashnikov? Or a BMW?"

"Sshsh, Eva," Simone said. "Just do it. Then he'll see you've got nothing to hide."

They can make you do it. They can make you take all your clothes off, and they can even stick their maggot fingers up your arse if they want to. They can make it so you got nothing of your own, even your own arse. Free country? *Bollocks.*

So I turned out my pockets, and Detective Sergeant Maggot went through everything.

Would you like it? Well, would you? If you've got to explain every little ball of fluff in your pockets or your handbag or your home? They can make you if they want to. It's up to them, if they decide they want to. It's your turn. So they give you a tug and they make you explain every sodding item in your possession. It ain't up to you. *You* can't decide. Oh no. And you're lucky if you get away with your arse intact. Believe.

There it all was, on the table—my skinning knife, the sheath, my tobacco tin, money, snot rag, torch, keys, Swiss Army knife, short-handled screwdriver, tin of flea powder.

"Why've you got two knives?" Detective Sergeant Maggot said. "What's the skinning knife for?"

"Hush," said Simone.

"Fresh meat," I said. "For the dogs."

"Have you got a receipt for it?"

"No."

"Show me all the locks these keys fit. Every one."

See, he was saving the best till last. That's what the politzei do. They pretend they're interested in what's in your tobacco

261

tin, and they'll go on and on about it till you're climbing the walls. It's only when they've scraped you off the ceiling that they'll start talking about the money.

And all the time Detective Sergeant Maggot was asking me about the matches, candle stub, stock cubes, I keep in the tobacco tin, his little assistant maggot, Detective Constable Oily-Rag, was rummaging through the rest of my belongings. And every now and then she'd bring something else and put it on the table—like another torch or my sponge-bag or a box of tampons.

You can't concentrate. DS Maggot's firing questions, questions, questions while you're trying to see what DC Oily-Rag's up to. That's how they try to trick you.

"Let me get this straight," DS Maggot said, "you keep a wire saw, waterproof matches, et cetera, in this tobacco tin because you're afraid of a nuclear accident or an earthquake or something. Am I hearing correctly?"

"I ain't afraid of nothing."

"It's okay, Eva," Simone said.

"The SAS manual says it's a good idea," I said.

"You're winding me up," he said.

Then DC Oily-Rag threw my dirty old jeans on the table and said, "There's something in the pockets, Sarge."

That gave me an awful fright. I was scared I'd forgotten one or two of those dung squillions when I changed to my brand-new zippy strides.

What they found was my lucky piece—the ten pence that old lady dropped for me when I was waiting to ask Harsh to be my personal trainer. Except he wouldn't and he just gummed off about toothbrushes, so it wasn't lucky after all. The other thing they found was the lottery ticket. The real one. And that *was* lucky because it reminded me of my story. And it proved to

Simone I was telling the truth. 'Cos now she could see with her own eyes I was the sort of person who went in for the lottery.

"That's mine," I said. "You ain't taking it."

"Shush," said Simone. "No one's taking it."

"Haven't you checked the numbers?" said DS Maggot. "Maybe you've won a million."

"Not with my mojo," I said. "If there was any good mojo going I wouldn't have you bastards crawling all over me."

"Eva," said Simone, "shut up. Just answer the questions. I'm exhausted." She was talking to me like I was a baby. And the politzei was letting her do it. They never told her to go away. They thought I was so stupid I needed a responsible adult along to hold my hand. Which shows how stupid they are.

Simone wasn't the only one who was totally butchered. As the night went on DS Maggot and DC Oily-Rag got more and more tired too. It was their own silly faults. They was trying to wear me down so that I'd crumple when they got to asking about what really interested them. They forgot they was dealing with a trained athlete. They forgot that I'm used to being up all night.

So when Detective Sergeant Maggot decided to talk about the bent money I could of laughed, 'cos actually he knew less than nothing. I knew he didn't know piddly-pooh because of the questions he didn't ask. He didn't ask about God Greg. He didn't ask about a red Carlton. He didn't ask about a Puma sports bag.

What he had was one measly twenty-pound note which he said I bought a burger with, from John's Burger Bar. That's all he had.

I said, "You turned me place upside down 'cos I bought a burger? One stinking burger. I s'pose if I bought a pizza you'd of sent me to prison."

He and Simone said, "Shut up," together.

He didn't know about the rest of it. He didn't know about Hanif and Value Mart. That's what surprised me. The Enemy wasn't the one who dobbed me in. If she dobbed me in he'd of known about Hanif's and the Army Surplus store and Value Mart. But he didn't. So she wasn't the one and I was amazed. It must of been Burger Bar John. The sod—he can swing before I eat another of his smelly old burgers.

So it was morning before I got to tell the story Simone and God Greg wanted me to tell. I thought I told it pretty bloody well. But DS Maggot was scratching his stubble, and DC Oily-Rag was yawning, and Simone was rubbing her eyes by the time I finished.

"Keeping you up, am I?" I said.

"Shut up," they all said together.

"'Cos I got to feed my dogs," I said. "They ain't ate since yesterday morning, and they've spent the whole night cooped up in your van. I ought to get the RSPCA onto you. I don't s'pose you even gave them any water."

"Shut up."

That's a fine way to talk to someone in her own home. I was almost as knackered as they was but I wasn't letting my guard down. For one thing, I was rageous. I mean, it was my home they was trashing. It wasn't Simone's. It wasn't DS Maggot's or DC Oily-Rag's. It was me they was tearing open with their questions. Not Simone, or Maggot or Oily-Rag. Who the hell did they think they was telling to shut up? When all I was doing was answering, answering, answering their stupid questions.

Maggot said, "This woman in the market? She gave you money for luck? You expect us to believe that?"

"You lot never believe anything," I said.

"How much?"

"What?"

"Money."

I looked at Simone. I'd forgotten.

"How much?"

"Dunno," I said.

"Don't ask her," Simone said. "She can't count."

"*Can*," I said. "What d'you mean I can't count?"

"So how much?" said Maggot.

"Er . . ."

"Come on."

I looked at Simone again. I couldn't remember what I told her.

"Sixty-seven?" I said.

"Sixty-seven pounds?" said Maggot.

"A hundred?" I said. "Um. And sixty-seven?" I was looking at Simone and she was looking back, but she wasn't telling me if I was right or wrong.

"A thousand?" I said. They was doing my head in. "Could of been fifty-seven thousand. No. A thousand and fifty-seven. I mean sixty-seven. I mean, a hundred."

"Christ," said Maggot.

Simone said nothing.

"How much did she give me?" I asked Simone. "I got to feed the dogs."

"I wasn't there," Simone said.

"I *can* count," I said.

"Of course you can," she said.

"I just forgotten."

"I know," she said. "It's all right. Maybe it'll come back to you if we wait."

We waited, but I couldn't think numbers. All I could think of at that moment was Wozzisname and that was the worst possible thing to think of.

"I *can* count," I said. "Why did you say I can't?"

"I was wrong," Simone said. "I'm sorry." She was tired too. She said, "Do you think, Detective Sergeant, that Eva could feed her dogs now? Could we have a word?"

"We *all* need a break," Maggot said. "She can feed her dogs if she puts them on a leash and keeps them under control. Besides, there's one place we haven't searched—the dog pen."

"Ramses won't like that," I said. "Dogs is territorial. Why should Ramses put up with having his home trashed any more than me? You got a warrant?"

"Shut up," said Maggot. "I don't need a warrant to search a doghouse."

"That's not fair," I said. "Dogs got rights. I'll get the RSPCA on to you."

"Shut up."

Simone was looking at me like I was soft in the noodle. She didn't understand, and she didn't say nothing to stop them neither. So we all got up and went out.

It was daylight and the rain was coming down in strips. Even the politzei looked miserable. The manager and the foreman were still hanging in, answering this and that everytime the troops found something dodgy.

When the men turned up for work they went through the politzei grinder one at a time, and then the manager or the foreman sent them home again. We'd been royally shafted. I thought that when this was over I'd deep-fry Burger Bar John upside down in his own chip pan and stuff his ears into one of his own soggy buns.

The dogs was in a terrible strop—except for Milo who was so pleased to see me he stood on his hind legs and gave me a morning wash. His stand-up ear looked a bit chewed. He spent the night cooped up with Ramses and Lineker and I spent the night cooped up with Maggot and Oily-Rag so I knew how he felt.

I fed them and gave them water. Then I had to put them back in the van.

"Not Milo," I said. "He's only a pup."

"A *what?*" said Oily-Rag. "He looks like a small horse to me."

"He's too young to take chokey," I said. "I'm keeping him with me. He won't bite no one—he's a dead loss as a guard dog so far. He won't even bite *you*."

"Oh for God's sake," said Maggot.

"Herf," said Milo, looking pitiful. He was good at that.

"But keep him on the leash," said Maggot.

"Hip-herf," said Milo.

"Shurrup," I said. "He talks too much. I dunno what to do about that. Guard dogs is supposed to be silent and deadly but he's always got something to say."

"I wonder who he takes after?" said Maggot. "Right, let's look at the pen."

So we tramped through the rain and the puddles to look at the pen.

There wasn't nothing in the pen to look at except the old fridge I keep the dogs' feed and brushes in. It's only a pen. It's got an awning I rigged up to the doghouse and a mat under it so the dogs can sit out if they want to, even if it's raining. Maggot looked under the mat and Oily-Rag emptied all the Bow Chow rusks on the floor.

"Now they're spoiled," I said. "You're supposed to keep dog biscuits dry and hard. It's for their teeth and gums. You're taking food out of my dogs' mouths and you ought to be ashamed."

"Shush, Eva," said Simone. "Let's get this over with."

They went into the dogs' house. They turned their beds over. They shook out the bedding and I hope they caught fleas. I wished my dogs was free to protect their own territory, 'cos I couldn't. Nobody listens to me. I should have a lawyer. My dogs should have a dog lawyer.

"Shut up," said Maggot.

But he didn't find nothing. He didn't find no Puma sports bag filled with bent squillions. Did you think he would? Get a brain. I ain't stupid.

"Where can I wash my hands?" said Oily-Rag.

"Ssh-ssh," said Simone 'cos she thought I was going to tell her to wash her hands in the same place she put her enema. But I wouldn't soil me lips.

What? Tell the politzei useful information? I wouldn't even tell them their own names. I didn't tell Detective Sergeant Chapman of the Fraud Squad his name was really Maggot of the Turd Squad, did I? No. I got my pride.

They didn't leave till nearly midday. Then they got into their vans and cars and went back to the cesspit they came from. They took the manager with them. But they didn't take me. And they didn't take Ramses and Lineker.

They didn't take the yard foreman neither.

"Frigging Frieda," he said. "Ever been grateful you're only small fry?"

"I ain't small anything," I said.

"Well, that's my job down the garbage chute," he said. "Yours too."

"What you talking about?"

"No one's going to pay you to guard an empty yard," he said. "And an empty yard's what's going to be left by the time the cops sort out the bent gear from the straight."

"That ain't *fair*," I said.

"Don't shout at me," he said. "When was life ever fair to the likes of us?"

"But I always did my job."

"Pull the other one," he said. "You spent half your time out on second-wagers and the other half in the boozer."

"Did *not*."

"So where did all those cassette and disc players and stuff go?"

"Ask those thieving crows you work with," I said. "*I* don't touch nothing that ain't mine." Well, not much. Not enough to notice.

"Hah!" he said. "And what about the fire extinguisher? I was looking for that only yesterday."

"What would I want a fire extinguisher for?" I couldn't look at Simone. She was sitting on the step to the Static with her head in her arms.

"I dunno," he said. "What would you want with any of the things you pinch? To sell in the market? You know your business. I don't. But that fire extinguisher's got the name of the yard scratched on it. I thought you had more sense."

How was I supposed to know that? It was dark when we bundled Wozzisname into my sleeping bag. I wasn't looking for no scratched names. I only wanted something heavy to weigh him down so he wouldn't float in the Thames. It wasn't my fault.

I was glad Simone wasn't listening. She'd of been scared. She couldn't deal with Wozzisname. Think of the trouble we'd be in if I hadn't looked after everything the way I did. I wasn't going to tell her about the name on the fire extinguisher any more than I was going to tell her about the squillions in the Puma bag. She's too sensitive. She needs someone to protect her from the ugly facts of life. It's a good job she's got me.

Her eyes look like a foal's eyes when she wakes up. She raised her head and said, "Has everyone gone?"

I gave her a mug of tea. Everyone was gone. Even the foreman. There was only her and me and the dogs left.

269

"Still free," I said. We'd been so close to pokey I could smell it.

"No thanks to you," she said. "When will you ever learn to keep your mouth shut, Eva? You were foaming. I thought one of your dogs had given you rabies."

"I didn't say nothing," I said. "I never say nothing to the politzei."

"Jesus!" she said. She sipped her tea and I thought we was going to settle down to a nice chat when God Greg came sailing into the yard in the good ship BMW. He stopped right in front of the Static.

"Simone, you poor child," he said. "You look exhausted."

"What about me?" I said. "I spent all night keeping you out of trouble. Don't I look knackered too?"

"Shut up," said Simone. "For the last time, Eva, just shut up."

"I'll take you home," Greg said. He got out of the car in his big black coat and hat, and he held the door open for her. Like he had manners—don't make me spit.

She looked at him with her foal's eyes, as if it was him who'd been up all night with her, keeping her out of trouble, instead of me. She got up off of the Static step.

I said, "I've lost my job 'cos of you. My home's been trashed 'cos of you. I've had maggots all over my yard, my *life*, 'cos of you."

"You'll be compensated," God Greg said. "Come, Simone."

"You and your bent money," I said. "I wouldn't touch either of you with rubber gloves on."

"Be very careful about what you say to me," he said. He was holding the car door for Simone. She bent her head and climbed in. She didn't even say good-bye.

Greg said, "Be almost as careful about what you say to me as you are, and will be, when you speak *of* me. Do you understand?

My young associates gave me a very detailed description of the person who stole the car and the sports bag. And I have to warn you, Eva, I find the likeness to be uncanny."

"Bollocks," I said. "They're piddling in their pants."

"They may well be afraid of me," he said. "I'm not denying that. But they are showing more sense than you. You may have convinced your sister of that absurd story about a lottery ticket, and who knows—the absurd *is* sometimes the truth. But, Eva, be very careful what you say to me. I am not so easy to convince and I have a very long arm."

He closed the door on Simone. He went round the car to the driver's side. He got in and drove off. And Simone drove off with him. I couldn't even see her face behind the tinted glass.

Chapter 29

I hope Greg explodes. I hope the bastard he was doing a bent-dosh deal with sticks a sawn-off shooter up his big greasy nose and blasts his big black hat into outer space. Who does he think he is? Who does he think I am?—treating me like that—coming between me and Simone. After everything I done for him.

See, he thinks he's God Almighty and he thinks I'm lower than a worm. But he doesn't know, and now I'm not going to tell him. Ever. He can light a fire with ice cubes before I tell him I could of done a bent-dosh deal with him myself.

Yes I could. I still got his sodding Puma bag, except I don't know what it looks like now. And I still got his bent dosh, except it's a bit more bent than it used to be. A *lot* more bent, actually. It's still in the back of the red Carlton car. Well, not *the* red Carlton, but one just like it. It's in the one Milo chose for me when he lifted his leg on the rear wheel and showed me that the old mojo stuff was still working.

I couldn't just throw them squillions away, could I? They was much too pretty to throw away. So I kept them, and the Puma bag and the red Carlton. And if God Greg ever gives me any more grief I'll load them all up on a trolley and wheel 'em along to the politzei cesspit and give God Greg all his grief back.

Don't think I won't. I'd chew on a crowbar before I let the politzei use me, but they wouldn't be using me, would they? I'd be using them, and God Greg don't deserve no better. He can go mouldy in the cooler like the rest of the rotten meat.

He's so stupid. The squillions was right under his nose when he came to fetch Simone. Actually, they was right under Simone's arse when she sat on the Static step. And they was right under Maggot and Oily-Rag's big feet when they was invading my home.

What do they look like? Well, I dunno really, except they're bent. Crushed, more like. Quite small—the size of a big door step. I had to put that red Carlton through the crusher three times to make it small enough—just the right size to stick outside my front door. And with a sheet of hardboard and a rubber doormat on top I'd made meself a nice front doorstep. The rubber mat has "Welcome" written on it. But don't you believe everything you read—if your name's Greg or Maggot or Oily-Rag or Burger Bar John or Andy or Ma you ain't welcome.

I bent down and turned the welcome mat upside down. There wasn't nothing written on the backside.

And I was glad I did it 'cos the next person to stand on that mat was The Enemy and she is another one who ain't welcome.

She said, "You're still here."

"Where did you think I'd be?" I said. "Banged up in pokey? You'd like that wouldn't you?"

"Believe it or not, I wouldn't," she said. "I didn't inform on you. Maybe I should've, but I didn't."

"I know. It was Burger Bar John. The creepy sod."

"Well, maybe," she said. "Have you sorted everything out with the police?"

"You never sort it out with them," I said. "Never. They're always round the next corner, waiting."

"I mean, are you in the clear?"

"Dunno. They went away. They didn't take me in."

"I expect you're all right then. I'm glad." She stood there, all ruled lines and buttons—typical lady copper.

"What're you waiting for?" I said. "I ain't asking you in for tea and fancy cakes."

She looked round the yard. It was empty and silent.

"What're you going to do?" she said.

"What makes it your business?"

She sighed and said nothing. Then she turned away and started to walk back to her white Peugeot.

I said, "I ain't drinking no more."

She turned back. She looked at me but she still didn't say nothing.

"You thought I couldn't give it up," I said. "Shows how much you know. I'm in training again. I'm an athlete. I can give it up whenever I want to."

"Good for you," she said. "Tell you what, Eva, if you can stay clean and dry for six weeks, come and talk to me or Mr. Schiller. Perhaps we can find something for you."

Six weeks! Who did she think she was kidding? What would I eat in the meantime? What would Ramses, Lineker and Milo eat? Six weeks is forever when you got nothing to eat. Six *hours* is forever. That's The Enemy for you. Stuff her.

I looked at the money in my pockets. There was a five-pound note, coins and a lottery ticket. And that was supposed to see me through six weeks. Yeah, *right*. And then perhaps, maybe, The Enemy *might* find something for me—if, perhaps, maybe, might. Oh, I could count on The Enemy all right.

I was standing on bent, crushed squillions and all I had in my hand was a measly five-pound note. Ain't life a joke?

There was enough in my hand for some bread and beans, so I went out. And I met Keif coming in. Well, he would be coming in, wouldn't he? He didn't know I was down to my last fiver, did he? He didn't know I was out of a job. He didn't know I wasn't rich no more, and it's only rich women who get all the visitors.

"Hey, pretty pudding," he said. "How's it hanging?"

"It ain't hanging," I said. "It's dangling from a broken thread. Look around."

"Shit," he said. "What's happening here?"

"We was raided last night. Politzei closed the yard, so I ain't got a job no more. And if I ain't got a job, you ain't got a job. So you can sling your hook."

"Tough," he said. "Man, that's tough. What you going to do?"

"What do you care?" I left the yard gate unlocked. I didn't care either. "I can't pay you no more," I said, "so buzz off."

"You know it ain't like that, babes," he said. "C'mon, admit it—you know I ain't like that."

"Everyone's like that," I said. I showed him what I had in my hand. "That's all I got," I said. "Five quid and a lottery ticket ain't enough for a personal trainer."

"It ain't enough for dinner neither," he said. "Come on, I'm buying."

"That's a first," I said. "You never bought me nothing before."

We walked up Mandala Street and I didn't even slow down when we got to the Fir Tree. I walked right on by. See? I told you I wasn't drinking no more and I meant it. If I say I'm giving it up, that's what I do.

"Okay, safe," Keif said. "I ain't giving you no hassle about that. No need for shouting."

We went into the caff on the main road, and I ordered

sausage, eggs, beans and chips. No burgers. I've given up burgers too. I don't care who cooks them, they'll always remind me of Burger Bar John.

We sat down at a table by the window and waited for the food. When it came everything felt better. You can't be too blue with half a pound of sausage, egg and chips in your gob.

"Tell you what," Keif said, "my dad was well impressed with you."

"I should fucking well hope so," I said with my mouth full. "I saved his little Keifee's arse, din't I?"

"Dunno 'bout that," he said. "But you were impressive. All that stuff you said about believing in it—about wrestling like you mean it—when you was in that ring I believed."

"For true?" I said.

"My dad said a girl like you ought to do something serious—like boxing."

"Wrestling's serious."

"He meant something you can make a living from."

"I can make a living wrestling," I said.

"Can you? Did you ever?" he said. " 'Cos the money ain't great. And it don't seem to me there's enough women for you to fight. Not twice a week like the men do."

"You're a bright little ray of sunshine," I said. 'Cos he was bringing me down. Usually he annoys the shit out of me but he doesn't bring me down.

"Oh, I get it," I said. "Mr. Deeds kicked your arse out of the wrestling game. You're blue 'cos you're on the dole too."

"Um, well . . ."

"Go on. You can tell me."

"You wrong again," he said. "Mr. Deeds thinks Muhammad Wily got potential or what. Didn't want to tell you. I got my job if I want it. But he blaming you."

"Typical," I said. "Blame me."

"Now, now, honey-bear, it ain't so bad. I ain't going back. My mum, she'll kill me if I go back. She don't like that scene at all. And my dad thinks I better work with him, at his gym—training all the youth."

"Oh well, t'riffic. That's *you* sorted. Mr. Deeds takes what *I* want and offers it to *you* on a plate. And you don't fuckin' want it."

"Knew it'd make you sad," Keif said. "What I think is—you should work for my dad too, make a wage, pay your personal trainer. I should go back into a non-contact sport, like decathlon. Serious this time, no schoolboy stuff. I used to be good at that."

"Oh yeah?" I said. "Ain't you full of surprises today. Nice to know you're good at something other than talking the hind leg off a donkey. If you got paid for exercising your mouth you'd make a fortune."

"Hey, yeah, chicken-little," he said. "I could be a DJ. Yeah, you got good ideas, babe." He grinned that piano grin.

Don't you just hate it when you cheer someone up by mistake? When you ain't got a future and someone else suddenly sees his and it's all fizz, buzz and bubbles?

I finished my chips and looked around for more. If this was going to be my last good feed I wanted it to be big.

"You want all your chips?" I said.

See, I'm all give and no take. I give Keif all these good ideas and what's he give me? He doesn't even give me the chips off his plate. I got to ask.

"Still hungry, cherry-o?" He pushed his plate over. He said, "You like my rap the other night? Wasn't that something? Yeah, man, I'll do a bit of DJ-ing—make money in no time."

"Don't mind me," I said. "I got stuff to do too. My sister's going into business for herself. I told you—we're going to start a fitness centre."

277

"Yeah?" he said. "You sure about that?"

"What you know about it?" I said. "What you heard?"

"Nothing, babe," he said. "Only, is fitness really her scene?"

"Why not? She's a model. Models got to get in shape."

"Yeah but, well, not that sort of model."

"What you know about it?"

"Hey, chill. I don't read that sort of magazine myself but you see them around sometimes."

"I don't read women's mags neither," I said. "But you still got to be slim and fit if you're modelling handbags or lipstick."

"It ain't women's magazines," he said, "and it ain't handbags."

"Well, lipstick, whatever."

He was staring at me with Cousin Carmen eyes, which made me shiver. But he said, "Okay, baby-buns, lipstick, whatever."

"Models got to be fit," I said.

"Okay, child," Keif said. "They got to be fit."

"So?"

"So, nothing. Just thought it wasn't your scene. Just thought you might like it if I put a word in with my dad. It's a proper gym—all weights and punch bags. There's a pool there too and a basketball court. All sorts of good gear. But, like, if you prefer the glamour game . . ."

I finished his chips. I was still hungry. "Well," I said, "Simone ain't in business yet. So I got to find something temporary."

"Now you talking," he said. "And mebbe I'll be working there too. Just temporary. And I got to get you running again."

"No running," I said. "I fucking hate running."

"Skipping then. You got to work on your lungs. I was watching you, night before last. Lotta raw power, lotta speed, but it ain't no good if you out of breath."

"Wasn't out of breath," I said. "I want some pudding."

"Fruit," he said. "You don't want that sticky pudding. You going to eat good hard apples from now on."

"Bugger off," I said. See, he always thinks he knows what's good for me and he's always wrong. Sticky pudding *is* good for me. It keeps the cold out, gives me energy. Apples make my teeth ache.

"Apples ain't sweet enough for you?" Keif said. "You eat what I tell you, then *I'll* be your sugar. I sweet enough for both of us."

But I wasn't listening 'cos I suddenly had a thought about the yard. See, it was *my* yard now. The owner wasn't coming back. He'd be in Spain or Bermuda if he had any sense. He'd let all his employees take the heat and he wouldn't come back till it was safe. At least, that's what I'd do if I was him.

So I'd have the yard all to myself. Just me and Ramses and Lineker and Milo. I'd paint the Static and put some glass in the windows. And Simone could come and stay. And maybe I'd plant a tree so she could look out of the window and see something growing. She's sensitive so she probably likes trees and flowers. The yard could be a home for the two of us.

I'd go out to work at the gym, and my personal trainer would get me ring-ready. He could come round sometimes and give me a back rub with those voodoo digits and Cousin Carmen's embrocation. But only if he promised not to annoy Simone. Oh yes. I could see it all.

"Apples?" said Keif. "I ain't gonna waste time training you 'less you change your diet."

"Okay, apples," I said. "But I want some sticky pudding first. After that you can buy me all the apples you like. And while you're doing that I'm going to check out my lottery numbers. I feel some good strong mojo coming my way."

Cody, Liza.
Musclebound.

MYSTERY

$21.50

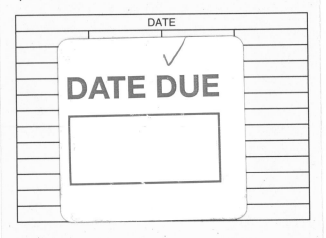

DATE					

09-97